PRAISE FOR NIKKI TURNER

#1 Essence *bestselling author*

"Always surprising, Nikki Turner's prose
moves like a Porsche, switching gears from tender
to vicious in an instant."
—50 CENT

"Nikki Turner has once again taken street
literature to the next level, further proving that she
is indeed 'The Queen of Hip-Hop Fiction.'"
—ZANE, author of *Dear G-Spot*

"Another vivid slice of street life from Nikki Turner.
You can't go wrong with this page-turner!"
—T. I. on *Ghetto Superstar*

"Few writers working in the field today bring
the drama quite as dramatically as Nikki Turner....
[She's] a master at weaving juicy, 'hood-rich sagas
of revenge, regret, and redemption."
—Vibe.com on *Forever a Hustler's Wife*

"USDA hood certified."
—TERI WOODS, author of the True to the Game trilogy
on *Riding Dirty on I-95*

Relapse

Nikki Turner

A NOVEL

ONE WORLD TRADE PAPERBACKS
BALLANTINE BOOKS · NEW YORK

A One World Books Trade Paperback Original

Copyright © 2010 by Nikki Turner

Published in the United States by One World Books, an imprint of The Random House Publishing Group, a division of Random House, Inc., New York.

ONE WORLD is a registered trademark and the One World colophon is a trademark of Random House, Inc.

ISBN 978-0-345-51105-8

Printed in the United States of America

www.oneworldbooks.net

2 4 6 8 9 7 5 3 1

Book design by Laurie Jewell

This book is dedicated to

Marc and Christina Gerald—

I wish you many years of love and happiness.

&

To everyone who has ever been addicted to love

and experienced a relapse or two!

A Special Message from Nikki Turner
to Her Readers

Dear Loyal Readers,

I'd been trying to pen this letter to you for a while, and for the life of me, I couldn't figure out why it was so hard, because I love sharing my writing experiences with you. Then it hit me: this letter was my final chance to add my two cents to this novel, and writing it meant I would finally have to let go of something that is so dear to my heart—like a mother who cries on the first day of school when the bus pulls off with her child. I have special connections to all my babies, and this newborn is no different.

Like with *Black Widow,* the concept of this story had been in my heart, mind, and spirit for a very long time. I felt that both male and female readers could relate to it, and the overwhelming response I received from family, friends, and readers when I explained the plot was encouraging and such a blessing.

Ashanti sings in "Baby, Baby, Baby" that "like a drug you relieve my pain." Everybody, at one time or another, has been a fool for love. Has experienced the highs and lows of a relationship, the fiending to be with that person, the withdrawal after a breakup, and finally the Relapse.

I knew someone whose life seemed so together; she was a powerful person with lots of money, success, and fame. But one harsh word from the love of her life would just shut her down. I've been there too, and so have many of my friends and family, so this idea of having a relationship become an addiction is something I just had to dig into.

Initially, I wanted to write about a new male character, but I love listening to my fans and you all sent lots of messages asking about Lootchee and wanting more of the inside scoop on him. So I decided to incorporate him into *Relapse* and show a different side of him than what you saw in my previous novels.

This book was on a really tight schedule, and once I received my edits, I had the privilege of revisiting my characters with a fresh eye and doing a lot of rewriting and moving things around. The extra work really enhanced the story, but racing against the clock was no joke. After days operating on little to no sleep, the book was finally completed. I had only four hours to shower, pack and get to the airport to go to one of the most mysterious places in the world, Marrakech, Morocco to witness the matrimony of two very special people: my agent, Marc, and his fiancée, Christina. I had the time of my life, learned so much, rode a camel (can you imagine me on a camel?), and yes, brainstormed a new project while I was there.

Yes, this book has definitely given me great rewards. It's helped me face some of my craziest addictions, and I hope it does the same for you—if not more.

So, without further ado, I introduce you to the newest baby, *Relapse!!!* Fingers crossed that you love her as much as I do!

Much Love,
Nikki Turner

My name is Beijing Lee . . .
And I'm an addict!

My drug of choice isn't cocaine, heroin, prescription pills, alcohol . . . or any other mood-altering drug. The intoxication that I'm hooked on has a stronger hold on me than any of those drugs ever could. Sometimes it brings out the very best in me, and at other times the absolute worst.

Some of my friends have called my problem an addiction to please, but that's not it. I'm simply, absolutely addicted to a man. It's not the sex or his money that has me hooked. It's so much deeper than that . . .

Relapse

"Bye, Dad." Beijing planted a kiss on her father's cheek before jumping down from his tow truck for her monthly visit with her mother, Willabee.

"If you need anything, be sure to give me a call on my cellular phone." Sterling hated letting his little girl go. Willabee and her oldest daughter Paris not only lived on the wrong side of the tracks, they were riding the train in the wrong direction as far as he could see. If he had his way, Beijing would never have contact with any of her kinfolks on her mother's side of the family. But Sterling didn't have his way. Those were Beijing's peoples, and he didn't want to make his only daughter resent him by forbidding her to visit her biological mother and older sister.

"Yes, Daddy. I will."

"If for some reason you can't get me on my hip, call the office to have the dispatcher radio me."

"Daddy, I know the routine." Beijing smiled. "Stop worrying, Daddy. I'm not a lil girl anymore."

"You may be ten years old now." He squeezed her nose. "But fifty years from now you will still be my little girl."

"Daddy, you gotta let me grow up."

"In due time, but I don't want it to happen too fast. Now, one more kiss, on the other cheek this time." He bent down and Beijing kissed his left cheek before he walked her to the front door of her mother's place.

Willabee swung the door open before they reached the porch. "Hello, my little princess cream puff." She reached out to hug Beijing.

"Hey, Momma," Beijing asked while in her mother's arms. "Is Paris here?"

"Yup, she's in her room, baby."

Beijing idolized her older sister. Paris was ten years older than her and everything Beijing aspired to be when she grew up.

Whenever Willabee had one of her mental episodes, it was Paris who looked after her, and Beijing knew that her sister would never steer her wrong. Although lately Paris didn't keep her hair freshly done the way she used to, or her clothes as crisp, and her once shapely body no longer filled her clothes the same way, but none of that mattered to Beijing, who still adored her big sister Paris.

"And how you, Sterling? Is that a new truck you got?" Willabee peeped around Beijing's father to look at the new flatbed truck.

Sterling considered his baby's mother, Willabee, a lame excuse for a parent. Every time Sterling thought about the fact that he'd been with this woman his stomach turned. What in the world had he been thinking? Or which head had he been thinking with? No man in his right mind would have taken on Willabee and all her baggage and bullshit. She had a child, a mental condition, a mountain of debt, and no job, but a body and beauty to die for. He blamed it on the marijuana and that's why to this very day he said no to drugs.

"I can't complain," Sterling answered as he placed Beijing's overnight bag inside the house. "I will pick her up at three o'clock tomorrow."

"Okay bye, Daddy," Beijing said as she rushed past her mother and straight to Paris's room.

"Oh, Sterling, you don't have to come so early." Willabee asked for a little extra time with her daughter but Sterling wasn't having it.

"Have her ready at three tomorrow," he said firmly.

"Oh, don't worry." She waved her hand. "I will."

Sterling sat in his truck gazing at the house, praying the entire time, as he always did, that God would be his eyes for him and watch over his baby girl. Each and every time, God had answered his prayer. Hopefully, this time wouldn't be any different.

Three hours later Beijing was sitting on a dingy sofa that was riddled with holes, the white cushioning inside trying to escape. Paris had taken her to a house that smelled like a dirty locker room, and the rank odor was seeping into Beijing's throat. She peered over her shoulder every now and then to look at her sister, who stood in a cramped kitchen with peeling wallpaper. It wasn't really her sister that Beijing was watching, but the man with whom she was having a conversation. Beijing was trying to figure out what they were talking about and could tell by their expressions and gestures that it was intense. Beijing wanted to turn the volume down on the outdated floor-model television so that she could make out what they were saying, but she didn't want to appear to be too obvious. Suddenly both her sister and the man she was talking to looked at Beijing and locked eyes with her. Beijing quickly turned back around so Paris wouldn't yell at her later for being nosey and sticking her nose into grown folks' business.

Paris turned her attention away from her little sister and continued her rap with the man she had come to see: Chimp, an old cocaine dealer with bad teeth, bad hair, bad breath, and even worse fetishes.

"I don't know about coming off a whole half of zone," Chimp said. "That's seven hundred bills."

"Don't try to play me like that, Chimp, we both know that yo' shit got bake on it," Paris replied rolling her eyes.

Chimp cracked a crooked smile because Paris was telling the gospel. He whipped all his coke into crack with baking soda, and he was damn good at his craft. Because of the highly addictive nature of the drug and his skill at cooking it up, his customers always came back. If those same patrons knew that they were actually buying more Arm & Hammer than cocaine, they probably would not have been so loyal.

"Look, you wasting my time. I got what you want, you in or out?" Paris taunted as she put her hands on her hips.

Chimp stared Paris up and down, mildly upset because she knew his MO. Once upon a time, Paris had been a breathtaking beauty, and even though she had fallen off a bit, she was still easy on the eyes with her dark skin, full eyes, high cheekbones, and petite frame. But today, Paris wasn't his preference; he knew she had been tricking with all the boulevard fellas, and he wanted something a little more fresh.

He peeped over the top of his glasses at the young girl sitting on the soiled sofa.

Watching him, Paris felt a sickening ache deep down in the pit of her stomach. The feeling was partly out of disgust for his perversions, but also because of her shame for what she knew she was about to do.

Torn between her love for the coke and her love for her sister, all sorts of questions filled Paris's brain. *What kind of big sister would do a thing like this to her little sister?* she wondered. What kind of person would do this to another person period? But especially to her own flesh and blood?

Before Paris could answer the silent questions in her mind, the feeling in her stomach was quickly replaced by the euphoria of being that close to having fourteen grams of crack in her possession. She pushed any noble thoughts she may have had away. Now it was time to step up her game and close the deal.

"Look, she's a ten-year-young virgin and I'm giving you the pleasure of busting her little ripe cherry." Paris moved in closer. "I ought to be charging you the whole zone for this once-in-a-lifetime opportunity. You know that don't you?"

Chimp bit down on his bottom lip so hard that he broke the skin, coating his mouth with the bitter flavor of his own blood. "Okay, aight, we got a deal. One hour with little Miss Marker for the half. Deal?"

Paris looked at her little sister, who was none the wiser about what was about to happen to her. No one else had to know.

But someone else did know. Mike had been in the bathroom, sitting on the throne, taking a dump, counting the money he had just collected from Chimp earlier. At seventeen years of age, Mike was a lot more advanced than most kids his age. With the help of his older cousin, Qwon, from Queens, New York, Mike had put a decent portion of Durham, Greensboro, and Raleigh in a chokehold from the time he was fifteen. After exiting the bathroom, he managed to hear the end of Paris and Chimp's conversation. He heard enough to know what was about to go down. Mike had heard the rumors of some of Chimp's sordid affairs in the street, but had never really put much stock into them until now.

"Paris, I'm hungry. Can we leave now? Stop at McDonald's or something?" Beijing called out from the living room. Looking from the kitchen, all anyone could see was her big doe eyes peering over the back of the couch. Innocent eyes. If Paris and Chimp had their way, those eyes wouldn't be so innocent for long. Staring into the eyes of the soon-to-be victim, Mike couldn't walk away.

"Oh yeah, Lil Mama, you gon get a Happy Meal all right."

Chimp rubbed his manhood and licked his chapped lips. "And I'm going to see to it myself, you pretty little thing you."

Repulsed by the comment, Mike's stomach turned, and he walked up to Paris and spoke in a low and deliberate tone. "Take your sister and get the fuck out of this house before I break your fucking neck."

Beijing appeared to be oblivious to what was taking place. "Take this and go buy your sister something to eat." He pulled out a twenty-dollar bill and handed it to Paris. Then he grabbed her by the arm, and he said, "And that's for the kid, not for yo' fucking habit, and I mean that shit."

Fear settled in Paris's eyes as she slowly took the money and Mike released her arm.

"Hold on, Mike," Chimp blurted out. "I respect you and all, but you need to tend to your own bizness and leave mine alone, lil bro. I can fuck who I want, when I want, how I want, and I'm fittin' to do something real good and nasty to that young tenderoni there. I'm about to make it official."

No one noticed that Beijing was suddenly all ears as to what was going down in the kitchen. They were all consumed in their own role in the vile scene that was taking shape.

The intense scowl etched into Mike's normally handsome face should have been enough to let Paris know that he wasn't bullshitting, but her craving for the drug overrode her common sense. Mike's twenty-dollar bill for a damn Happy Meal didn't stand a chance against what Chimp was offering. Chimp was oldschool and had a reputation in the game, and at the end of the day, if Mike wanted to keep his pockets lined, he needed Chimp. Feeling the odds were in her favor, Paris stayed put.

"Chimp is right, Mike," Paris said. "Maybe you should just stay out of this."

"Yeah, you've handled your bizness up in this joint, lil bro," Chimp added. "Now let me handle mine; *my* bizness, not yours."

"Too late, maggot, I'm making it my business, and don't ever call me lil bro again. It's disrespectful to both me and my mother."

"Whatever, man." Chimp waved his hands at Mike. "I'm going to fuck that sweet lil thing and you can put up three grams to watch if you want to. Fuck what ya talking 'bout, sheeid—"

Not Beijing, not Paris, and even more so, not Chimp, ever saw where the seven and a half inches of finely sharpened steel had come from before it plunged into Chimp's stomach. Chimp went from arrogance to agony in record-breaking time, and before he could react, Mike jerked the blade upward with a force so brutal that it ripped cleanly through Chimp's skin. He gave the knife a twist for good measure. Blood flew from Chimp's body, splattering all over the refrigerator, the stove, and the cabinets of the small kitchen before Chimp collapsed to the floor.

When Mike turned his eyes to Paris, she stood with a blank expression on her face. Then the lights seemed to switch back on in her eyes, and she grabbed the crack cocaine off the counter and galloped past Mike out the back door, leaving her little sister in an apartment with the body of a man who had just been murdered and his executioner.

Mike and the ten-year-old girl stared at each other for what felt like forever. Finally, Mike walked over to her and asked calmly, as if he wasn't covered head-to-toe in blood, "What's your name?"

She stammered, "B-B-B-Beijing."

"That's a pretty name." He remained cool. "Are you okay, Beijing?"

"Y-yes." She nodded her head.

"That's good." Then he asked, "Do you know what happened here?"

"Uh-huh," she spoke timidly. "You kilt the man in the kitchen with your knife."

"Do you know why I did that?"

Beijing paused and thought for a moment before speaking. "My sister was going to let him do something really bad to me?" she said, gazing into his eyes.

"That's right," Mike said. "He was a bad person and was going to hurt you."

"Are you going to get in trouble for what you did to him?"

The irony didn't go unnoticed. He had probably saved this young girl's life. Now if she described Mike to the police she could end his.

The scowl was long gone from Mike's face and was replaced by his boyish smile. "Not if you don't tell anyone."

Again Beijing paused and thought for a moment before speaking. "Then I won't tell anyone. Ever. I promise. I won't. Cross my heart and hope to die."

CHAPTER 1

All in a Day's Work

Beijing surveyed the lobby of the Tabby Hotel, making sure that all her guests were comfortable.

The toilet paper heiress was sitting in a comfy maroon chair with her prized teacup Yorkie cradled in her arms. The well-groomed, silky-furred dog was licking the salt off his owner's margarita glass. An older couple, who looked like ordinary travelers but were really dripping rich with old soft-drink money, played a game of backgammon at a mahogany game table in the corner by the bay window.

Then there was one of her favorite clients, Natalia, who had been living in one of the Tabby's penthouse suites for six months paid for by her boyfriend, business tycoon Seth Soberman. The Russian beauty was drop dead gorgeous, with flowing blond hair, although she had quite the wig collection as well. Her beautiful green eyes were framed by lashes that seemed as long as her slender legs. She had no career, and wasn't exactly certain about what she aspired to do with her life, but the one thing she was sure of was her love for Seth.

Beijing had just finished seeing to it that all the stores Natalia wanted to shop at today knew she was on the way when Beijing's eyes roved across the marble floor, through the custom-made bar, past the bellman's stand, beyond the giant fish tank to land on a man in khaki pants that were too short, a white polo shirt, and deck shoes. He tried to come off as nonchalant but instead stuck out like a rock in a glass of water.

Beijing strolled over to further inspect the man. "Hello, sir. Is there something that I can help you with?" she asked politely while checking him out.

"No, just waiting for a friend," he said, shifting his leg in front of the black bag by his feet.

"Would you like for me to give your friend a buzz for you to let them know you are waiting?" she offered.

"No need. I don't mind waiting. I'm a patient kind of guy," he said with a dry smile.

Beijing paused briefly, and then said, "Okay, no problem." She sensed that he was up to no good. "Well, if you need anything, come and see me," she added.

As she walked away, she heard his cell phone buzz. She lingered over a plant pretending to check to see whether it needed to be watered while she listened to the one-sided conversation.

"Yeah, he's here. He's definitely here. I heard the limo driver outside bragging that he picked him up from the airport. Yeah, the 'friend' is here, too. Ole Johnny boy is as good as busted."

Beijing made a mental note to herself to scold the limo driver but smiled at the tip she'd just gotten from her ear-hustling. She was now certain that the guy in the lobby was one of the paparazzi with big plans for her famous guest, Johnny Wiz, to be his next meal ticket.

It's not going down today. Not today, not on my watch, Beijing thought as she punched in her security code to open her office door.

Beijing was a jack-of-all-trades who more than lived up to her title of concierge-at-large for the Tabby chain of hotels. She went to extreme measures sometimes to satisfy the extraordinary requests of her high-powered clients, ballers, and anyone else rich or famous who strolled through the door of the Tabby Hotel. She went to great lengths to make sure her clients' stay was as comfortable and as enjoyable as possible. Between her thousands of contacts and vast resources, she could get anything accomplished.

Johnny Wiz was a music industry mogul. The man, in some way or another, touched over 50 percent of everything that got played on the radio, and this week he happened to be her client.

She picked up her office phone and called Johnny's room.

"Hi, Johnny. It's Beijing. I wanted to warn you there's a guy down in the lobby with a camera bag and he's definitely not taking pictures of the beautiful skyline," she said.

"Shit," Johnny exclaimed. "The piranhas will never give me any peace."

Beijing heard an exaggerated feminine voice in the background ask, "What's wrong, honey?"

"Damn paparazzi are downstairs wanting to steal a picture of me with you," he told his friend, and then he asked Beijing, "Any suggestions on what to do?"

"Don't you worry about a thing. I'm on top of it as we speak. Just don't open the door for anyone until you look through the peephole and see that it's me," she warned.

Beijing knew that the feminine voice in the background didn't belong to a woman. Johnny Wiz's secret rendezvous was with a flamboyant two-snaps-and-a-shake male companion, and they had been spending a discreet, quiet, cozy few days together. However, the paparazzi had plans to share their lurid affair with the world. Rumors about Johnny's sexuality had been floating around the industry for years, and a photo of him with his secret lover would command big bucks from the tabloids.

After Beijing hung up with Johnny, she called her partner in crime.

Seville was Beijing's first cousin, and the closest thing to a real sister that she would ever have. Their fathers were brothers. When they were young, they saw each other for two weeks every single summer and every Thanksgiving when Beijing and her father would visit his brother, Jimmy, in Charleston, South Carolina.

The two girls had always been as thick as thieves when they were young and had gotten even tighter as they got older. Seville's boyfriend and the love of her life had recently been transferred to a plant in Germany, and as fate would have it, Seville got a job there, too. Her boyfriend's contract had a little over a year and a half left, and Seville had agreed to be there with him for the long haul.

Seville was due to leave for the big trip in a few more days and had been packed and ready to go for over a week now. Beijing couldn't get time off work, so the cousins had agreed that Seville would hang out today at the Tabby with Beijing. While Beijing put in her hours at the hotel, Seville chilled in her cousin's luxurious suite and enjoyed all the amenities of the five-star hotel. After Beijing got off work that day they would spend time together.

Beijing let her fingers do the walking and her mouth do the talking when she called upstairs to her suite. "Seville, I need you to come down to my office. Time for you to work off all that luxuriating you've been doing." She added, "Oh, and wear something sexy and chic."

Ten minutes later, Seville slipped into Beijing's office through the back hallway looking stunning in a shoulder-baring top, sandals, and skintight jeans.

After Beijing explained the situation to her, Seville said, "Girl, that damn Johnny Wiz! I can't believe he's bi, but then I shouldn't be surprised that he would think nothing was off limits to him with that ego of his. And you were keeping his secret from me?" She raised an eyebrow. "And I really can't believe you are going to help that cocky asshole. After the way he treated you yesterday?"

"My job is to assist him. He's in my care until he leaves this hotel. And I don't want it to ever be said that I allowed a scandal to happen because I didn't like the way a client spoke to me," Beijing explained, leading Seville back into the hallway with a quick look to make sure none of those bottom-feeding scandalmongers were in sight.

"As cocky as he was, I would let him get caught," Seville said, following her.

Beijing shot a look at her cousin and Seville knew Beijing meant business, so she changed her tune. "You know I got yo' back. But I am only doing this because of you, not to help that self-absorbed booty bandit."

"Well, let's put the plan in motion. I will call you when the coast is clear and then you take the freight elevator and meet me upstairs, Room Nineteen Thirty-four."

When Beijing arrived at Johnny's room, it was apparent that he was worried. He looked vulnerable as he paced the floor and continuously peeped out the window. *This is not the same arrogant man from yesterday—not the way he's on edge sweating bullets,* Beijing thought.

"Calm down, everything is going to be okay," she assured him.

Beijing turned to Johnny's lover. "Will you please put this on?" She handed him one of the hotel housekeeping uniforms she had grabbed on the way up. There was a knock on the door. Beijing checked the peephole and saw Seville standing in the hallway, twirling a finger in her long hair. She quickly let her into the suite.

Seville strutted through the door swaying her hips from side to side, looking fashionable and seductive with a twist of class.

Beijing made her introductions. "Johnny, this is my cousin Seville, your date out of here."

Seville was the perfect person to play the role. She stood five foot nine, with a long black deep-wave hair weave. She didn't need the makeup that she painted on her mocha skin, but it made her eyes stand out. She was beautiful.

Johnny's eyes met hers. "Thanks for coming to help me wiggle out of here," he said sincerely.

Beijing could see the relief overtaking the worry on his face when she began to explain how they were going to maneuver out of the hotel and to the airport. "Beijing," he said nervously, "the reason I don't want anyone to know about this is because of my mother—"

Beijing stopped him. "You don't owe me, or anyone else, an explanation. It's simply nobody's business what you do. Johnny, I am here to make your stay here and your transition home as smooth as possible."

He took a deep breath and smiled at her.

"Thank you, Beijing."

"My pleasure, Johnny."

"Do you think this will work?" he asked, still somewhat unsure.

"Of course it will," Beijing said with confidence.

"If it does, you know I will owe you big-time," Johnny Wiz said. He pulled a wad of folded cash from his pocket and started counting out hundred-dollar bills. "Take this," he said with his hand full of money, extended toward Beijing.

She shook her head no. "I can't accept that."

"You have to, you saved my ass; this is only a small token of my gratitude."

"Johnny, it was my pleasure, and if you want to do something nice for me, just refer another client or two my way."

"You can bet on that," he said smoothly.

She looked at him with a smile. "Now let's get you to the airport."

Before they left the room, he reiterated, "Beijing, I am in deep debt to you. Please, if you need anything, and I mean anything, don't hesitate to call me."

Beijing was at her post at the front desk smiling as Seville played her part as Johnny's girlfriend, sashaying through the lobby like a stuck-up celebrity princess.

While Beijing watched the taillights of the car move farther and farther away, she wanted to pat herself on the back, proud of the publicity stunt that she had pulled. *I swear, every day I get better and better at this.* She turned around and saw the reporter angrily pick up his camera bag and head toward the door after Johnny and Seville drove away.

"Didn't your friend show up?" she asked.

The jilted paparazzi snarled at her, "No, he didn't. I'm actually going to leave."

"Well, before you go, why don't you have a drink on the house?" She asked for his business card, then led him to the bar and told the bartender to pour the man a drink. That was Beijing's MO. She had beaten the man at his own game, gotten his contact information, and even given him a consolation prize. *You's a badass bitch,* she said to herself, stroking her ego. A huge smile spread over her perfectly symmetrical features as she thought about how, just moments ago, she'd put the brakes on a would-be national media-story-of-the-year about how one of the most powerful men in the music business liked to pack sausages in his lunch box on his downtime.

Beijing went back to her office to take a breather. She looked around the luxurious room with the view of the waterfalls outside. This was her dream life, her dream job: to work in hotels and make everything right for people who traveled. When she was young, she had traveled damn near all over the continental United States, Canada, and Mexico, and even to the Caribbean with her stepmother, Greta. Greta would encourage Beijing to do all the organizing and find out all the places that they'd want to see. Through those childhood experiences she learned how to get around in strange cities and communicate with people from all facets of life. Who knew that she'd turn her passion into profit?

"Daydreaming on the clock, I see." Her thoughts were interrupted by a voice.

It was her boss, Thaddius Collier, the owner of the Tabby. Thaddius had grown up with a silver spoon in his mouth, but he was taught at an early age that he had to polish it himself. Before his tenth birthday, his father had taught him the ins and outs of the stock market and the basics of business. When Thaddius turned eighteen, his father sent him to Morehouse instead of Harvard or Princeton where all his friends were going. Although one of the Ivy League schools would've looked better on his résumé, Mr. Collier wanted his son to know what it felt like to be in an environment where he was a minority. Besides, a son of his would never need a résumé, he would be sitting on the other side of the desk.

When Thaddius turned twenty-five, he received his first fortune the old-fashioned way: He inherited it. With his own money to do with as he pleased, he opened his first hotel. He named it after his mother, Tabitha, and just like his mother his hotel would be eclectic, modern, and classy. And the Tabby was indeed in a class of its own. It was the playground for a lot of new money and young socialites.

This hotel chain was Thaddius's baby and he treated it as such. He oversaw the operation of each and every hotel, and his relationship with Beijing was special. He had handpicked her to handle the extreme demands of his rich and famous guests. In return, in addition to her healthy salary, she received a spacious one-bedroom suite at the hotel with a view to die for. Since she had taken the job, not only had her Rolodex grown but she and Thaddius had become good friends as well.

"You did well here today. As always, I'm so impressed with all the rabbits you seem to pull out of your hat."

"Thank you. That's why you pay me the big bucks."

He chuckled before speaking. "That brings me to the reason I'm here. I have a special assignment for you."

Beijing grabbed her pen and turned to a fresh page in her notebook. "What?" she asked.

"Jamie Tiller. You remember him, don't you?"

"Yes I do, the big-time investment banker who met his girl-friend at the bar."

"How do you manage to remember each and every client? I'm always moved by your photographic memory."

Because I am that bitch. You don't get it! I'm just that good, is what she wanted to say, but instead she replied, "It's what I do."

"However, your personal life is nonexistent."

"It's nonexistent because I have no personal life," she stated.

"You need to get one. You make enough to buy one," he joked.

"I'm going to ignore your corny digs and get back to business. So, I know he's having a surprise engagement party for his girl-friend on Tuesday night."

"Yes, but he will need you to fly to Las Vegas—on his jet, of course—to pick up the ring from Harry Winston."

"No problemo. You know I love Vegas. When do I leave?"

"I'd like to have the ring here no later than Monday evening."

"Do you mind if I leave Friday night after I drop off Seville at the airport? The big fight is in Vegas on Saturday, and I would love to go and maybe pick up some new clients for the Tabby."

"I think that's a wonderful idea. Do you have tickets?" he asked, and then shooed his question off. "It doesn't really matter if you do right now, because I know you will get them."

She lit up like a Christmas tree at the thought of the fun she was going to have in Vegas. "I'm happy to go and even happier that I'm going in the private jet. Thanks for such a great opportunity."

Thaddius finished giving her the details for the coming weekend and exited her office. Ten minutes didn't go by before he popped his head back in. "Hey, you should go sit down in the restaurant and have a steak dinner tonight. You seem to always have room service."

"Maybe I will. I haven't had a good tender piece of meat in a long time."

"You need some excitement in your life. While you're in Vegas, you should take advantage of the spa. You never get a moment to take care of you since you are always so busy taking care of everyone else."

"Thank you again, Thaddius."

At the end of the day, and to commend herself on such a good job, she took Thaddius's advice and ordered a scrumptious steak dinner, compliments of the Tabby. As she took the last bite of the juicy filet mignon, her phone rang. It was Johnny Wiz.

"Hi, Beijing."

"Hello, Johnny, how was your flight?"

"Worry-free, thanks to you."

"Not a problem."

"I wanted to tell you thanks again and to remind you if there is anything you ever need, please call me."

"All in a day's work."

CHAPTER 2

A Knockout

The MGM in Las Vegas was crammed with Hollywood's elite. The hotel was hosting the biggest fight of the year, and the atmosphere crackled with electricity. It was a sold-out event; everybody who was anybody was there, and everybody that wanted to be somebody was hating on those who were.

"May I see your tickets, please, ma'am?" the young usher asked. He was tall and had his long hair pulled back into a ponytail. The two ladies handed him their ticket stubs. He took a quick glance at the tickets then back at the attractive women.

"Follow me," he said after pulling his eyes away from the girls. He led them to their seats.

"Girlllll," Rayna squealed after the usher stopped at one of the aisles and pointed toward their ringside seats, "these seats are top-flight. A bitch is close enough to land a punch her damn self." She shot a short jab, as if to give her approval. Then she asked, "How'd you manage to cop tickets like these?"

Beijing was sidetracked scanning the room with her trained eyes, making mental notes on who was there, whom they were with, which ones she'd dealt with, and the potential clients she'd like to meet.

As she nonchalantly looked around, she made eye contact with a boxer, Taymar, who was there as a commentator on the fight. She had hosted him when he was at the hotel, and not only did two of his girls end up fighting over him, breaking furniture and lamps and spilling liquor all over the rugs, but he had skipped out, leaving a bill of over sixty thousand dollars. Beijing smiled on the inside because she knew that Taymar thought he had seen a ghost. After all the people he had faced in the ring, at that very moment he was scared shitless not knowing if Beijing was going to come over and embarrass him in front of the boxing officials.

"I thought I told you," she said, turning to Rayna for a brief moment, "I did a favor for the trainer of one of the boxers once or twice. After he found out I was a huge boxing fan, we stayed in touch. I can get him to give me a light workout routine for you, if you'd like," she added while giving Taymar the evil eye.

It was no secret; Rayna had been struggling to maintain a "society-approved" weight for years. Truth was: she was tall and naturally big-boned, and she carried her weight well but was still self-conscious.

Rayna was about to take Beijing up on the workout routine offer when she saw the ponytailed usher return with two fine brothers in tow. The usher pointed to a row behind them for the two handsome guys to sit. Rayna gave Beijing a nudge with her elbow to get her full attention, then gestured toward the duo. They were making their way into their seats when Beijing glanced at the fellas.

Both of them wore clean, tailored suits and exotic-skinned shoes. One was about six foot four, the complexion of a midnight sky, his suit barely able to conceal his powerfully built physique. But it was the partner who stood out. His skin was the color of lightly toasted bread, sprinkled with cinnamon. His red hair was cut low, waves orbiting his scalp like his own private solar system. With all that was going on around him, he walked like he owned the big arena and all that was in it. Beijing thought he came off as sexy and confident.

When the ring emcee began to announce the fighters, Beijing forgot all about the man responsible for the brief palpitations of her heart. The theatrics that were about to take place in the center of the ring now monopolized her attention.

"In this corner fighting in blue trunks and weighing in at one hundred seventy-two pounds is Billy-the-Bullet Bevins. And in this corner fighting in black trunks weighing in at one hundred seventy-one pounds is the undefeated world champion, Jack Be-Quick Thomas." The crowd leaped to their feet for the champion; most of them were there to see him put on a can of whip-ass.

"Let's get ready to rummmmmble," the announcer said, and the fight began.

"I told you Be-Quick was going to beat that boy's ass," Beijing overheard the wavy-headed man sitting behind her say after the bell rang to end the first round.

"Be-Quick is that dude, girl," Rayna said, still at the edge of her seat from all the excitement.

"Girl, it's only the first round, we still got eleven more," Beijing retorted. She was pulling for Bullet, the six-to-one under-dog. She was still smiling, though, because the fight had just begun, and from the looks of it, it was going to be a good match. "It's far from over." Beijing sat back and waited for the second round to start.

Be-Quick danced out in the second round the same way he'd ended the first: a flurry of hard jabs and three-punch combinations.

"This is going to be the easiest fifty thou I ever made," Red Head said to his friend. The two slapped hands so hard it sounded like a small firecracker exploded.

Beijing was serious, concentrating on the brawl. In her eyes, Be-Quick was throwing more punches, but Bullet was blocking most of them and when he did counter he was hitting with blows.

"Oh shit," it seemed like the crowd exclaimed collectively when Bullet caught Be-Quick with a vicious right, dropping him to the canvas.

Beijing jumped from her seat screaming. "That's right, that's what I'm talking about. Hah, never bet against the underdog."

"One . . . two . . . ," the referee was counting, unable to conceal the shocked expression that had enveloped his face. When the fighter wobbled to his feet, the ref stood in front of Be-Quick, reaching for the fighter's gloves. Be-Quick wasn't that quick.

"Let me see your hands," the experienced adjudicator said. He took one look into Thomas's vacant eyes and stopped the fight.

After most of the fans got over their initial shock, they started cursing the third man in the ring for stopping the bout. Surely Be-Quick would have recovered from that lucky blow, people were saying to whoever would listen, while others were applauding and jumping up and down in pure exuberance.

"A knockout," Wavy Head said offhandedly.

Beijing turned around, sweeping her long, silky hair from her shoulder. "Actually, it's not a knockout," she said, speaking to Wavy Head for the first time, "it's a TKO."

"I wasn't talking about the fight," he tossed back with an easy smile. "I was speaking of you."

Beijing blushed at the guy. He had caught her off guard. She was trying to think of a quick comeback line, but it didn't help that people were exiting in a hurry. It was time to go party, either to celebrate the win or sulk over the loss.

Beijing glanced over and saw Taymar shaking people's hands. She wanted to approach Taymar about the hotel's money. Then Wavy Head reached out and touched her arm. A tingle ran through her entire body.

Damn . . . I guess too much time with a vibrator makes me forget how electrifying the touch of a man can be.

"Excuse me, miss," he said, "my name is Lootchee." He handed her the back of a matchbook with a phone number scribbled on it. "Whenever you feel up to it, give me a call. I would love to take you somewhere, show you a nice time." He spoke with the confidence of a man who was used to having his way.

A nice time, is he talking 'bout fucking? Damn, girl, get yo' mind out da gutter!

"I'm sorry, but I have a man," she said instantly wondering why she'd told that bald-faced lie. She hadn't had a boyfriend in a couple of years and wasn't looking for one, either.

"Just keep the number in a safe place," Lootchee said, penetrating her eyes. "Maybe you won't have that problem much longer." Before she could respond, he stepped off. She looked back over to her task at hand and that quick, Taymar had pulled a Houdini, disappearing into the crowd.

I'll see that clown later, she thought.

At the end of the aisle, Lootchee looked back at her and winked. Beijing was still standing in the same spot trying to figure out what her next move would be.

CHAPTER 3

Torch It

Everybody was running around the hotel with their heads cut off as they prepared for the big engagement party. Beijing was glad that she'd gotten the ring safely to the Tabby and into the hands of Mr. Tiller. Because the hotel was shorthanded, she decided that she would help out in the lobby.

"Girl, who is that?" April, who worked as a front-desk clerk at the hotel, jumped straight into groupie mode when a tall, slender, dark-skinned guy with a big diamond earring in each of his ears, wearing a ridiculously big medallion on a platinum chain, entered the lobby. "Look at the way his waves are in his hair. He must be a basketball player because he's so tall and delicious looking." April answered her own question.

Unaffected by the man's appearance, Beijing nonchalantly informed April, "He's probably one of the rappers coming into town for the concert tomorrow."

Some of the biggest stars in the business had been through the

Tabby's doors and Beijing had been right there to greet them, so she wasn't inclined to make a fuss over a celebrity. Besides, as the hotel's VIP concierge, she'd seen or heard stories through the housekeeping staff of just how trifling some of these stars really were behind closed doors.

"Girl, do you see that big-ass chain around his neck?" April shook her head. "Umpf, umpf, umpf. One diamond could pay my rent and my car note if I had a car." She chuckled and nudged Beijing on the shoulder. "And he fine too, girl, he could get it."

"Aprillll, hello, Ms. Thing, you don't even know him. He could be a mass murderer, or a serial killer, and you talking 'bout hopping in the bed with him." Beijing shook her head.

Even when she was a rookie to this business, new to being in the presence of the stars, diplomats, millionaires, and plain old rich bitches, Beijing never considered dropping her panties just to get some of their paper. Even after hearing how some of the housekeepers could damn near retire with some of the money they got off eBay for selling some of the stars' left-behinds, she still never considered stooping to go through their garbage and whatnot. If nothing else, Beijing had a code.

None of that seemed to affect April, who had been working at the hotel even longer than she had. You would think she'd be immune to all the glittery dust by now, but nope, she was still blinded by it.

As the man strode over to the front desk with his superstar walk, April lusted over him. "Let me go check him in and offer him an upgrade." April winked. "And see what else I can offer him, if you know what I mean," she snickered.

Beijing rolled her eyes as a slight smile graced her lips.

"Hey, you got to see all those superstars in Vegas over the weekend when you went to the fight," April said. "Now I'm going to work on making some of these dreams come true for my superstar guests."

Beijing went over to her workstation and worked on her clients' requests.

"Do what you do, and I am going to do what I do. Who knows? This may be my ticket up out of this hotel." April moved to her computer. "Josh, I got it," she said to her co-worker, who was about to check in the man whom she felt was her key to early retirement. "Welcome to the Tabby Hotel, where we make allllll of your dreams come true."

The man gave April an up and down. He didn't seem too impressed.

"Key please. My promoter, Wildcat Productions, should have made a reservation for me. Name's Teflon the Don or it might be under Don Sessions," he shot off.

April wasted no time calling up the reservation and handing two entry cards to the arrogant man.

"Is there anything else I can help you with?" she asked suggestively.

"I just found out my promoter's limo driver was involved in a five-car accident about thirty minutes ago," he said. "I need a car and a driver. I can't be cabbing it around this town or trying to find my way in some damn rental car."

"Oh, no problem," April said, smiling so hard it looked like her cheeks would burst. "I will get Beijing on it. She's the concierge who deals with all of our VIPs."

As Beijing listened in, she remembered that all the car services in town had been booked for months because of the CIAA national basketball tournament. April didn't stand a chance of finding a car for their demanding client. Beijing stood up and straightened out her sleek hip-hugging black skirt.

"Sir, all of the available limos have already been booked, but we have a fella that we call in these instances. He has an SUV that will be more than suitable, and he'll be happy to drive you wherever you need to go."

After looking at Beijing for a few moments, from her head to her toes, Don said, "Well, that will work. I'm about to take a shower and swap out the gear I got on, and then I'll call down and let you know when I'm ready."

"Great then." She flashed her pearly whites at him. "We will be looking forward to your call."

"And I will be looking forward to you answering, then—" He lit the room up flashing a smile full of white-gold teeth at her. "—wit yo' cute self," he finished as he walked off toward the elevators.

Beijing was standing next to April pretending that she didn't see April's jaw just about bouncing off the floor. She redirected her attention to another client who had approached the desk while Don headed toward the elevator with his key in hand.

"Mr. Bitz, I have your reservation set for five PM for dinner at this fabulous restaurant that your daughters will love. I managed to get you four comp tickets for that show." Mr. Bitz had informed her earlier of his needs.

"Wow," he gleamed. "That show has been sold out for months. My girls are going to be so pleased. You are making me a real cool dad."

"I am happy to do what I can. But you must be done with dinner no later than six forty-five, because the show starts at seven fifteen and the ride over to the theater is fifteen minutes. Your tickets and backstage passes will be waiting for you at the box-office will-call window."

Mr. Bitz reached into his wallet and pulled out a few hundred-dollar bills. "For you."

"No, it's my pleasure," Beijing said.

"I insist. Those tickets were impossible to get and sold out in a matter of minutes. Months ago. How did you do it? This is going to be the first step of getting me in the good graces of my girls. Since the divorce, their mother has turned them against me, so I am trying to piece our relationship back together."

"Well, getting tickets to the concert of the hottest girl group out is going to be a good start." Beijing smiled. "There is nothing like a bond between a daughter and her father. Trust me, I know."

Beijing knew firsthand of the connection that a father could have with his daughter. She sure had a close-knit relationship with hers. He had raised her from birth, and though she was pushing thirty and had been out of his house for years, she still depended on him for those jewels of wisdom that helped her along the way.

"So, Superwoman, lucky you, your time is almost up here."

Beijing looked at her Movado watch. "You are right. Time flies when you're having fun."

"Yeah, I wish I could say the same, I have three more hours to slave."

"It's not that bad."

"It's not that good, either," April was quick to counter.

"What are you going to do when you get off work?"

"Girl, you know I'm getting out of this place. I'm going over to check out that new restaurant the Vines to see if it's going to be a place we send guests. I went over there for the grand opening but haven't been since, and I'd love to check things out now that the hype has settled down."

"I don't blame you, I wouldn't want to deal with the party, either. But the folks are not that bad."

Beijing talked to April until her time on the clock ran out, and she headed upstairs to shower and change out of her black concierge business suit into something more comfortable for dinner.

As soon as she hit the lobby, the first person she saw was Don. She could see by the look on his face that he was stunned by her transformation.

"Damn, baby, you were already looking good but goddamn you could be a man's muse for real." Her body seemed poured into her indigo blue jeans, which she topped with a teal blouse. Her long silky black hair flowed down her back, and her dark chocolate skin didn't have a blemish in the world. Her full eyes appeared to be looking right into his soul.

Beijing laughed. "Thanks, I guess I'm supposed to take that as a compliment." Then she asked, "Did you get all squared away?" Beijing looked at Don, and he, too, was looking good. It was just something about this magnetic energy that he let off.

"Naw, I didn't, dude said it would be a couple of hours before he could get here. I'm ready to get out of this hotel now, though. I'm trying to go with you."

She laughed it off. "It's against policy," she said, but thought about how nice it would have been to have him join her for dinner. After all, she was going to eat alone.

"But you off the clock and it's just dinner. Shit, you even tried to get somebody to take me around but it didn't happen. I mean, what, you got a hot date?"

"Actually my dinner date just called to say she couldn't make it."

"Well, it's an innocent date and I'm good company. Plus I'd hate to tell your boss that you left me standing on the curb."

She took a deep breath. "I guess it can't hurt anything. Come on."

As she started out of the lobby, Mr. Bitz's daughters walked quickly past her in the same direction, with him in tow. Beijing had a grin on her face thinking of how her own father would sometimes try to keep up with her. As the girls passed, they said "Thank you, Beijing," in unison.

"You are so welcome."

"Thank you, you are the best!" Mr. Bitz said to her while running after his girls. She smiled at the compliment, but the smile was quickly interrupted by April.

"Beijing, can I speak to you for a minute?" April said, tapping her on the shoulder.

Beijing turned. "Certainly." The two turned their backs away from the counter.

"While you were so busy planning dinner dates with our guests, the credit card Don's promoter put on file to pay for his expenses was declined," she said in a harsh tone, then rolled her neck in a matter-of-fact way. "So that nigga ain't got no damn money," she concluded.

But the money didn't matter when you were just lusting over him, huh? Beijing looked at April but didn't express her thoughts. *Bet your ass would have still hopped in bed with him, even if he was penniless.*

Beijing could tell that April was only throwing dirt on Don because he hadn't paid her any mind. Most of the time the guys who came into the hotel were head over heels for April. She was super sexy in a hootchie sort of way and her cat eyes seemed to hypnotize men into doing her bidding. And it didn't hurt that she threw herself at them. She might as well have had FUCK ME FOR FREE tattooed on her forehead, because that's pretty much all that ever happened. She usually got nothing but a cheap meal and maybe an entrance to one of the hot clubs. She mostly would end up with an empty pocketbook and a wet ass.

"It doesn't mean that he's broke because the promoter's card was declined. It's not his. But I will check on it, April," she assured her co-worker as she walked away.

Once she'd strolled back over to Don, he asked, "So where are we off to? I mean, it really doesn't matter to me, it's basically wherever your heart desires."

"Well, there is a new restaurant called the Vines that I was invited to a few weeks ago, and the food was so scrumptious. I would love to go back there again. Let me tell you all about it. The—"

"No need to," he said, cutting her off. "I said anywhere your heart desires."

"Okay, but it's kind of pricey."

"If you like it, I love it," he said. "There's nothing to debate."

Beijing hesitated in light of what April had just told her. But, she thought, the promoter's and Don's pockets were two different things. Besides, she was willing to go Dutch. She didn't expect him to pay for her meal. Then again, the restaurant might comp her meal, which sometimes happened because they knew she would recommend their establishment to her clients.

Beijing led Don to her parking space near the front of the hotel, where she kept her father's vintage 1979 Lincoln Continental Mark V Bill Blass Edition that he had fully and lovingly restored. It wasn't the most expensive car on the road, but it was distinctive and it could flat-out run at 120 mph and make you feel like you were floating on air.

She got behind the wheel, and Don slid into the passenger seat.

"Nice ride, baby," he said. "Damn, and you got a CD player in here?" He leaned in to figure out how to slide his CD into the player.

"Thanks. Since I blew up the engine in my car, my daddy lets me use this. I keep telling him that I'm going to get something newer but he reminds me that restoring this car was a labor of love for him. It means a lot to me, and even more to Daddy. So, I'm driving it for the time being until I do figure out what I really want."

Beijing coasted out of the parking lot and didn't say much to Don, because she was enjoying his rhymes coming from the stereo. Impressed with his skills, she bopped her head to the tracks of the two songs he chose for her to listen to. He then turned down the volume to get to know Beijing a little more.

"So, do you like working at the hotel?" Don asked.

"Yes. It's cool for now but I have dreams and aspirations bigger than this hotel."

"Like what? Being the wife of a big rap star?" he teased.

"Not even." She smiled. "I want to own a concierge business that caters only to the wealthiest and most exclusive patrons."

"Count me in as one of your clients."

"No doubt." Beijing cranked up the volume, wanting to hear

the last song over again. Don looked out the window until the track ended.

"Would you mind pulling over to that gas station?" Don said to Beijing. "I need to grab some Blacks and a pack of gum." As Beijing pulled over, he asked, "You want anything?"

"No, I'm okay. I don't want to spoil my appetite."

Two minutes later Don returned with a look of disappointment on his face. "They don't have any Blacks. Ima walk over to that other station around back. Wait here for me."

"You sure you don't want me to just pull over there?"

"Nah, I'm good. Just chill for me here."

Beijing thought it was kind of odd that Don wanted to walk, but she didn't make a big deal out of it. She used the time to run tomorrow's schedule through her head.

Nobody but the clerk was in the store when Don walked up to the gas station counter.

"Let me get a pack of Blacks and all the money you got in that register."

"W-w-what?" the attendant stammered.

Don pulled out a Glock from his waistband and calmly stated, "Don't make me repeat myself."

The attendant had only been working at the Shell station for about thirty days, and he had no intention of losing his life over someone else's paper. He reached beside the register, grabbed a plastic bag, and started filling it with money.

After the attendant handed him the bag, Don casually walked out of the store as if nothing had happened. To the common observer it looked like nothing was going on, but George wasn't common: He'd worked as a security guard at Bank of America for the past four years, and he had seen the entire transaction between Don and the store attendant from his pickup truck in the parking lot.

Don noticed the toy cop in the gray truck when he stepped out of the store, but he kept it moving all the same. When he got back to the spot where he'd left Beijing, he found it empty. The gray pickup truck was trailing closely behind him. Don picked up his phone and called Beijing.

She answered on the second ring. Don looked around and asked, "Where are you?"

"I drove down the street to the BP to get gas; that's the only brand my father uses in this baby."

"I'm coming to you. Don't move," Don said before breaking out in a jog. He noticed the pickup still trailing, and the driver on the phone. Don didn't have to be a rocket scientist to know that the Good Samaritan was talking with the police.

Don made it to the BP gas station, out of breath, and jumped in the passenger side of the Lincoln.

He hit the dashboard with the palm of his hand and demanded, "Go, go, go! Get out of here! Someone is following me!"

"What's going on?" Beijing asked, confused. "Why would someone be chasing you?"

"Long story," he said. "Right now I need you to drive." They peeled out of the BP parking lot and hopped on 85 South with the pickup on their tail. "Speed up, girl, we need to lose that damn truck, and quick," Don insisted.

Beijing was scared to death, but she pushed that car like she was trying to get a NASCAR deal. The front end of the luxury vehicle rose up and the speedometer read 130. After a while she didn't see the truck in the rearview mirror anymore, and Don told her to take the next exit.

They got off, and then got back on heading in the opposite direction. "You can slow down now, I think we're good."

"What did you do back there?" Beijing asked, still shaken.

"Somebody tried to rob me," Don lied, "and I shot the dude."

"Why didn't you call the police?"

" 'Cause I'm a convicted felon," he said. "They'll lock me up for having a gun."

Beijing had calmed down until she saw a police car parked on the side of the highway. "There's the police," she said, using her eyes and head to point them out in the mirror.

Damn, Don thought, *I'm busted.* From the far left lane they drove past the police car, careful to observe the speed limit, and to their relief the car stayed put. *My lucky day,* Don thought, *they didn't pen me.*

"There's another one," Beijing said calmly, although she was scared shitless on the inside.

Just like the first one, this one stayed put. They rode past four more cruisers and all of them did the same thing: remained at the side of the road.

About two minutes after passing the sixth cop car, Don looked in the side mirror, and what he saw made his heart drop: All six police cars were right behind them.

"Shit!" Don yelled.

Beijing was tired of being on the wrong side of this cops-and-robbers shit. "I'm going to pull over, Don."

"Just keep on driving until they hit their blue lights," Don reasoned, but inside he knew he was done.

A highway sign said that they would hit the Charlotte city limits in nine miles. Don took another look in the mirror. "I don't believe this shit."

"What?" Beijing asked.

"They gone."

Beijing didn't know what to do. On the one hand she was relieved and on the other, she was paranoid. Once she reached the city limits she pulled over and called her father. Her heart was in her panties as the phone rang. She explained to Sterling, blow by blow, everything that had transpired that night. She could hear the hurt and frustration in her father's voice when he said two words before ending the conversation: "Torch it."

CHAPTER 4

Faking the Funk

Beijing stood on top of the hill out in the boonies, watching her father's custom car go up in flames down below. She shook her head. "I don't fucking believe this shit." She dropped her head. "I can't believe it." The car was in a full blaze.

"I apologize." Don turned around to look in her big pretty eyes when he spoke. "I promise I'm going to make it up to you. I mean it." He sounded sincere, but Beijing was too pissed to even care.

"Whatever," Beijing said and put her hand up as if she wanted him to talk to the hand, not her. She wasn't in the mood for empty promises.

"I swear on everything I love that I will somehow get you a new car."

"The fucked-up shit about it is," she said, frustrated, "it isn't even my car. I keep telling you, it's my father's." Then she screamed, "Goddamnit!" and popped Don upside his head with her pocketbook like an old lady fending off a would-be thief.

Don let her take out her frustrations on him. Tears were forming in his eyes because he felt so rotten inside for his actions.

"You going to sell that chain? Surely those big-ass diamonds can bring in some cash." She poked him in the chest. "That's what you gonna do."

"Actually they ain't really worth much of nothing," Don admitted.

"Probably not as much as you paid for them, but I'm sure they are worth something."

Don dropped his head and his ego and said, "Whatever we could get for the best cubic zirconia that money could buy, and you are welcome to it."

"What?" Beijing almost broke her neck when she rolled her head to take a better look at the chain and pendant. "What did you say?"

"You know the saying: Fake it till you make it. This is the perfect example of that." He lifted up the big cross medallion. "I'm on my way up the road to stardom but I ain't there yet."

"This necklace is fake?" She spoke slowly in disbelief. Then she walked off, saying, "Come on." She almost stomped her foot, but she didn't. "Shit!"

Beijing was disgusted with him. She bit down on her lip, not knowing how to fix the situation. The sad part was, she couldn't even call her father to get his input. She didn't see the need to worry him any more with this foolishness.

"I'm going to have to pimp your ass out or something," she said, shaking her head and crossing her arms. "Sure hope you got some gold dripping from that dick of yours 'cause you might be holding a sign that says WOOD FOR SALE. 'Cause you *are* going to buy my daddy a new car. I don't give a fuck if I gotta take it out yo' ass."

From the tone in her voice Don knew she meant business. He followed Beijing around like he was her little puppy dog.

"I'm going to have to call us a cab," she told him, "since the car we arrived in is up in smoke."

The ride back in the cab was awkward. The cab's air conditioner was broken. The windows were steamed, but Beijing was cold as ice.

Once they arrived at the hotel, she didn't speak to him until the elevator opened on his floor. "Don't call me. I'll call you," she snapped.

"Beijing, I want you to know I'm really sorry."

"You sure are," she said as the elevator closed.

Hours went by and he kept calling her. She stuck her cell phone under her pillow and tried to ignore it so she could think clearly. Finally, the fifth time her cell rang again, she snatched it up and answered. "Didn't I tell you not to call me!"

"Baby?" It was her daddy on the phone.

"Oh, Daddy. I'm . . . I'm sorry. I thought you were this lame guy who keeps pestering me," she said.

"I'll kill him if he bothers you, Beijing, baby," Sterling said in his gruff voice and was dead serious about it. Her father was no joke; he had killed a dude or two back in the day when he was hustling in the streets. Though Sterling had been walking the straight and narrow for almost thirty years now, make no mistake about it, he had no problem busting a cap in anyone who fucked with his daughter.

"No need." Beijing had taken her dad's comment as a joke but had no idea that to her father it wasn't. "He's harmless except that . . ." Just then someone knocked on the door of her suite.

"Dang," she muttered. "Hang on a second, Daddy." She was glad for the interruption because she wasn't really in the mood for the lecture that she knew her dad had prepared for her. She opened the door and there stood a bellboy holding a bouquet of a dozen white roses.

"For me?"

"Yes, ma'am," the young man said. "I tried to call up, but your room line was busy."

"Yes, I have it off the hook," she explained and then stood in awe of the beautiful flowers. "Who on earth?" She looked at the card inserted among the beautiful flowers knowing good and well that broke-ass Don hadn't sent them. Or had he used his last dollar trying to make it up to her? She found the card.

> *I can't stop singing your praises!*
> *You are the best. Call me if there is anything you ever need.*
> *Definitely indebted to you!*
>
> > *Your friend,*
> > *Johnny Wiz*

Beijing tipped the man and closed the door. She had a big smile on her face as she picked up the phone.

"Daddy, are you still out of town?"

"Yes, baby. I'm on the road now. I don't get home till next Tuesday." Sterling's tone was still calm as always. That was his demeanor all the time, but Beijing knew a lecture was on its way.

"Mmm. Okay. Well, I hope you're having a nice trip."

"We still need to talk about the ordeal."

"I know. Can we talk about it when you return, because I don't want to really talk about it over the phone?"

"You are right, over dinner when I return. However, I want you to know that I spoke to Greta and she has reported the car stolen."

"Yes, Daddy." Trying to get her father off the phone, she added, "I just want you to know that I love you."

"I love you, too, baby. I gotta go now. Bye."

Beijing hung up and stuck her nose into one of the big flowers. It smelled so sweet. She realized that Johnny might solve a couple of her problems. She did not think twice about calling him.

"My lovely Beijing," he answered, "I take it you received the flowers?"

"I did. And how absolutely beautiful they are. Thank you so much, but you really didn't have to."

"No, thank you, Beijing. You spared me a lot of pain and embarrassment, and if there is anything that I can ever do, big or small, please don't ever hesitate to ask."

"Well, Johnny." She paused to get her nerve up. "There kind of is."

"Anything," he shot back quickly. "You want my firstborn named after you? You got it."

"That won't be necessary, Johnny," she said, smiling, as she continued to build up courage.

"Good, because as you know I probably won't have any." Johnny laughed for a second, loving that he could be himself with Beijing. "How about a trip to your namesake, Beijing? I hear the weather is gorgeous this time of year. Have you been there before?"

"No, I haven't."

"Do you want to go?" he asked.

"I would love to, but that's not it."

"Just know I would send you to Beijing or to the moon for that matter, if you wanted to go. Let me know when and I will let you know what time the shuttle leaves!"

"I know you would, Johnny, and I *really* appreciate you offering to do so."

"So, if I can't name my firstborn after you and you don't want to take me up on my offer to go to Beijing, the moon, or Saturn, all that's left is the shirt off my back."

"I'm good with shirts right now." She smiled again.

"Then what is it? I'm all guessed out." Johnny wasn't usually this generous, but Beijing was different. She was someone who'd helped him without expecting anything in return.

"Well"—she took a deep breath—"I feel extremely awkward asking you for this."

"I'm all ears and eager to please," he said in a reassuring voice.

"This is totally out of character for me."

"No, no . . . spit it out, or I am going to start guessing crazy things . . . like maybe you want to ask to have a threesome with my lover and myself perhaps," he joked.

"No, that's not it either." She smiled again.

"Then do tell," he demanded.

"Well, I hate to be like so many other people who ask you for things, but I won't bore you with the events surrounding why I need this favor." She took another deep breath and inhaled a little more confidence and a bit of cockiness. "And maybe after this call, you may owe me another favor because actually, I got something on my hands that I am pretty sure can bring us both some big revenue."

His silence made her continue.

"You know I'm not the one to ever BS you, and I know people are tracking you down all the time begging you to put any and everybody's momma on, but for real, Johnny, I have a rapper that's the hottest thing since the hookers out at All-Star weekend trying to make a dollar out of fifteen cents."

"Ooouch now, that's hot. When can I check him out?"

"He has some music that I can email you."

"Then what am I waiting for? You should have sent it as soon as you got it," he said.

"I really need a deal for him, Johnny," she said, putting on her damsel-in-distress voice.

"Send over the music, and if he's half of what you say, on the strength of you alone, I will do it. Not for him, but for you."

"Give me a few minutes and consider it sent," Beijing said, feeling better already.

"And let's be clear, this is your baby. If it's what you say it is, I will break you off a piece for bringing it to me."

She called Don as soon as she hung up with Johnny. "Look, bring me some music up here. I have this guy that I want to send some music to, possibly get you a deal."

"That's a good look, Beijing," he said to her excitedly. "I really appreciate anything you can do."

"I'm still mad at you for that bullshit but at the same time, if I can help you I will. Come on now, because I got this guy waiting for me to email the music to him." Within minutes, Don delivered the music.

Beijing downloaded the songs to her computer and emailed them to Johnny. It had been a super-long day and it was already after midnight, so she wasn't expecting Johnny Wiz to call back. She took a shower and dozed off to sleep, only to be awakened by Johnny. As soon as she answered the phone, there was no *hello,* no *I'm sorry for calling you so late,* no salutations at all, he only said, "How come you never mentioned to me that hidden among your many talents was a good ear for music?"

"So you like it?" she questioned, still half asleep, but quickly waking up.

"From the sound of it, he seems to have great potential and it helps that he has you on his side. He nor I can't go wrong."

"So will you give him a deal? I'm asking you to give him a nice deal because he needs to take care of something that is important for me," Beijing said.

"Why don't you understand my love and loyalty for you, Beijing?"

"I do. You are proving it now, once you say yes about this deal," she said with a light giggle to try to soften the moment up.

"I will have him flown in tomorrow to do the preliminaries." *Damn, is my luck this good that I could possibly get Don a deal just like that? So easy? Am I really that good?*

"Tomorrow he has to open up a concert here in Charlotte."

"Okay, how about Monday, he's on the first flight out of there. As a matter of fact I want you both here. I am flying you in as well."

"Thank you so much, Johnny." It was Beijing's turn to be grateful.

"He must be special to you," he said, glad to be able to repay Beijing.

"It's not like that, but he does have talent."

"Well, consider him a part of the Wizard Entertainment Group from this day forward. I got him, and I am going to play fair with him too."

"Thanks again, Johnny."

"You can thank me when he goes double platinum," Johnny said. Then he chuckled. "After all, that's what I do. I create superstars, baby."

Beijing smiled at Johnny's cockiness.

"Johnny Wiz at your service, baby. Now, is there anything else I can do to help make your life easier?"

"No, you just did it all."

"Are you sure? Going once, going twice . . ."

"Well, there kind of is, but I just didn't want to ask for too much."

"I'm in a real good mood right now, so lay it on me."

"I mean, since he's now *your* artist, I do need the Wiz's credit card number for his room at my hotel because the card number the promoter has on file was declined. I can get a nice discount rate but I can't get it for free."

"Done. Whatever it is, I will have my office take care of it."

"You are the best."

"Now, after this deal is done, we are going out to celebrate."

"Count me in, Johnny. I can't wait."

When Beijing delivered the news to Don about who she was negotiating with he almost passed out. But this was only the beginning. There were still a lot of things to iron out.

Beijing knew she had to make sure that Don had his ducks in a row when dealing with Johnny. She had heard that he was the king of fucking musicians with no Vaseline, and though Johnny was doing her a favor, and Don was anxious to make the deal happen, she knew she had to be smart.

Beijing was thumbing through her Rolodex in search of an entertainment lawyer who could go through Don's contract with a fine-tooth comb when Dennard Dunlap came to mind. He and Beijing had dated back in high school. An occasional phone call or card over the holidays had been the extent of their communication since. Between their two sets of parents, however, they had kept up with each other's whereabouts. Dennard had moved to Atlanta and become a successful lawyer. He dealt with mostly people in the music business, mixed in with an actor or two here or there.

Beijing was mildly surprised by how happy he sounded to hear from her when she called him.

"Beijing, so nice to hear from you. You know I think of you all the time."

"That's really nice." Beijing didn't know what else to say; she hadn't really given him much thought besides when she ran into his mother every now and again.

"As a matter of fact, I'm going to be in Charlotte this weekend, are you there?"

"I am, and that actually works out for me, because I would like to enlist your services for a friend of mine. He has a contract that I would love to have you look at for me."

"Of course, anything for you. Shall we chat more over dinner this Saturday then?"

"Only if you let me pay," she suggested.

"Well, we'll flip over who will cover the tab afterward."

Beijing had still had the taste of the Vines restaurant cuisine in her mouth since earlier in the week when she and Don had planned to have dinner there, but because of their detour, they'd never made it. She made up her mind that she was going to enjoy tonight to the fullest. When she brought the brand spanking new Lexus to a halt in front of the Vines, the valet sprang up from under the huge black awning toward the driver's side of the car.

"Good afternoon, ma'am," he politely greeted. "Would you be using valet parking today?"

He was a young kid who barely looked old enough to drive.

Beijing gave the young attendant a once-over. "You do have a permit, don't you?" she playfully queried, still holding tight to the keys.

The boy shot her a youthful smile. "I sure do, ma'am, I get that a lot."

"Just be careful," she said before reluctantly relinquishing the keys to the luxury sedan. Shouldering her bag, Beijing stepped toward the entrance of the restaurant.

"Welcome to the Vines," the hostess sang from behind the podium. "Do you have a reservation?"

"Yes." Beijing returned the girl's smile. "It's under Lee."

She checked the list and then led Beijing to a secluded table where her dinner companion was waiting.

Dennard got up from the table and gave her a big hug. He still looked the same: a hair over six feet tall, Mr. Goodbar–colored skin, and perfect white teeth, although he was dressed a little better than back in the day. By the way his tailor-made suit clung to his body, Beijing surmised that he couldn't have put on an ounce of weight since school.

"Good to see you, B," he said, after releasing his embrace. "You look even more gorgeous than I remember. Why," he asked with a crooked grin, "did we break up anyway?"

"It probably had something to do with all those other girls that were running behind you that you had such a problem saying no to," Beijing teased, still blushing from his compliment.

A few deep lines materialized across his forehead as if he was thinking, then he smiled again. "Oh yeah. I somehow forgot about that."

They both laughed as they sat down, shared a few stories, then ordered from the silk-clothed menus. He had the surf and turf and she had the crab salad while they shared a bottle of Merlot.

After dinner, Beijing got down to business. She opened the compact briefcase that was on the floor by her feet and removed a small stack of papers, paper-clipped together in a pink folder. "This is the contract from Johnny Wiz that I want you to check out.

"The contract is for a friend of mine," Beijing continued as he browsed through the paperwork. "As you can see, it's from the Wizard Entertainment Group. I just want to be sure everything is what it should be." She watched his brow furrow as Dennard concentrated on one of the pages.

"That Johnny Wiz can be a sneaky bastard when he chooses to be," Dennard replied after closing the folder and taking a sip of wine, "and from my personal experiences, that's more times than not. He's like the Don King of the music biz."

She laughed at his joke and said, "That's why I wanted you to check it out." She leaned a little closer and lowered her voice. "My friend has so many people trying to get in his pocket, I wanted to bring this to someone I know I can trust."

"I'll be sure to take a good look at it," he assured her, tapping the document with his fingertips. "Let me hold on to it for the weekend, and I'll send it back Monday with any changes I deem pertinent. Okay?"

"Perfect."

"Good, now how about another bottle of wine?"

"If I didn't know better, Dennard, I might think you were trying to get me intoxicated." Beijing chuckled softly.

"That's what first attracted me to you, B. You almost always know better, but on those occasions when you see fit, you're not afraid to throw caution out the window."

"And I always thought you were just head over heels in love with my body," she said with a smile that was brighter than the four-foot chandelier hanging above the table.

With the help of Dennard and because Beijing had Johnny by the balls, she was able to get Don an advance on his advance. They picked up the sizable check from Johnny's Atlanta office.

"You are so damn lucky," Beijing said as they left the office and got into her rental car.

"And now this. The day I met you, girl: that was my lucky day."

"You got that right," Beijing said. *I wish I could say the same,* she thought to herself.

CHAPTER 5

The Boss Bitch

"Sit tight, Don," Beijing said before hopping out of the Lexus, "I'm going to go in and make sure this dude got the bread."

"You sure you don't need me to go with you?"

"Naw." She shook her head. "I got this." She reassured Don she had the situation under control and had all the backup she needed as she put her white pearl-handled .22-caliber in her bag.

"Aight, gangsta boo. If you ain't back in ten minutes, I'm coming in."

"You better not." She shot him a look and reminded him, "You are the talent."

Don watched with an admiring eye as she sashayed into the back door of the Atlanta strip club to handle their business with the owner. Beijing had earned Don's love and his trust. In his eyes, having her in his corner made him a privileged man.

It had been a little over nine months since Beijing had come into Don's life, and she had been a godsend. He had no idea what he did to deserve such an angel on his side. There was no doubt, he was a lucky man. Not only was she drop-dead gorgeous, but she had turned his life around. She had skyrocketed his career, taking his fame, bank account, net worth, and heart off to unimagined heights. It seemed that she waved a wand and damn near fixed every situation in his life—all *except* for one demon, which was beginning to spiral out of control.

What had started out as recreational weekend use of "heron" had now turned into a major habit. The truth was that habit had been in his life long before Beijing ever entered into his world. His addiction went back years, to a time when he was in his mother's basement with Kim, his then girlfriend of three weeks.

Things were getting kind of hot and steamy and he said to Kim, "Let's get our freak on." Don was rubbing his hands together smiling like a thief in an empty jewelry store. "My mother ain't going to be home until eleven."

"Shit, you ain't going to last no more than fifty seconds," Kim declared. "That shit was kind of cool at first because I know my pussy be the bombastic, but you can leave that quick-draw-and-shoot shit to Billy the Kid and the rest of dem cowboys."

That hurt Don's feelings. He was busy picking up his ego off the floor when he noticed that Kim had pulled a ten-dollar bill from her pocketbook and carefully unfolded it.

"What the fuck is that?" Don asked trying to forget about the attack Kim had just made against his manhood.

"Magic powder." She smiled before scooping a little of the powder off the bill with her fingernail. Kim lifted her nail to her nose to inhale. "This is exactly what you need to keep yo' shit hard. That is . . . if you really want to keep fucking this good pussy?"

Ever since that day not only was Don's nose wide open for what was between Kim's legs, it was open for the magic powder as well. The funny part was that after a month and a half, Kim was out of his life but the heroin wasn't. Though he just about broke his neck to keep the drugs under wraps, since his newfound stardom, the money and the ready availability of the drug caused his use to escalate. He could never share all of the details of his drug use with Beijing. Most of the time he stayed in denial about it, but Beijing wasn't slow. She knew what was going on with him. She constantly reminded him of the rehab programs that she had researched for him, and he knew that it would make her happy if he pulled it together. He wanted to do whatever he could to make her happy, but something about that dope had a greater hold on him.

Don saw Beijing making her way back over to the car. "So, I got the dough, and Wild-Bill said he's only two minutes away."

He motioned for Beijing to look. "There he is."

Beijing redirected her attention to Bill. "You are late. I'm docking your pay." She wasn't intimidated by the big, burly darkskinned licensed security guy. "It doesn't make any sense, all those people in there and the people in the front of the club and I got the world's hottest rapper out in the car, with no hired protection."

"Sorry, I had to stop and get something to eat."

"Nigga . . ." She playfully bopped him upside the head, and then said in a firm tone, "The next time you show up late and have me waiting on you, you are not going to have a job and you can take that to the bank."

"B, I apologize."

"Yeah, aight, but I still mean what I say." Then she turned back to Don and said, "They got a lil dressing room for you to chill in until it's time for you to go on. So, let's go in."

"Aight baby, you da boss." Don smiled because it turned him on how Beijing handled her business with him on the front line and behind the bedroom door as well.

They entered through the back door of the club, and Beijing led them past the half-naked women running to their workstations. Before going to iron out details with the DJ, Beijing got Don settled in the back room, which had dancers' outfits and shoes piled in a corner. Don couldn't really enjoy his spliff from shooing off the strippers wanting to get to know him better, get his autograph or number, or give him some head. They had swarmed around him like gravy on a biscuit.

He calmly and kindly rejected all the half-dressed women. "Baby, it ain't that type of party. I got a girl, I'm cool," he said in between pulling on the blunt.

"Damn, leave the nigga alone. I swear, y'all bitches got a club full of paying motherfuckers, let the man finish his blunt so he can help us all get dis paper. Plus he don't want no stinky, drunk Ecstasy-taking broads, no way," one girl said.

The other girls sucked their teeth at her outspoken comment while Don gave the dazzling beauty a smile and said, "Good looking."

"I dance before you go on," she said. She was dressed in all-blue patent leather. She had on a thong and a bra that looked like a turtleneck with a bunch of splits in it. "Since I'm the feature dancer and rake in the most money here," she boasted, "they want me to open up for you."

"That's what's up," he said not really caring one way or the other. He was zoned out in his own world.

"This is actually my dressing room that you're using."

"Sorry for the inconvenience," he said, "but I 'preciate the courtesy all the same, ya heard." The headline stripper left to finish getting ready to do her set about five minutes before Beijing came in.

"Coming to the stage is the dazzling Dazzle," they heard the DJ call over the speaker.

"Aight," Beijing told Don. "Showtime after the next song." He blew his smoke in the other direction, away from Beijing.

"Cool, baby."

He put out the blunt, stood up, and followed Beijing. Bill was on both their heels as she led him to a spot on the side of the stage where he could see the crowd without being spotted. He and Beijing both watched Dazzle perform. She was five foot eight with perfect skin a shade softer than a chocolate Yoohoo. Her blue contact lenses and blue eye makeup sparkled under the ideal condition of light. Proportioned at 36-26-44, her body could drive some men to commit acts they otherwise wouldn't dream of. Some said she was a gift from a higher power, perhaps stripper heaven.

Dazzle contorted her thickness into all types of erotic poses. Her flexibility was amazing. The crowd was loving it. "Damn." Both Beijing and Don looked at each other in amazement.

Don had a group of horny, sexy, seductive girls preparing to get naked surrounding him crammed into the small space on the side of the platform. Not only the blunt he had smoked but the bass in the song that the DJ was fading into the end of Dazzle's song had him feeling intoxicated.

Beijing handed Don the microphone, and he took the stage. Don knew that in a strip club if a person didn't have a fat ass on that stage, they weren't going to get any respect. Within five seconds of touching the stage, the DJ used the instrumental of a bass heavy beat to momentarily jolt the crowd to life, forcing the attention of every single person to the stage. Don nodded a couple of times and began to spit with a flow that was a hybrid of Young Jeezy and Jay Z. Don eyed Beijing for approval. She gave him thumbs-up and a reassuring nod—and he ripped the club apart. Every table in the place was empty. All the people in the club were on their feet dancing while a small band of female strippers had surrounded the club for "the take-over," forcing the fellas to make it rain on them with money. But by the time Don was finished with his performance, he had the club patrons making it thunderstorm with cash.

As soon as he was off the stage, he had a one-track mind. Don was trying to take a sniff of the powder he had creased in a crisp Franklin before Beijing showed up. He was greeted by Dazzle.

"You rocked dat shit," she said, putting her paper bag full of money into her locker and securing the lock.

"You did yo' thing too, boo," he replied, trying to get rid of her so he could take his edge off.

"I know. Told you I was the best one around these parts. I think I'll make a nice accessory to your stage performance," she boldly stated. "Maybe a few videos . . . I can put together a fresh routine for all of your songs. What do you say?" she asked.

"You gotta talk to my baby, Beijing. She's not only my wifey, but she's the boss too."

"I'm going to find your boss lady right now."

"And shut the door on your way out."

By the end of the night, the girls might have flocked to throw pussy at him like a feline giveaway at the ESPA, but Don wasn't fazed by any of it. Beijing was his queen, and there was no girl on earth that could fuck with her. But there was a boy running a close second, that went by the name of Heron.

Don took a sniff of the magic powder, and fell deep into a dope fiend nod.

CHAPTER 6

The Burning Bed

Over the next few weeks Don was swamped with all kinds of paid gigs. When he wasn't performing he devoted the rest of his time to putting in work at the studio. Finally Beijing and Don had arranged for a quiet night in to enjoy each other's company and watch the premiere of Don's new video.

"Is there anything else you need before I leave, baby?" Beijing yelled to Don as she wrapped her scarf around her neck and put the strap of her Gucci pocketbook on her shoulder. She was going to get some takeout, maybe some Chinese, and then come back and cuddle up in her boo's arms, and together they would watch the video. She could not believe the way things had happened for them. He had blown up overnight, he was on everybody who was anybody's remix, his single was number one on the charts, and now his video was about to premiere . . . and the checks were rolling like cars to the drive-thru at McDonald's. Damn, life was good.

"Baby?" she called out to him again. After he didn't respond the second time, Beijing walked back into the bedroom to see what was consuming so much of his attention that he couldn't answer her. *Probably has the volume on the TV turned up too loud,* she thought, but after entering the bedroom and laying eyes on him, Beijing shook her head in disappointment.

With the aid of about half a dozen pillows, Don was propped up in the middle of the queen-sized cherrywood bed. His arms were folded and ankles crossed. His head angled forward, bobbing on its skinny neck. Don's eyes were closed and a lit cigarette dangled from his full black lips. To a person who didn't know any better, he appeared to have dozed off, but over the past couple of months Beijing had learned a lot from observing Don, and boy did she know better.

Minus the cigarette with the inch-long ash on its tip, she had seen it all too many times before. Don was nodding off once again, and it damn near broke her heart.

Beijing pinched the cigarette from his mouth; before she could make it to the ashtray on the nightstand, some of the ashes barely missed the end of the bed on their way to the tan-carpeted floor.

"Don," she said, shaking him. "Wake up, Don, wake up. Honey, wake up." She tapped him roughly, several times before getting any type of response.

When his eyes popped open, they were red and glassy. The pupils were tiny pins. "I'm not asleep, baby, I'm just watching the tube," he said and pointed to the television.

"Look, man, you got to stop this bullshit." She leaned over on the bed to look him in his face. "That shit isn't healthy, safe, or sexy for that matter."

"You overreacting, I'm just a little tired—that's it, that's all," he repeated. "Thought you were going to da sto'."

He didn't want to get into that *other* conversation with her because it always started an argument. They saw it two entirely different ways. With her it was simply "Say no to drugs"—that was it, that was all, no ifs, ands, buts, or supposes about it. And in his eyes, everybody in the entertainment business got high off something, one thing or another—at least all the people in his circle did. Everybody that is . . . besides her.

Beijing despised drugs with a passion. She had seen firsthand what drugs could do to someone. In her eyes, drugs made people lie, steal, cheat, kill, sell themselves and the ones they loved. Her sister was still lost in the eye of the drug storm, and Beijing wasn't going to get sucked into it, in no way, shape, or form.

She sucked her teeth at his lame excuse but left it alone for now. "I am, that's why I was calling you. Do you want me to bring you anything specific back?"

"Naw, I'm cool." Don grinned. "What time is it?"

Beijing glanced at her Movado watch. "It's six fifteen."

"Dat late already?" He didn't give her a chance to respond. "Then you better hurry up and get back so we can watch the video together. Girl, you know how much we worked to make this shit happen." Johnny Wiz had made good on his word in the nine or ten months since Beijing had asked for his help. He had made Don a superstar who was on his way to becoming a megastar, just as he'd promised. Beijing played a major role in every step of the way, as Don's assistant, publicist, stylist, manager, and every other hat he needed her to wear. Somewhere along the journey to stardom, she had fallen for Don. He was talented, sexy, and treated her like a goddess—that is, until the dope started getting in the way. She had been hoping and praying it was just a temporary phase.

"I'm not going to miss it," she assured him. "I'll be back well before seven thirty."

Don looked into Beijing's eyes, then pulled her down to the bed. "Come here, my sweetness." He took her into his arms and gave her a huge hug. "And I'll be waiting for you with open arms when you return," he said in that cool way he had of speaking. Then he broke the spell of the sweet moment and started channel-surfing with the remote control in his hand, his eyes riveted on the television.

"Oh, umm, if dat nigga Deuce, ummm, don't hurry up and show, I might need you to stop off somewhere and pick me up a lil some to hold me over till he get here," he said casually.

"No you didn't! ARE YOU FUCKING CRAZY?" Beijing screamed at the top of her lungs. "I ain't no fucking drug-runner, nor mule, no trafficker, and I damn sure ain't no damn drug transporter, Don." She couldn't believe that he had the audacity to ask her to pick up a package of drugs for him. "Oh, I know good and well your ass is high as gas, asking me some shit like that."

Without giving him time to say another word Beijing was on her heels and out the door. Don was on the doorstep, saying something as she was about to back away in her Lexus. She rolled down her window to see what he wanted.

"Don't be late either, because you always late. Beijing, I really need you to be on time," he pleaded.

"I will be."

On her way home from the restaurant, her phone rang.

"Hello?"

"Hello, Beijing. This is Dazzle, the dancer you met at the strip club."

"Oh yeah, how are you?" She remembered the woman, who had a body like a superhero.

"I'm fine. Is this a good time?" Dazzle asked.

"I can spare a couple of minutes for you." Beijing knew that Dazzle was following up with her to see about performing on the road with Don.

"Well, I won't take up a lot of your time. I've heard of you and saw how you operated that night I met you and I would love for you to manage me."

Beijing was shocked. "I really don't know much about the adult entertainment business."

"You seem to know business, and it's clear you know entertainment. I think you could do something to help me get us some money."

"I don't know." Beijing was baffled.

"Look, you just need to think about it. I got a lot of talent," she confidently said. Then she whispered as if someone was listening in on their conversation, "Look, I'm not in denial, I don't have much education and I need money. I'm not going to front like I dance to put myself through school or the baby needs shoes—nope, none of that. I dance because I like nice shit and you need money to get it. I'm not ashamed to say that my only assets are that I got a pretty face and a drop-dead body. And the bottom line is I will use what I got to get what I want."

"I hear you," Beijing said, after the brazen confession, "and I could respect you knowing what you want." She didn't agree with Dazzle's thoughts about herself, but she drew the conclusion *To each her own.*

"There are a lot of pimps in this industry," Dazzle broke the temporary silence. "I am looking for someone who could point me in the right direction and not exploit me while doing it. I believe that person is you."

"Why do you think I'm the person for you?"

"People talk. I've done my research, and I saw firsthand how you handled Teflon the Don's BI."

Beijing didn't know what to say, but she did know pussy was power and she could see with her own eyes that being in the right place at the right time could generate a nice piece of change. Beijing didn't overlook the fact that Dazzle's tricks and treats might come in handy to her one day.

Before Beijing could speak, Dazzle said, "Look, before you say no, just think about it and keep me in mind. After all, you are *the* concierge to the rich and famous and the go-to person for a lot of things for a lot of people. So put me on your roster of things you may need to produce."

Beijing felt odd, but she agreed. "I will definitely keep you in mind if anything arises."

After they agreed to stay in touch and ended the odd call, Beijing looked down at the dash for the time

"Okay. Thanks again for thinking of me," Beijing said in a mystified tone.

The digital clock in the car glowed 7:03. Time was slipping through Beijing's fingers.

As if it had a mind of its own, her right foot pressed down on the accelerator a little harder. She was about to make a right off Lennox when her cell phone rang. The Lexus rounded the corner with ease as she pulled up in front of the building.

Beijing's bladder was begging to be relieved. She jumped out, slamming the car door with one hand and clutching two bags of Chinese food in the other, rushing to the condo. She put her key in the front door lock, walked in, and immediately realized that something just wasn't right. She sniffed the air.

Smoke . . . and when there was smoke, there was always fire!

Beijing dropped the Chinese food, not caring the least bit where it landed, and rushed down the hall toward the bedroom where the foul odor seemed to be lurking from. The freshly buffed hardwood floors caused her to lose her balance and slip.

Bam! She hit the floor hard. Face-first.

"Shit!" she screamed.

As she rose quickly, her balance was off, causing her to twist her ankle and break the heel on one of her new to-die-for Giuseppe Zanotti shoes in the process. Her ankle throbbed as she held on to the wall.

At first she thought the wastebasket was responsible for the stench. Then she looked and realized that it was the comforter on the side of the bed closest to the wall.

"Oh my God!" she yelled, but neither her high-pitched scream nor the fire disturbed the slumbering Don. "Don! Don! Don!" she called out to him, but he was oblivious. *I will deal with this motherfucker later,* she thought. First she had to deal with the emergency at hand.

She needed to get the fire out before it spread to other parts of the house. There was no time to try to locate a fire extinguisher, but thank God there was a vase filled with roses on a table next to the television. Beijing grabbed the vase, throwing the flowers to the side as she hopped over to the trash can. She emptied some of the water from the vase on the small fire and then got more water from the sink, along with a towel, to extinguish the rest of the fire on the comforter.

After conquering the potentially disasterous situation at hand, a tightening in her bladder reminded her about the other emergency that had her racing into the house in the first place. Just as she started running like a track star toward the bathroom, knocking down any- and everything in her path, her body chose not to cooperate. She could not control her bladder anymore.

She screamed in momentary defeat, "Fuck me! Will you just fuck me all over please! This is some damn bullshit." She peeled off her soaking-wet panties along with the rest of her clothes and got some clean towels from under the sink, where she noticed the fire extinguisher box sitting all the way in the back. She took one of the towels and wiped up the mess she'd made, then placed one on the edge of the tub for when she got out of the shower and the other on the sink for just in case. The entire time she lathered up and rinsed off under the hot water pellets shooting from the showerhead, with tears in her eyes she cursed Don out.

All of it was his fault: the condo almost burning down, her breaking her heel of the shoes that she just had to have—and only got to wear one time, the food landing all over the place, her urinating on herself and on the floor . . . hell, in her mind the list could go on forever.

Beijing stepped out of the shower feeling better than she had before she got in, but not a lot better. At least her ankle didn't seem to be damaged too bad; it just hurt like hell. She reached for the lavender-scented baby oil, squirted a substantial amount on her washcloth, and began to use it to dry off and moisturize her body at the same time. The water magically vanished, and in its place a beautiful sheen appeared, causing her chocolate-brown skin to radiate with what appeared to be an inner glow.

Don walked past her as she left the bathroom to go into the bedroom and get dressed. "What happened to the damn food, baby? Shit's everywhere."

Before she could respond, Don had softly shut the bathroom door behind him. "We got two minutes before the video jumps off."

"Don, are you even concerned that you almost burned the house down?"

He ignored her and didn't say a word. She decided she'd approach him when he came out of the bathroom.

After sliding on a pair of Seven jeans and a camel-colored shirt that was the same color as the stitching in the jeans, she went to brush her hair in the bathroom, but the door was locked.

She banged on it and then screamed, "Why'd you lock the door? Open the door, Don." She tried banging again, but there was no response. So she kicked the door. As she waited, she caught a glimpse of the smoke detector on the ceiling in the hall.

"You took the fucking batteries out of the smoke detector, Don?" she asked.

She could hear him inhaling what she knew was *that shit* up his nose.

"You need to stop that shit!" Beijing screamed from her side of the door.

"Don't want to stop" were the words that came from the other side. After two or three more snorting sounds, he shouted, "You should try some of this here shit"—another sniff—"you know you like its benefits."

He had to be talking out of his ass. She sighed. "What benefits?" she asked. "That shit don't even work for you no more. For real," she shot back at him, wanting to bruise his ego.

"Don't be modest. You ain't that modest when I be putting the wood down on you for hours at a time. You know you like the perks of the dope dick."

"I just can't believe you are addicted to that shit. That shit is disgusting and it makes you look bad. Dude, you ain't even aware of your surroundings."

"One thing for certain," Don reasoned, "you may be on the other side of the fence one day."

"Don't hold your breath," she shouted and went into the bedroom to gather some of her things up, throwing everything that would fit into her overnight bag.

"Yes, you will." He took another sniff. "You gonna need something to lean on one day. Believe that shit! Everybody needs something to escape at times."

"You got me mixed up with one of dem hoes or one of your groupies!" She was going to start in on him, but she realized that the only important thing was getting him help before he really hurt himself. "Real talk, Don, you really need to go to rehab!"

"I'll wait until the day come when we can go together," he sarcastically said to her.

Beijing was so pissed off, she stormed out of the house without even realizing that she'd forgotten her purse. The car door was unlocked so she put her bags in before returning to the house. When she stormed back in to get her Gucci bag, she saw that the bathroom door was now slightly ajar. She couldn't resist peeping through the opening.

"I can't believe this shit," she murmured.

Don was still in the bathroom sitting on the toilet, pants all the way to his ankles, but what she couldn't believe—or didn't want to believe—was that he was sitting on the porcelain throne with yet another lit Newport stuck in his mouth, and he was semiconscious at best. Somewhere in his mind he was wrestling with the heroin, and the drug must have been winning. The drug must have finally pinned him down to the proverbial mat because—*Bam*—a loud noise arose when he fell off his throne, passed out.

Beijing rushed in and put out the cigarette from his mouth for the second time that day. "This shit is fucking over. You can kill yourself on your time, but not on my fucking watch." She *knew* he was in no condition to understand but she had to get it off her chest. "I'm done, finished, out of here. I refuse to let you take me down that road with you—willingly or unwillingly. Audi 5000!"

Beijing took one last look at the man she thought could possibly have been the man of her life before making her final decision.

She recited the words at the top of her lungs as she wrote them out in her mocha lipstick on the mirror: *Good-bye, Don. Holla back when you get to rehab!*

Then she walked not only out of the room but out of the house and out of his life.

Don called Beijing later on that same night, but she didn't want to hear any of his lame excuses. After answering her phone, she screamed, "Don't fucking call me back until you carry your junkie ass to rehab."

CHAPTER 7

You Are Fired

Beijing missed the hell out of Don. It had been two weeks, three days, and four hours since she left him OD'd on the bathroom floor. When he wasn't high, Don was one of the most fun and loving people she had ever been around. Before the breakup, he would call her from six to sixty-six times a day to keep her up on his every move as well as tell her all the breaking news around the world. But Beijing knew that she did not want to get caught up in his madness. She thought about what the old folks would always say: *The best cure for the ex is the next!*

Beijing had to do something to get her phone ringing again and get her mind off Don or she would drive herself crazy.

"Girl, why you so quiet," her girlfriend Rayna asked Beijing over the phone. They had been friends for a little over two years and talked about everything and everybody.

Rayna and Beijing met at self-defense class. Beijing's father had convinced her that the class would be a good way for her to learn to protect herself since she was traveling around the country by herself. Rayna was there trying to shed both a few pounds and her frustrations.

The cardio that the instructor put the class through was such an intensive workout that it kept Beijing's body in tip-top shape. However, Rayna was a different story. Rayna was a brown-skinned girl who rocked a short Halle Berry haircut, and though she appeared to be very confident and have it all together, the truth was that she was obsessed with losing weight and had tried anything and everything from B_{12} shots to Slim-Fast, Fen-Phen, and any and every other kind of diet and diet pills. Rayna had even gotten liposuction a couple of times, and while the results were fabulous it didn't fix her issue. Her problem was that she loved good greasy food, and especially junk food, and would eat it in excess, knowing that it was bad for her health and her waistline.

"No reason." Beijing lied as she used her shoulder to hold the cordless phone while she opened up the curtains in her hotel room, which she had made her home, to let some sun into both her suite at the Tabby and her life.

"Tell that nonsense to somebody that don't know any better," Rayna shot back.

Beijing admired the Charlotte skyline through the window. "You think you know me so well." She smiled as she quickly became bored with the view, picking up her cell phone off the nightstand. Beijing pushed the button that brought up her contacts while she listened to Rayna invade her business.

"I do—" Rayna paused. "—too well. You thinking about that damn Don, huh?"

"Nope, actually I'm trying to find someone to get my mind off Don."

"What about Larry Love?"

"Hell naw." Beijing sucked her teeth and twisted her face up like a foul odor had assaulted her nostrils. "Now, how does that sound? If I am trying to get my mind off a damn near double-platinum rapper, why would you think a wannabe rapper would be a sufficient substitute?"

"You right." Rayna chuckled at herself. "Especially one that has never done as much as a high school talent show." They both laughed.

Beijing continued to scroll through her contacts list, and she wasn't coming up with anything.

"Girl," Rayna said, breaking the silence, "I know somebody you should call."

"Who?" Beijing asked, not quite enthusiastic, since Rayna wasn't the best at relationships herself. Her baby's father had dragged her through the mud and back again. They had a dysfunctional relationship that centered on money. They hustled together by all means necessary: ride or die, hook or crook, lie, cheat, beg, borrow, or steal. If it could get got, then it was good as gone as far as those two were concerned. When the relationship was good, it was very good, and they were Bonnie and Clyde at their best. But when it was bad it was the War of the Roses. Though Beijing didn't know all the details of Rayna and York's relationship, she knew that it was tumultuous.

"The dude from the fight," Rayna added. "Tell me you still got his number."

"What guy?"

"The guy who had you all googley-eyed when he tried to put his mack down on you at the fight."

Beijing laughed out loud. She would have been lying if she said she hadn't felt the attraction when the guy spoke to her. But the truth was that it was a really great idea, and Beijing knew that she had his number buried in her wallet somewhere.

"Girl, I'm serious, if York didn't have me under ball and chain, I would have tackled his ass. Promise me you are going to at least call him."

"It's been a long time since that fight, though, almost a year. He probably don't even remember."

"Trust me, girl, the way he was eyeing you, you are tattooed on that dude's brain. And if he has amnesia, you make him remember."

Still a little unsure, Beijing said, "I hear you but still, I don't know about this."

"Gurl, just call him. I know he will remember," Rayna assured her friend. "I am not saying that you have to marry him or anything. I'm saying that he's someone to get your mind off what's-his-name." She promised Rayna that she would.

Beijing felt reluctant about calling Lootchee. As she stood looking out the window, sipping on a glass of wine, her phone rang.

"Good afternoon."

"Yes, my name is Macy-Rae and I am calling on behalf of Mr. Teflon the Don."

"Yes, is everything all right?" Beijing asked, concerned. She thought that this might be someone calling from a drug treatment program.

"Yes everything is fine. In fact, it's wonderful, marvelous, and life couldn't be better for him or me."

"Oh great, I'm so happy for him." She wasn't sure what the woman was talking about and paused as she thought about the last time she'd seen Don.

"Ain't no need for all the small talk; we ain't friends nor am I interested in trying to be your friend," Macy-Rae said, cutting through all the pleasantries. "I just need to figure out how I can meet up with you or give you an address so I can get all of his paperwork and personal documents from you since he don't fuck with *you* anymore."

Beijing was stunned at the angry woman on the other end of the phone. For a split second she was tougue-tied, and Macy-Rae knew it too. Before Beijing could respond, Macy-Rae added, "Yeah, we thank you and appreciate you for the deal and all, but it is what it is. You are old news and I'm the headline in Don's life."

Beijing had no idea why this chick felt it necessary to call her talking smack, but she did know that she wasn't in the mood for it. "I'd rather be old news than an old ho any day," she shot back.

"Bitch, you don't understand who the hell you fucking with. While you calling me a ho, I'll whip your mother . . . fucking ass," Macy-Rae screamed into the phone.

"Are you serious?" Beijing laughed.

"Dead-ass serious, bitch! Keep playing with me. I'll beat you down and then drag yo' ass like a mop."

"Now, that is funny. I'd like to see that day." Beijing was roaring in laughter. "Hell, I'll pay to see that day," she taunted.

Most of the time Beijing could find humor in everything, but not this day. After dealing with her psychotic mother her entire life and her crackhead sister's bullshit for many years, dealing with very high-strung, demanding clients was a breeze—that's what made her so good at her job. And the times she felt like things were too out in left field—crazier than normal—she would just try to laugh it off.

"You better watch yo' back," Macy-Rae warned.

"Look here, Ms. Whatever-the-fuck-your-name-is. I'm a busy lady and I don't have the time or inclination to play with little girls who swallow cum for a living." Beijing had had enough of the foolishness. "So until you get that dick out of yo' mouth and talk like someone with some sense . . . take Michael Jackson's advice and beat it, bitch!" And then Beijing ended the call.

After that heated discussion, Beijing was ready to call Lootchoo. She hesitated, holding the phone in her hand for several seconds. Then it rang again, from a 215 number she didn't recognize. Philly, she thought to herself. She answered, "Hello."

"By the way, bitch, Don said that yo' ass is F-I-R-E-D! Your services are no longer needed, beyotch!"

"Yes, honey, but I still get paid my fifteen percent, that's indefinite, baby girl. So you enjoy working for free while I reap the benefits, boo." Beijing hit END on her cell phone. That was enough motivation to finally make her put in the call to Lootchee.

CHAPTER 8

The Pimp Hand

Roy was six foot two, light-skinned, with wavy black hair. Though he lived a life of luxury, he'd never worked a real job a day in his life. And the only thing smoother than his baby-bottom-soft hands was his rap. He was a true ladies' man, and he made sure that they paid to play—usually big bucks, no whammies.

Roy had met Gia a little over six months ago, and surprisingly he hadn't been with anyone else since he'd bagged her. Why would he? Gia was everything he needed in a girl. At twenty-five she had her own beauty salon, her beauty and body were off the chain, and she had a rich brother who adored her and gave her anything that her heart desired. If she thought it, her brother bought it, which was even better for him, because after the brother gave her everything there was only one thing left to give her: wood.

From time to time Gia would get straight disrespectful out of her mouth, but that was nothing Roy couldn't deal with. In fact most of the time her quick wit and sharp tongue were kind of cute, but on the rare occasion that Gia did pluck his last nerve, he quickly shut her down with a slap or two. In his eyes it was nothing that she didn't have coming. Afterward he would sex her down real good—not forgetting to lick her clit a little longer than usual while telling her how sorry he was for having to hit her. "You know you brought that shit on yourself," he'd tell her. Not counting the beat-down he gave her last night, he only had to put his pimp hand down twice, so things couldn't be better for him. Roy had been in Gia's ear for months to persuade her to convince her brother to put him down. Roy wasn't sure what her big brother was into but he knew that it was something heavy—and that bro had money out the ying-yang. Just judging by the money he gave Gia, it seemed like his bank account was big enough to choke a horse.

Roy was leaning against the breakfast bar in the kitchen of Gia's condo eating a bagel when Gia's brother rolled up outside to give her a Gucci bag that he had bought hot off a booster coming straight out of Saks. He walked over to the window and saw them talking. Shortly afterward, Gia brought her new gift inside the house and went back out for work.

A few minutes later, the phone on the wall rang. Roy knew it was going to be his lucky day when he heard it was her brother on the other end. "You busy?" Bro asked when Roy picked up. "I got some'em I want to holla at you about . . . that is, if you like money."

"Naw, man, I ain't never too busy to holla at family," Roy replied, smiling like a cat in a room full of birds.

"Bet, it's eleven now. I'll meet you at Sis's house about one."

True to his word, there Bro was.

"So, what was it you wanted to talk to me about, bro?" Roy said, barely able to hide his excitement.

Not wasting any time, Gia's brother said, "I want to show you this." He reached in his waistband and began to pull something out.

The nine-inch barrel of the .41 snaked out of his pants like a steel cobra. When the mouth was finally released it reared down in an arcing motion, hitting Roy across the left side of his temple. *Whop.*

Roy grabbed his face with both hands, collapsing to the hardwood floor like the little bitch he was. Instead of being thankful for being smacked and not getting a cap busted in his ass, he attempted to ask, "Why you hit—"

Before he could get the words out he felt size-twelve Timberland boots do a B&E to his mouth. The impact was so great it knocked out two of his front teeth, sending them flying across the floor like a pair of dice in search of a point. The next time the boot visited his face, it broke his jaw.

"I don't like men who pick on women! The next time you stupid enough to put yo' hands on my sister, you won't be this lucky, ma'fucka! Ya heard me?" Another foot to the stomach came with those words. "I said did you hear me?" Bro asked.

Balled up in a fetal position, with blood and tears pouring from his face and mouth, Roy said "Yes" in between sobs.

"Yeah! What? Motherfucka!"

"Yes," he sniffled, "Lootchee"—his lips were trembling—"I heard you."

Lootchee was walking out of the condo, hoping that he didn't have to kill that fool Roy next time.

His phone rang and he picked it up. "Yeah," he answered as he got in his car. No sign in his voice that he had just pistol-whipped a man a minute ago.

"Hello, can I speak to Lootchee please?" Beijing said in her sexiest voice.

CHAPTER 9

Pissing Razors

"This is Beijing. You met me a while back at the fight in Vegas," she added.

Lootchee was silent for a minute, so Beijing continued. "I'm sorry to call like this and I know you probably met so many girls that weekend."

"Ahhh, yeah . . . ," he said hesitantly. He smiled as he thought about all the exotic beauties he'd met that weekend.

"It seems like you're trying to place me. Give me your email address and I'll send you a picture to help you out."

"Is this your number?" he abruptly asked when he saw a police car driving past him going in the direction of Gia's house.

"All day, every day."

"Bet. I'ma going to call you right back in a short."

"Okay. No problem." The conversation was over as quickly as it began. *Damn, that was fast,* she thought to herself.

After an hour had passed and Lootchee had not called back,

rejection began to set in. Beijing dialed Rayna back and explained what happened.

"Girl, he gonna call you back. Did you tell him that you were the girl he called a knockout?"

"I didn't get a chance to."

"Well, you should've."

"Rayna, listen to me. The dude had me off the phone damn near before I could remember what number I dialed."

"The nigga was probably in the middle of someting like counting money." Rayna was trying to make light of the situation. "Look, just give him a while. He will call." Rayna was just as excited as Beijing was, anticipating the phone call. She assured Beijing that Lootchee was a busy man. "He'll call."

Beijing's phone rang about an hour later, just as Rayna had predicted. It was him.

"I apologize for not being able to call back sooner but something came up that needed my immediate attention," Lootchee said. He wasn't lying. He had to run out and buy a laptop and have someone create an email account for him. He didn't want Beijing to know that he not only didn't use a computer, but he barely knew how. That's the type of guy Lootchee was, it was just too hard for him to say that he didn't have email.

"Here's my email address," he said before reading it from a piece of paper.

"That's not a problem," Beijing said, like she hadn't been the least bit worried that he wouldn't call back. "I'm sending the pictures now. My hair was different when I met you, though," she lied.

"I'm sure you are a looker, no matter how you dip your hair," he flirted.

She could hear the smile in his voice and reminisced back to the first time they had met in Vegas. She had to admit that the man had game.

"Peace this, ma, I'm still not done with the matter that came up, but I truly apologize. I'm going to call you back the minute I'm free," he said before adding, "and can I share a secret with you? I don't need a picture or video to remember the fight or the knock-out," he said before ending the conversation.

Before she could put her phone back onto the charger, her work cell rang.

"Hello, this is Beijing."

"Beijing, this is Peter Bitz. A while back, I stayed at the Tabby in Charlotte and you took great care of me."

"Yes—yes, of course. How are you, Mr. Bitz?" Beijing said through her earpiece as she looked in her Franklin Covey planner to see if he was due to come back to visit.

"You took such great care of my girls and me when I was there and you seem to be a resourceful young lady. I don't know if you moonlight or not but I could make it worth your while, if you could get the Carowinds Amusement Park to open up for my girls and me. They want to go, and the last day of the season was yester-day."

Beijing's mind started racing. "Is there a particular day you have in mind?"

He told her the days that he had his girls, and Beijing jotted them down.

"Okay, I will get to work on this."

She hung up the phone, began to search her extensive and in-tensive Rolodex, and finally found what she was looking for: Cameron. Cameron was the great-grandson of the man who created and owned the amusement park. Cameron tended to frequent various Tabby hotels. No matter who his hotel VIP concierge was, he would always ask Beijing to give the orders to his host. Beijing kept his secrets: He was a mess indeed who loved wild sex and orgies.

Beijing dialed his number. As the phone rang, she reflected on the first time she'd met him.

Cameron had been in his penthouse suite for over a week with several women and a sandwich bag of E pills, celebrating his eighteenth birthday, when he'd called Beijing.

"I need to speak to you in private," he said.

Only minutes before he rang her, Beijing had just said to one of her co-workers that she had never had a client so low-maintenance and easy to work with.

She quickly went up to his room, and was directed by one of the girls to the bathroom. She entered and he stood there hung like a horse, holding his wrinkled-up penis in his hand and pants down to his ankles. Her first instinct was to flee the room but she remained calm.

Beijing was shocked at two facts: The myth about white boys having little dicks wasn't true, and he wasn't shy at all. "My dick feels like it's spitting hot coals when I piss. I think I contracted a bad case of the clap."

Never heard of a good case, she wanted to say, but he continued to speak. "I was told that whatever I needed, you could get it at the drop of a dime. I need this shit fixed by the next time I take a fucking leak." He looked her in the eyes and swallowed. "Discreetly of course."

Beijing nodded. "Yes, of course. I understand completely."

Within the hour, Beijing had not only arranged for a doctor to set up shop in the penthouse to administer penicillin shots to Cameron and all his girls and write a few prescriptions for the antibiotic, but she'd provided condoms to them as well. Since then Beijing had been his favorite host.

"Cameron, I need a favor." She cut to the chase because she could hear in the background that wherever he was, the party was about to get going. "I need you to get your people to open up the amusement park for three of my guests."

"Beijing, anything for you. Take this number. I'll call Chris, the general manager, and tell him to make it happen for you."

"Thank you so much, Cam. I owe you."

"You damn right you do, and you can pay up tonight because I am actually at my buddy's house in Charlotte."

She was almost afraid to ask, but he told her, "I want you to turn me on to one of those beautiful black women, like in those rap videos. The ones with the big butts." He made the request like he was ordering up a sandwich from a deli.

Beijing moved the phone away from her ear. She could not believe what she was being asked, but she wasn't surprised.

Only a person with more money than he could spend could be so insensitive, Beijing thought, but she said, "Careful not to bite off more than you can chew."

He laughed. "I got a big appetite."

"Okay, let me call you back, I have just the girl in mind."

Beijing searched for Dazzle's number and gave her a ring. Dazzle answered on the first ring, no hello, just a simple, "Is this my favorite manager with a gig for me?"

Beijing smiled at her salutation. "Indeed it is, and actually I need a favor for a favor."

"Sure, what type of job?" Dazzle asked.

"Basically, I have this filthy fucking rich white client who wants a shot of black pussy," she said, holding her breath hoping that Dazzle didn't mind sexing up a white boy.

"Okay, not a problem at all. Never did a pink dick before but hell, dick is dick. When? Where? And I guess he'll let me know how much, huh?"

"Right away, and the place is to be determined."

"Well, get me details."

"And there's one small problem."

"What? Don't tell me there's two of them?"

Beijing laughed at how free-spirited Dazzle was, talking about engaging in sex with a complete stranger like she was planning on hanging out with an old friend. "There is no budget . . . but hold on, I'm going to pay you out of my own pocket, so we'll have to meet up afterward."

"Okay," Dazzle said with no hesitation. "But Beijing, don't worry about it. If the dude ain't paying you, then I don't want you to have to pay me out of your own pocket. I got you on the strength."

"Good looking out but I want you to do a good job because he's one of my clients who is doing me a favor."

"I got you. I'm going to turn him out so that he understands that once he go black, he ain't never going back."

They shared a laugh and a few more minor details.

Beijing hung up the phone with Dazzle and began trying to think of situations where she could help the woman make money and elevate her career. Then she called and got all the particulars from Chris. He confirmed that he would open up the park for her.

Beijing gave Mr. Bitz back the good news. He was pleased once again with her services and reminded her that if there was anything she ever needed, she should call him.

Damn the power of pussy! Every badass bitch need a good ho on her team. She sat in amazement at what she had pulled off in a matter of minutes.

Before she could pat herself on the back, the phone rang again. This time it was Lootchee.

"Is this my knockout speaking?"

"It is, it is me," she said in an upbeat and confident cadence.

"So, tell me about Beijing Lee?"

She thought for a few beats before answering. "Well," she said, "I enjoy traveling. I speak a few different languages, love to read novels and biographies, like walks on the beach, good food, and some people say I am generous to a fault, but I don't think so." She paused to catch her breath. "I'm a people person. But enough about me, tell me something about you?"

"What's there to tell? I would much rather hear about Beijing."

"Nope. That's not going to work. Tell me at least three things about you."

"Okay," he said reluctantly. "I own a chain of Laundromats. I love sports . . ."

"That's two," she said.

"And I would like to get to know you better." And that was the truth. If the photos she'd sent were anywhere close to being accurate, the woman was gorgeous and just the way he liked them: dark smooth skin, long hair, and sexy with dreams and aspirations.

"What's the funniest thing that ever happened to you?" she asked. They both shared a funny story, falling into wild laughter.

It didn't take long for Beijing to bring Lootchee out of his comfort zone and loosen him up.

Lootchee looked at his watch; it was three twenty-five in the morning, and they'd been talking on the phone for hours. "Damn, time flies. This is a record for me."

"What is?"

"Being on the phone with someone, hell anyone, this long. It seems like I just picked up the phone ten minutes ago."

Lootchee continued, "I want to see you in person. Make the reservations and hop on the plane to Dallas. I'll take care of all the expenses."

That caught her off guard. She had to admit that she was enjoying the conversation and was looking forward to meeting him maybe one day soon—but not this soon. "That sounds very thoughtful and sweet of you, but—"

"No buts," he cut in. "Be spontaneous and just do it."

She said, "I have to be honest with you, Lootchee."

"Please do."

"I'm uncomfortable getting on an aircraft to go see a strange man in a strange city."

"Ain't nothing strange about me, girl, but this lil bit of change I got?"

She laughed at his cockiness.

"I do feel like I know you well already. People I have known for years ain't ever got this much time from me over the horn."

"Talking on the phone and talking about coming to Texas are two completely different things," Beijing reasoned. "But the feeling is mutual."

"I'll let it go for now, but I got one question." He asked, "how in the hell you manage to get better tickets than me at the fight?"

"Darling, I have connections in high places," she said in a very provocative way. She knew she had captivated him when he chuckled a bit before speaking to her.

"I believe you." Then he came back with, "It takes one to know one."

"That's for sure."

"But for real, your man was one of the boxers or something?" He drew his conclusion but she knew by the way he said it that he wanted her to explain how and where she'd gotten the tickets. "Because besides the press you had the best seats in the house. You can tell me who that someone in a real high place is who admires you."

Is he trying to figure out if I have a man? "If I told you I'd have to kill you."

"Okay, I like your style."

And I like yours too. "All right, all right, all right, I got the tickets through work."

"Where the hell do you work? For the boxing commissioner or something? I'm curious to know what you do for a living."

"I'm the best concierge you'll ever meet."

"The average concierge doesn't get tickets like that."

"You better bet that I'm not your average concierge," she said with great confidence. "Some call me a concierge-at-large, while others call me a VIP hotel host. I work at the Tabby and I make a lot of things happen for a lot of 'important' people, with no questions asked and no explanations needed."

"My kind of girl," he assured her. She didn't need any assurance; she knew that she was the best at what she did. "Well, in my parts they'd call you a whale wrangler, bringing all the big money whales into the hotel, making sure they come back time and time again."

She laughed at how Lootchee defined her job.

"I gotcha and I like a resourceful woman."

Beijing smiled. She knew the combination of her playful wit and seductive tone of voice demanded his utmost attention.

They continued to talk through that night, and the next. They talked about where they wanted to go with their lives and all the things that they had in common and all the things that they didn't have in common.

"Who's the closest person to you?" he asked that second night.

"My cousin Seville hands-down is my very best friend. She's in Germany right now and won't be back for another eight months. We talk all the time, but it just isn't the same." She sighed.

"Maybe you can go and see her," he suggested.

"I would love to, but I work too much," she admitted. "But even if I could get a couple of days off, who flies to Germany for a two-day visit? I'm actually counting down the days until she comes back."

"Well, when she returns be sure to introduce us."

"I will," she agreed.

"What about the rest of your family and friends?" he questioned.

"You don't want to know about my dysfunctional family."

"Aren't they all?"

"Some more than others," she said, sighing again.

"Tell me more. I want to know who my future in-laws may be," he joked.

Beijing obliged. "Well, my father and stepmother, Greta,

raised me. My father, God bless him, is a workaholic, but he loves me. He has been everything I could have wanted or needed in a father." Beijing said.

"Okay."

"Greta and I are really close, and though my daddy loves me, she was the one who really raised me, who really took the time out."

"Where's your real momma?" he asked.

"She's around, trying to make it, but she sometimes has a hard time. She gets sick on and off."

"I'm sorry to hear that."

"But for the most part, she's alive and kicking it, and yup, a mess, but most of the time in a good way." She decided to change the subject. Lord knows she didn't want to have to tell him that her mother was mentally ill, among other things, and have him come to the conclusion that the fruit maybe didn't fall far from the tree. "What about your parents?"

A few beats went by before he gave a deep sigh. "I don't really like to talk about it. They are no longer with me anymore."

"Both of them?" she asked.

"Both of them," he echoed. The tone in his voice told her it was an extremely touchy subject and to move on.

The next night Beijing realized that during all of their hours of conversation, she never asked him an important question, so she called him.

"Hey you." They had last spoken less than an hour ago.

"Hey baby."

"Real quick, I have a question."

"Shoot," he said, "I don't have anything to hide."

"When's your birthday?"

"Funny you should ask." She could hear him smiling. "It's today!"

"Then give me your address. Birthdays are important to me."

"No need to send me anything. I have all the creature comforts a man could want. Maybe even enough for ten men, baby, so don't spend your hard-earned money on me."

"I have to get you something for your birthday and I don't mind spending my hard-earned money on something worthy of it," Beijing insisted.

"Well if you must insist . . . I'm having a big birthday party on Friday night. I would love for you to be my date."

"I'm there," she said a little too fast. *What the hell am I thinking?* she asked herself. She took her foot out of her mouth then asked, "What's the dress code?"

"I just need you to make motherfuckers and they two-bit bitches envy me when they lay eyes on you."

"And I can do that."

CHAPTER 10

To Die and Go to Hell For

After Beijing accepted Lootchee's invitation to fly out to Texas for his party, she spent the rest of the week making sure that her appearance would be perfect. She consumed not only her life but the lives of Seville and Rayna with all the particulars of what she was going to wear.

Though it was only 1 PM in Charlotte, it was already 7 PM in Germany when Beijing called her cousin for help. "Girl, you need to virtually help me out!" Beijing told Seville. Beijing was standing in front of her closet with her open suitcases on the bed, feeling like she would never be ready.

"Don't tell me I got to be the hoochie for another queer celebrity," Seville said. " 'Course that was a nice tip Mr. Wiz gave me. Takes a gay man to know that diamonds really are a girl's best friend."

"No, I need you to help me get fabulous, gorgeous, and beautiful for a trip to Texas. Rayna's going to meet me at the mall. I really don't have anything to wear."

"First of all, you are already beautiful, and next, you can't fool me, you have plenty to wear. You just want something new."

"You gonna have to stay up and help me get it together."

"You know I got your back. You just have to really describe everything with detail so I can try to picture it."

"I'm going to have you on the phone the entire time and I will have Rayna take pics of stuff and send them over the phone."

"Okay, but you better keep Rayna away from the chocolate store!"

"Girl, that cold Germany weather got you being cold as ice."

Beijing and Rayna were like the Barbarians descending on Rome when they went through that mall. They hit Neiman Marcus, Macy's, and Saks as well as all the specialty shops.

"Do you really need six more pairs of shoes?" Rayna asked as Beijing sent the salesgirl back for another pair of stilettos.

"A woman needs sixty pairs of shoes at least," Seville said. "You just jealous 'cause that no'-count man of yours ain't flying you to Texas. By the way, how come we've never met him? What's his name? Tray? Troy?" Beijing laughed it off, but didn't repeat that comment to Rayna—she had been playing mockingbird.

"Should I get these shoes?" Beijing described the shoes to Seville over the phone.

"No," Rayna said.

"Yes, definitely," Seville contradicted.

"You two are no help at all. Aren't you excited for me?"

"Oh baby, we are so excited for you." Rayna hugged Beijing.

"Yes, we are. Come on, get those shoes and get back to the room so we can get you packed. I got a feeling I'm going to be up all night."

Beijing laughed. She felt so lucky. She may not have a sister she could count on, considering Paris, but Seville and Rayna were better than sisters. And now she was going to see this delicious, sexy man. Rayna carried her bags for her like she was a princess as they headed out of the store and off to grab a bite to eat.

They all planned out every detail of every single outfit from the time she walked off the big bird until the time she would leave Texas. Neither of them minded at all; in fact they were excited that their friend was moving on to a new chapter in her life.

After the wardrobe was mapped out, Beijing turned her attention to her hair, her nails, and all the beautification one person could do including some new makeup, a manicure, and a pedicure.

Home Sweet Home. She entered her suite after another long day of shopping, carrying packages in both hands. Beijing's suite looked like a fashionista's heaven. Shopping bags from her numerous trips to the mall occupied every available space. *Damn, this shit is like a job in itself,* she thought to herself, exhausted but satisfied that when everything came together she would be hotter than a July picnic in Alabama.

Before packing she decided to take a nice long soak in a tub full of sweet-smelling bubbles. *Ooooh, that feels so nice,* she thought as she slid into the warm water. She loved a good bath and the way the bath oil made her skin feel silky and smooth. *There is nothing in the world that Calgon can't fix,* she thought as she relaxed.

Which was of course the precise moment her cell phone went off.

I am not getting out of this tub, she thought, letting the phone sing away in the other room. She lifted some bubbles to her face and blew. Then across the room the cell phone started singing again.

Can't I get any peace? At all? Leave me alone.

But there was something about that cell phone ringing that got under her skin and caused a bad feeling to come over Beijing. She raised her tired naked body from the tub, beads of water and suds racing down her smooth skin. Not bothering to grab a towel, she padded into the bedroom, leaving a water trail behind. She realized who it was and shook her head because she knew it was gonna be bad news. It was her mother, Willabee.

"What is it, Momma?" Beijing asked.

"Don't you 'What is it, Momma,' me," Willabee said. "I am calling about yo' niece." She went on, "The person you say you love so much. The little girl who you claim you bust your ass for so she can go to college and have a life better than your life, even though yo' life don't seem so bad to me. But that's not what I'm calling about to discuss this go-'round."

"Yes, Momma, what about Chyna?" Beijing asked, alarmed.

"She's over at Paris's place and I'm worried to death about her. They ain't answering the phone, it just—"

"You did what, Momma?" Beijing interrupted her mother in disbelief.

Willabee ignored the question and kept talking. "The phone over there is going straight to voice mail and nobody is picking up."

"How long you been calling?"

"About three hours. Plus Paris started getting in that shit again," Willabee said.

"What? Momma, I don't know why you would let Chyna go with Paris. The courts gave you custody of that girl. You aren't supposed to let her go over there and be around that druggie-ass bitch, and God knows what else she might be doing over there."

"Don't talk about yo' sister like that, baby. Paris was clean and had been for months. She was doing real good, then Chyna begged me to let her go over her mother's house. So I've been letting her go over there on weekends. You know firsthand I can't keep a little girl from her rightful momma."

Beijing knew that her mother was right. The more Sterling tried to keep her from Willabee, the more she yearned to be with her mother, but she knew her sister wasn't fit to have any little girl in her care.

"Momma, you must be off your meds again if you trusted Paris.

After what she tried to do to me?" Beijing's blood pressure shot up. "Do you honestly think she won't do something just as bad if not worse to her own daughter?" Beijing pulled on a pair of jeans and whatever shirt she could grab. She didn't have time to worry about how she looked; she had to leave right this instant to get her niece away from that damn Paris. "I'm leaving right now, Momma. It'll take me a couple of hours to make the trip. I want you to keep trying to get Chyna on the phone and make sure she's okay till I get there. And if anything goes wrong, you call the police." She raised her voice in anger. "I don't care if the bitch does go back to fucking jail." She meant every word of it.

Willabee was off her rocker most of the time, but this time she knew better than to challenge Beijing. "Okay, baby, I'll do what you say." Willabee hung up the phone while Beijing grabbed her keys and her purse and flew out the door barely touching the floor of the lobby. A few minutes later she was speeding down I-85, wishing this one time that she lived closer to her crazy mother and drugged-out sister.

Paris had been getting high off and on since she was fifteen, mostly on coke. She'd been to jail, drug rehabs, and counseling, but nothing seemed to slow her down; not for long anyway.

Paris was fresh out of jail twelve years ago when she met a hustler who went by the name of Boney-Slim. After doing ten months in the joint, Paris had gotten her weight back up and was looking like her normal beautiful self again. It had been a long time since her ass had been that phat. Boney-Slim liked what he saw and didn't waste any time getting her back into drugs and in the mix planting a baby in her stomach. Though the drugs were intentional, the baby was an accident.

Paris felt bad about what she had tried to do to Beijing all those years ago, so she named her daughter Chyna in honor of her sister. But Beijing never wholeheartedly forgave Paris and damn sure didn't trust her. Beijing strived to be Chyna's guardian angel and the one normal thing in her niece's life. She tried to do everything in her power to make sure Chyna would grow up to be a productive human being. It was hard when Beijing lived nearly two and a half hours away, but under the circumstances she did the best she could.

She arrived at the three-story rent-subsidized apartment building where Paris had lived for the past four years and got out of her car. She was on a mission and had a one-track mind, paying no attention to anything or anyone around her.

"Nice Lex," a guy getting out of a candy-apple-red late-model Cadillac said to Beijing.

"Thanks," she said to him and gave his 1988 Sedan DeVille Cadi with twenty-two-inch wheels a glance over. "Nice pimpmobile."

"Somebody's gotta do it," he agreed, heading in the same direction as she was.

There were five young cats sitting on the steps leading to Paris's apartment. They all had their pants hanging down off their butts and were drinking beer and smoking weed. As Beijing started to make her way past, the dude she'd spoken to earlier stopped to kick it with one of the young cats.

"Excuse me, excuse me," she said to the hoodlums-in-training, easing her way up the steps while trying hard not to tip anyone's forty over. At the top of the steps, she knocked on her sister's apartment door several times. She could hear noise on the other side, so someone was definitely home. She knocked harder as she smelled the strong aroma of marijuana smoke from inside the apartment. She imagined her niece inside, probably catching a contact high from the secondhand smoke.

Secondhand smoke is worse than actual smoke. I wish they'd hurry up. Her wish came true when a guy dressed in camouflage finally opened up the door. She marched right past him without saying a word. As she entered, out of the corner of her eye she saw Cadi-Man making his way up the stairs.

Once Beijing was in her sister's apartment she was disgusted.

"Yo, you here to get baby girl, ain't you?" Camouflage said with the butt of a blunt hanging from his mouth. Before Beijing nodded, he said, "Aight, hold up, let me finish rolling this L and Imma get her for you."

In a firm tone and with a stare that said *I'm not playing with you motherfuckers*, she demanded to know, "Where is she at? And where is Paris?" Beijing looked around in disgust. The place was filthy. Empty beer bottles and Doritos bags lay around and razor blades, plastic bags, discharged cigars, tobacco, ashes, coffee stirrers, and other trash was strewn about randomly.

There were two guys sitting on the living room couch in front of the small thirteen-inch television who looked like they had dozed off, but Beijing knew that they were high in the clouds by now. She had witnessed Don in that same type of dope nod.

"Lil Momma in the room. And Paris back dere handling her BI," Camouflage said as he put a cigarette behind his ear.

Beijing stomped down the hall, pissed off that her niece was in the midst of this madness. She tried to open up the first bedroom door, but the knob didn't move when she tried to twist it. It was locked. She banged on the door with all types of unsavory thoughts of what might be taking place on the other side.

"Chyna, Chyna, open up this door," she called. Her heart dropped and she began to shake the doorknob in a panic, nearly falling inside when it suddenly opened. Chyna was in the room alone. Feeling enormous relief that her niece was okay, Beijing took her in her arms and embraced her.

"I locked the door because I didn't want anybody to come in here."

"That's right." She smiled at her niece. "You are such a smart girl."

"Gram always tells me that I have to take care of myself when I'm over here because Momma is used to living her life without me and she may sometimes forget I am here."

"Where are your things? Pack everything up and let's—" Before Beijing could finish her statement, she was startled by a loud noise. She poked her head out the bedroom door to see what in the world had caused the commotion. The back bedroom door had been kicked in and was hanging off its hinges. She sucked her teeth. "What da fuck is going on now?" she huffed.

"Bitch, is you fucking crazy?" the owner of the red Cadi screamed..

"Motherfucker, get out of my shit!" a buck-naked Paris screamed back. "You don't live here, motherfucker." Paris tried to shove Cadi-Man out of the room.

"And my bitch don't either," he screamed, punching Paris in the mouth and then smacking the naked woman who had been lying in the bed with Paris. "Get the fuck up, Keonna. Now bitch."

Beijing could see from the doorway that there was a dude in the corner of the room with his pencil-thin dick in one hand and a video camera in the other.

"Nigggga," the guy said. He had obviously been watching the girls freak off. He continued in a slurred tone, "Ain't no need to come in here with that bullshit fucking up a nigga's ménage. If bitches wanna trick off, let 'em do it."

Cadi-Man hadn't noticed the man in the corner until he opened up his mouth for trouble. Cadi-Man pulled the longest pistol Beijing had ever seen and went upside of Video Man's cranium until he was beaten to a pulp.

Blood squirted from his head and mouth, splattering Paris's dingy white walls. Beijing gasped before turning to make sure that Chyna wasn't witnessing this mayhem. Only the Lord knew what her niece had already seen.

Cadi-Man's girl, Keonna, was screaming at the top of her lungs. "Ahhhhh! Please, stop."

Beijing turned back and saw that Paris wasn't fazed by the dude getting his ass pistol-whipped in her house and was using the opportunity to run through his pockets to find more of his drugs and money.

That's her MO. Beijing shook her head. *She got heart,* she thought of her sister, but wanted out of there.

"Shut the fuck up," Cadi-Man hissed at his girl. "This is the shit you make me do. This shit is yo' fault."

Keonna didn't respond. Instead she put on her clothes as fast as she could, hoping not to be the next victim of the pistol-lashing.

Meanwhile Beijing grabbed her niece's belongings, took Chyna's hand, and they got the fuck out of Dodge.

CHAPTER 11

Run, Bitch, Run!

Beijing sat in a plastic chair in Charlotte's airport staring out of the floor-to-ceiling windows at the planes coming and going. She reflected on how Chyna seemed unfazed by the entire ordeal the night before and made a mental note to herself to call Greta to have Willabee get the poor child some counseling. Then she thought about how Don had come and gone in and out of her life, and how his career had skyrocketed. Despite their differences, she sincerely hoped that he was getting the help he needed with his health and career.

As she waited for her flight to arrive, she noticed a guy watching her. He looked familiar, but she couldn't place him. As she tried to figure it out, her thoughts were interrupted by her ringing phone.

"Hi, TJ?" she answered after looking at the caller ID.

TJ was a guy who moved back and forth among Houston, Dallas, and Vegas. He could get concert and sporting event tickets in any city, state, province, or country. And he always had the best seats in the house. Beijing had made several large purchases from him for clients over the years, and he would call now and then to check on her, find out what she was up to, and remind her that he was still around.

"What up, Beijing! How are you? Haven't heard from you in a while."

"I'm great! I've been just doing what I do. You?"

"Me? I'm better than most, worse than some. Been running back and forth doing my thing; you know how I do."

"That's what's up." Beijing fed his ego. "I meant to call you because a girlfriend of mine was dating a guy out there in your neck of the woods and I wanted to know if you had any tea to spill on him?" TJ was a notorious gossip.

As far as Beijing knew TJ wasn't gay, but he always gossiped like a woman.

"What's dude name?" he eagerly asked. He couldn't wait to get into somebody's business. " 'Cause if the nigga is making any kind of noise in any of my zones, you better believe he's on my radar."

"I know, that's what I was thinking," Beijing said. "His name is, oh I got it on the tip of my tongue," she stalled, snapping her fingers as if she were trying to remember it. "Lootchee's his name."

"You fucking wit dat nigga?" he asked bluntly.

Damn! Beijing couldn't believe that TJ had snapped. Maintaining her cool, she said, "I told you, my friend is dating that ol' boy and she talks about him all the time. I just wanted to make sure he was okay."

"Ain't nothing okay about dude," he said. "He's rotten to the core."

"Wow! In what way?" Beijing was more curious than ever.

"He's just a nasty fucking nigga, that's all. He's fucked up."

"What's so messed up 'bout dude?" Her antennas were on full alert.

"The nigga is a manipulative, selfish motherfucka. Goes all-out to get anything he wants."

Beijing thought, *Is that all?* "Does he sell drugs?" she asked.

"I'm not sure. I've never heard about it if he does. But that means nothing. He's so intimidating that the people around him wouldn't let the cat out the bag if he did."

How could that cat not get out of the bag if it was true? she wondered.

"Well, thanks, TJ, I'll be sure to warn her."

"Do so!" he insisted, "but don't tell her that you got it from me."

Damn, Beijing thought . . . was that fear in his voice?

"Okay, TJ, you got it," she said before ending the call.

As soon as the line was clear, she immediately called Seville.

At times like this she couldn't wait for her cousin to return home. She thanked God for her cousin's Vonage line because as much as they talked, the long-distance bill would be a small fortune. "Soooo, one of my colleagues called me and he happened to know or know of Lootchee and he had nothing nice to say about him."

"Girl, I know you ain't listening to no nigga talking about another nigga. He probably want you for himself and mad that you don't want him."

"He said that Lootchee was intimidating and manipulative."

"So is Donald Trump. You spent hours on the phone with Lootchee; did he seem that way with you?" Seville asked.

Beijing ran her fingers through her hair thinking of the long talks she had with Lootchee. "No, not at all."

"Then fuck what you heard. All that matters is how he treats you."

Just then the announcement to board her flight came over the intercom. Beijing said, "You right, girl. Let me board this flight."

"You know the drill. Call me as soon as you touch down so that I know you're okay."

"Will do."

"Just have fun and try to block out the haters because you know they will be at the party," Seville said.

Beijing's flight arrived right on time. Traveling first-class definitely had its perks. Besides the comfortable roomy seats, champagne, and slightly better food, they were the first to board and the first to exit the aircraft. Beijing retrieved her small carry-on bag from the overhead compartment and stepped off the plane.

Lootchee admired her from afar; she was even more beautiful in person. Mesmerized by her full package, he watched with lust-filled eyes as she came down the escalator. Her jeans showed off her curves, and her olive-green wrap shirt revealed just enough for his imagination to go full-tilt. Dior sunglasses made her look like a superstar, his star. He waited for the escalator to descend, and like a perfect gentlemen he stood with a beautiful bouquet of roses.

Lootchee looked better than she had remembered. He looked good enough to eat and simply delectable in his money-green shirt, blue denim jeans with money-green trim, and sneakers to match. He beamed a perfect set of pearly whites at her.

"How was your flight?" His voice was deep and sexy.

Beijing was so busy staring at him she almost didn't hear him speak to her.

"Oh," she said, snapping out of her less than pure thoughts. "It was cool. Are the flowers for me? They're lovely!"

"Not as lovely as you are," he said. He put his arm around her waist and gave her a hug. His cologne did something to her. It was alluring.

"This is Steve." Lootchee nodded toward the man to his left. "Let him take your bags." Beijing handed her carry-on to Steve and then pointed out her other luggage coming around on the carousel.

Steve was six foot seven and black as a winter night on a Georgia back road. His head was almost perfectly round with a shine like it had just been waxed and polished. He scooped the two suitcases with one hand while Lootchee escorted her to the white Rolls-Royce Phantom. The car was beautiful. She had ordered Phantoms for a couple of clients, but had never actually ridden in one. Steve hurried ahead of them and opened up the door for the couple.

After putting the bags in the trunk, Steve slid his massive frame behind the steering wheel and peeled out with the precision of a professional driver.

Beijing sat back and enjoyed the smooth and luxurious ride. Once they got onto the highway, she asked, "So, what time does the party start?"

This time his smile revealed a tad of guilt. "There isn't one." And then he admitted, "I just wanted you to be here so we could spend time together."

"So you mean to tell me that Tuesday wasn't your birthday?"

"No, but I do have a special celebration planned for us."

Bitch, get the fuck out of this car and go home! This nigga is full of shit! Run, bitch! Run! She started to second-guess herself for flying all the way to Texas to meet a man she had only met one time for about thirty seconds and talked to on the phone for a few days. *What the hell was I thinking? Am I that desperate or hard up for a man? TJ was right about Lootchee. I need to figure out how the hell I'm going to bail.* When she turned to him, he met her gaze. His smile was mesmerizing and intoxicating in a way that made her tipsy. She felt her resolve melting with each passing second.

"What else have you lied about?" she pulled herself together long enough to ask, wanting to be upset but finding it impossible with such a charming free-spirited guy.

"Ouch, baby! *Lied* is such a harsh word. I just slightly misled you in order to get you where you needed to be." The words rolled from his mouth like chocolate from a fountain.

"And where is that?" she managed to ask.

"Right now . . . right here . . . with me."

CHAPTER 12

So Amazing

Beijing gazed out the window of the Rolls-Royce at the Dallas skyline, smiling on the inside.

"So where are we off to?" she asked.

"I thought I'd get you settled in at the house, and then we could grab something to eat."

Lootchee slid an arm around Beijing's shoulders. "You look so nice, so stunning," he whispered, but she could feel his breath tickling her ear.

She had no intention of being swept off her feet with a few well-placed words.

"Thank you—" she paused for a moment. "—but can you drop me off at the hotel I reserved? It's been quite a long day and I would like to take a shower and pull myself together. I've been in these clothes since early this morning."

Lootchee was offended. "Hotel room? I wouldn't hear of it. You're staying at my house," he insisted.

"That's not going to happen." She shook her head. "I would hate to think that you got me twisted with a chick who doesn't know any better. I'm not dumb enough to spend the night at no man's house I just met."

"I'm just trying to show you southern hospitality at its best."

"No matter how much he wines and dines me, I *do not* play that game." She scooted a few inches away from him in the backseat to let him know that she was serious.

"You're serious, ain't you?"

"As a heart attack."

"Then I guess you got me twisted also, because I don't deal with bitches, only with ladies. And I don't take rejection well either."

"You'll get used to it," Beijing said. *Let him be mad,* she thought. *He is not getting his way with me.* "I'm staying at the Tabby." She was playing this mental chess game with Lootchee and enjoying every minute of it.

"You know, I don't really like the way things are going at all, but I'm going to still respect yo' gangsta." He smiled. "Damn, girl. You are something else and don't let anyone tell you anything different."

Reluctantly, he instructed his driver to take them to the hotel.

The Rolls coasted to a stop in front of the Tabby of Dallas, the newest addition to the hotel chain. They were instantly met by a valet and a bellhop. Lootchee told them the car was fine while Beijing directed them to the bags in the trunk.

After checking in, Lootchee walked her up to her room and suggested that he'd pick her up in two hours for dinner.

"I'll be ready," she said, accepting the offer. Then shut the room's door, leaving Lootchee standing there with his hands in his pockets.

Lootchee arranged for them to have a private dinner at Arthuro's, an upscale restaurant.

"This place looks closed," she said.

"Not for us it isn't."

An Italian man with salt-and-pepper hair and a warm smile appeared in the doorway. "Lootchee," he said with a thick accent, "I've been expecting you. Good to see you again." He gave Lootchee a hug, patting him on his back. "Who's the lovely lady?" Anthony asked, looking at Beijing.

"This lovely lady is Beijing, so serve us nothing but the best, because she's very dear to me."

"Say no more." Anthony smiled. "Follow me."

The restaurant was beautiful, modern with an old-Italy feel.

"This place is gorgeous," Beijing said after being seated. "I hope the food tastes half as good as this place looks."

Once they were seated, Beijing noticed the surprised look on Lootchee's face when she ordered her food in Italian. In fact, Anthony and Beijing began talking about Lootchee right in front of his face.

"Can you clue me into the conversation?" he asked.

"He simply asked how long I had known you. And I told him it felt like a very long time."

Lootchee nodded. "You speak Italian?"

"Just a little," she answered modestly.

He smiled. "Impressive."

Six delicious courses and a bottle of wine later, Lootchee said, "Lady Italy, I have another surprise for you."

Five men made their way out from the back of the restaurant over to Lootchee and Beijing's table. It was New Edition. They were in town to perform at a throwback show on Saturday night at a local club that Lootchee happened to be promoting. He'd hit them with a few extra bucks for a last-minute favor to serenade Beijing at the restaurant.

"Beijing," Johnny Gill said in a deep baritone, "this song is for you." Music floated from hidden speakers, and the group sang their hit, "If It Isn't Love."

After the mini concert, the two enjoyed each other's company with nonstop chatter the entire ride from the restaurant to the hotel.

"What an amazing night. I've never had anyone serenade me before," she said back at the hotel.

"There's a lot of things you can experience with me that may be your first. Like you, I'm a very resourceful man," he said, "and can make things happen that are beyond your wildest dreams."

"I can believe that." Her eyes were gleaming. "This is a pretty nice start."

"If I ask you a question, will you promise to give me an honest answer?"

"If I can, sure I will."

His eyes grabbed her, pulling her full attention toward him. "Are you glad that you're here with me?"

The words eased from her mouth in a melody. "I am," she admitted.

Lootchee was delighted. "Music to my ears. Then everything I did was worth it." He gave his trademark smile.

"Oh, I almost forgot. I have something for you. Well, it was for your birthday but I guess I can give it to you anyway." Beijing reached into her duffel bag and removed a beautifully wrapped box. "Go ahead and open it," she urged him.

Lootchee took his time removing the wrapping paper from the flat, rectangular box, revealing a Gucci wallet inside. "I love it," he said. "I got a pair of Gucci sneakers at home that'll go perfect with it."

"Thank you." He gave her a big hug. "I'm surprised," Lootchee added, looking at her.

"Why?" she asked. "I came here thinking that I was going to your birthday party."

"Well, because besides sexual favors, women really don't shower me with anything. I usually just go cop whatever I want." He admired the wallet. "You know how to score big points, huh?"

"I'm glad you like it." Neither one of them spoke for a moment as each tried to figure out what to say next. "I guess this is good night," she murmured.

"Aren't you going to invite me in for a drink?"

"Of course . . . I'm not." She rejected his begging eyes. "I told you. I'm not some jumpoff that wants to give you some sexual favors, so see ya tomorrow."

"I'll be here first thing in da morning." He barely got the words out before the door to her room closed. He laughed at himself, not believing that he'd have to wait until the next day to see her.

CHAPTER 13

Ten Carats

Beijing lay in bed thinking of Lootchee and what a wonderful time they'd had. Sure she was a little peeved about lying about his birthday, but that seemed like something that could be over-looked. After all, he was being the perfect gentlemen and show-ing her a wonderful time.

She made a mental note to get Rayna a thank-you gift, because Lootchee was different from the guys that she usually dated.

This trip was just what she needed to get her mind off Don, his foolishness, and all the madness of work, she thought. If the rest of the weekend came close to tonight, it would be well worth the time.

A knock at the door brought her out of her thoughts. She slipped on a robe, tied the belt, and went to the door to peek out the peephole.

It was Lootchee.

"Funny, I was just thinking about you," she confessed.

"I've been thinking of you too." He looked deep into her eyes as if he was searching for something inside of her. "Actually"—he smiled—"you've all I've been thinking of. Can I come in?"

"I told you . . ."

"You told me tomorrow," he said, looking at his watch. "It's after midnight. It's officially Saturday. I promise I won't try anything."

Beijing threw reason to the side and listened to her emotions. She stepped away from the door. "Come on in, but you're not getting any."

"I'll be on my best behavior." Lootchee threw his right hand in the air before adding, "Scout's honor."

Once inside he said, "I'd like to lie down with you and hold you in my arms." Before she could speak he said, "I promise I will be on my best behavior."

She couldn't say no to him. He removed his clothes; she took off her robe and got under the blanket. Lootchee slid in behind her, wrapping his arms around her soft warm body.

"All we're going to do is spoon," she reminded him.

Beijing was enveloped inside Lootchee's strong arms when she was awakened by the hotel phone. She picked it up.

"Good morning, Ms. Lee. This is Roger from the front desk. There's a Mr. Lootchee down here in the lobby waiting for you."

Beijing's eyes went to the other side of the bed, then to the clock. The bed was empty and the clock glowed 6 AM. Last night was a dream!

"Tell him I'll be down in about forty-five minutes," she said sleepily.

Less than an hour later, she had showered, dressed, and was in the lobby, where Lootchee was having a cup of coffee and reading the paper.

"Morning, beautiful," he said with a smile. "How did you sleep?"

"Like a baby." She sat down across from him. "What do you

have planned for today, early bird?" she asked and then yawned, covering her mouth. "Excuse me."

"Early bird gets the worm," he quipped. "But to answer your question . . . we're going to Six Flags, shopping, a concert tonight, and I have a surprise for tomorrow."

"A surprise? I love surprises! Tell me."

"If I tell you, it's not a surprise." Then he gave her the rundown of the day's itinerary. "For starters, it's unheard of for you to be my guest in my town and not go to a Cowboys game. We play the Dead Skins tomorrow and I got a bundle on the big game."

"I've never been to a professional game before," Beijing admitted. Football wasn't really her thing, but she was willing to give it a try. "Just gotta get something to wear. You know the weatherman was all wrong about the weather."

"The only person who can give wrong information and still have a job," Lootchee said, "but we'll be at the Galleria when they open to do a little shopping for the occasion."

Once they were at the mall, Beijing was in her element. She tried on about ten outfits and decided to keep four. Then she and Lootchee argued about who was going to pay for them. He insisted that the least she could do was allow him to be a gentleman in his hometown.

"Thank you very much," she said, "but I can pay for my own clothes. You've done enough and I appreciate you." She gave him a hug.

Lootchee raised his hands as if he was surrendering. "You win."

After she sent the sales associate to search for a pair of boots that she'd seen on display, Lootchee said, "I'm going to step out for a minute to use the phone."

Beijing was admiring another pair of shoes as she said, "Okay, no problem."

No sooner had Lootchee left the store than he peeped this cat named Owen coming out of the jewelry store.

Owen and Lootchee had never liked each other. Owen was "the man" at one time. He owned a few car lots, among other things. He made plenty of money and had no problem spending it. And just as two billy goats can't stand at the top of the hill without butting heads, Lootchee and Owen were always trying to knock each other down.

Much to Lootchee's delight, over the past ten to twelve months Owen had fallen off in a major way. He still dressed the part because when he was getting it, the getting was good, but now his pockets were hurting. Owen walked past Lootchee with hate in his eyes and envy in his heart. Lootchee laughed and went into the jewelry store that Owen had just left.

"What up, Jo?" He gave the jeweler five.

"Nothing much, just trying to stay afloat."

"I feel that," Lootchee said. "I see ol' Owen just left. What dat nigga buying?" If it was anything worthwhile, he would buy a bigger one just for spite.

"Nada." Jo shook his head in disgust. "He returned a piece I custom-made for him. He asked me to lend him money on it till he can do better."

"Word, let me see the piece." Lootchee had heard stories that Owen had been strapped for cash and was spinning out of control but had not seen it firsthand.

"I feel bad for the guy because he has spent a lot of money with me," Jo said, shrugging, "but I'm in business. I just can't give my creations away for free." The Mexican man went over to the safe and pulled out a necklace. "Such a beautiful piece." He shook his head. "I think Owen is getting wasted on a regular basis. I can see it in his eyes,. He tries to hide it, but I know the look."

Just then Lootchee saw Beijing step out of the clothing store, looking around for him.

He stuck his head out of the jeweler's shop. "I'm over here, beautiful."

Beijing joined him in the store just as Jo handed him the necklace. "The heart pendant is made up of ten carats."

"Ten?" Lootchee was impressed. "Really?"

"Yup and the necklace is . . ."

Lootchee cut him off and asked Beijing a question he already knew the answer to: "Baby, how long has it been since our first call?"

"Today makes ten days." She smiled, thinking about the first night she'd called him.

"That's what I thought." Lootchee looked at Jo and said, "I'll take it." He instructed Beijing to turn around so that he could put the necklace on her neck.

"I can't accept that," she gushed.

"Sure you can. It's a sentimental moment. Now turn around," he instructed her.

"What do you mean, sentimental?"

"I mean it's significant. How could it not be? What's the chance that my main man Jo would have a gorgeous custom necklace that signifies our courtship—ten carats? A carat a day. It was meant for me to buy this for you today. I believe in fate."

Beijing smiled and took another look at the breathtaking piece of jewelry. The diamonds were so clear they looked like ice cubes frozen from the finest springwater. There was no denying that it was beautiful. She slowly turned around and let Lootchee clasp it around her neck.

"This is just so gorgeous. I don't know what to say."

"You don't have to say nothing. You don't even have to say thank you. Seeing you smile is all the thanks I need."

The timing couldn't have been better because just then Owen walked past the shop. He said, "Turn this way baby, so I can see how it catches the light."

Beijing turned facing Lootchee but in Owen's sight. She did as she was told, pulling her long flowing silky hair up off her neck.

Owen turned and stared from the doorway. His eyes were burning with hate when he saw Beijing wearing the necklace he'd had made for his mother.

Lootchee laughed.

CHAPTER 14

Club Celestial

After Beijing and Lootchee left the mall, they spent the day at an amusement park. The time seemed to fly by. Lootchee had dropped Beijing off at the hotel to change clothes for the New Edition concert. After he changed his own gear, he scooped Beijing back up and took her to Club Celestial.

As Lootchee pulled into his reserved parking space, people were treating him as if he were a movie star, running up to his car, greeting him, and giving him fives as he got out. Beijing was impressed at how people respected him.

A tall, handsome man spotted Lootchee getting out of his car. He stepped from behind the black velvet ropes, meeting the two of them at the curb.

"What's popping, my nigga?" They gave each other dap. The tall guy leaned over to Lootchee and asked, "Who's the honey? I never saw you bring sand to the beach."

"First time for everything," Lootchee said, and then he took

Beijing's hand. "This is Beijing. Beijing"—Lootchee moved his eyes from her to his man—"Jeff."

Beijing remembered him from the fight and gave Jeff a warm smile. Jeffrey couldn't help but notice that the lady was a straight dime, and he pulled his eyes away from Beijing before getting himself in trouble. He said, "The fire marshal already been here."

Lootchee looked around. "I can't tell." The music was still jumping from the inside. "Looks like the party's out here, not in there."

Beijing had to agree with Lootchee as she looked around. The place was jam-packed. People were standing all around in the back and front parking lots, conducting some sort of business, envious of those who were inside.

"Naw they partying like rock stars in there. We sold out, and the bar is bananas for sho," Jeff assured his partner with a nod. Beijing could only image the fun people must be having inside. The strong aroma of the marijuana hit her nose before she actually noticed the people who were smoking weed. There was no denying that Lootchee smelled it too.

"Sounds like everything going all right." Lootchee nodded.

"That crook wouldna gave a fuck if we had the entire Chinese Republican Army in that bitch after I put them Franklins in his pocket."

Lootchee smiled at his boy, but Beijing was thinking how she needed to have the fire marshal added to her Rolodex.

"The bar sales looking good, but man, I didn't even have to tell you that, you can tell by the looks of this crowd out here."

"Let's go in," Lootchee said.

"New Edition's inside. They haven't taken the stage yet, but they gon go on in a short," Jeff said.

Jeff led the way followed by Lootchee and Beijing, with Steve covering the rear. Beijing was confident and felt good as all eyes were on her checking her out hand in hand with Lootchee. As they walked past the long lines of people desperate to get in, Beijing felt sorry for the guy with the guest list. He was being bombarded by people claiming to be on it. Another girl was saying that she was on New Edition's VIP list but the guy with the list didn't see her name.

Beijing wished that all the people trying to get in could see the performance, but she was glad she was with the man throwing the event.

Once they broke the seal of the entrance, there were so many people stuffed into the huge club that it looked like sardines in a can. Lootchee turned to Beijing and said, "We going to the VIP area." He gave Steve a nod. Steve then squeezed his way to the front of the group and started elbowing his way through the crowd with Jeff, Lootchee, and Beijing right on his heels.

After they got about fifteen feet away from the VIP booth, they came to a standstill. Even though it was such a short distance, it turned out to be a chore to get to their desired destination. Steve was in front of them as they pushed their way through the crowded, smoked-filled, musty nightclub. Steve was inching his way one step at a time but not making much progress. Frustration set in for various reasons not only with Lootchee and company but with almost every person in that place, especially a guy named Boo.

Boo was pissed beyond pisstivity and he wasn't letting anybody cut in front of him. He was bothered that he had been at the club since 9 PM and the show had not started at 10 PM as promised. To top it off, his girl had stood him up, the event was oversold, everyone was jam-packed like circus clowns in a car, it was hotter than fresh-poured black tar, and he had big pellets of perspiration coming from every gland in his body wetting up his new linen outfit.

"Motherfucker, go to the fucking back," Boo screamed at Steve.

Steve ignored Boo at first and kept trying to inch by. Boo was about three inches shorter than Steve and ten pounds lighter. Boo was so amped by his frustration that he wanted to go toe-to-toe with somebody and it really didn't matter who. If it was a heavyweight boxing match, both Boo and Steve would have made the ticket. Boo turned around filled with liquor and mischief, wanting a chance at the belt, and Steve had given him all he needed.

Boo said "What's up" with a two-piece to the side of Steve's head and then again to the jaw.

Unfazed, Steve asked, "Are you crazy?" with three vicious blows of his own.

All hell broke loose and all Beijing saw were fists, feet, and elbows all over the place. Somebody caught Steve from the back with an Absolut Vodka bottle. The bottle shattered against his skull, sending him down to one knee. Then the situation got out of control and someone else hit Steve, sending him to the ground, and then out of spite people started to kick him. In the midst of everything, Lootchee let go of Beijing's hand and dropped the bottle-wielding chump with a flurry of blows to the head. There was no way Lootchee could stand by and watch his childhood friend get beat down.

Security guards came to break it all up, but they were unsure what was what and who was who. Tempers were still flaring and at that point the entire club was outraged. This one incident almost incited a riot. Somehow, through the chaos and madness, Beijing was sucked out the front door. She was shaken up but unhurt. She had no idea where Lootchee was. Her new outfit was ripped, and she had lost one of the Manolo Blahniks she had bought that morning.

After about twenty minutes of standing outside, scared to try to go back in, she managed to hail down a cab to take her back to the hotel. The first thing she did once she was back safely in the room was sit down with a glass of wine to clear her head. She could not believe that Lootchee had gotten in a fight . . . *at his own event!*

She plopped down on the sofa in her hotel room, thinking of

Lootchee, the night they had shared together, and how something so wonderful could turn into something so horrible. One thing for certain, two for sure, she was planning to be on the first thing smoking out of Texas in the morning and wasn't coming back.

Someone knocked at the door. She got up and looked through the peephole to see Lootchee standing there, looking fresh as the morning. She was shocked, happy, and mad all at the same time.

"What do you want now, Lootchee?" she asked through the door. She wasn't quite ready to forgive him.

"Will you let me in so I can explain?"

"What's there to explain? You left me for dead while you got in a fight at your event. What type of businessman does that?" She had her hands on her hips. "What type of man does that?" She asked the same question again, but she stood aside, waving him to come into the room.

"You can't expect me to stand by and watch my man get beat down, right in front of my eyes." He came into the room. "Just like I wouldn't expect you to stand by and watch Seville or one of your girls catch a bad one."

Lootchee had a point, but she didn't want to admit it.

"Hello, Earth to Gangsta Man," she said and waved her hand at him. "You had a date, a beautiful woman by your side, and you just started throwing blows like Mayweather."

"If I had my way, it wouldn't have gone down like that. Some things you just can't control in life. Where did you go anyway? You were supposed to help me," he said, trying to lighten the tension.

"You can't be serious?" She stepped back to the end table where her glass of wine sat and crossed her arms.

He nodded, looking into her eyes.

"If things were the other way around, I would've gotten dirty for you. Believe that. Anyway, I came here because I was worried about you. I couldn't stop thinking about you," he said, taking her into his arms and embracing her.

She didn't want to hug him back but she couldn't help herself.

"I was just thinking about you too," she said. "But as a businessman you can't think with your emotions. Please let this be a lesson learned. Violence isn't always the key."

"I get it. Teach! That's what I like about you. You want to make a better person out of me."

After she let go of him, she smiled.

They had a couple of drinks and soon were laughing about the whole ordeal.

"Is Steve going to be okay?" She was really concerned. "He took some nasty chucks to the head."

"He's a tough dude. I would've been stretched out in somebody's hospital room after some shit like that," Lootchee admitted. "I gave him the rest of the night off, though."

"How nice of you, what a great boss. Only the night off?" she inquired.

He put his hand on her leg. She could feel the heat through the robe's thin fabric. "Yeah, only the night because he's driving us to the game. I still want to take you with me to the Dallas game tomorrow."

Beijing covered the hand he had on her leg with her own.

"It's a date," she told him. "What time does it start? Because I have to catch my flight back to Charlotte at nine PM, which means I have to be at the airport no later than eight."

"The game starts at noon," he said excitedly. "I'll stay here tonight. When we get up in the morning, we can have breakfast. Steve will scoop us and take us to my place so I can get changed and then head off to the stadium."

Beijing gave him a *Slow down cowboy* look. "What do you mean . . . you'll stay here?"

"I don't want you to take this the wrong way but if I just wanted some pussy I wouldn't have to look long for it. I like you, Beijing. If all I get to do is hold you in my arms, I'll be a happy man. No strings attached," he said. "It would be a pleasure if you allowed me to hold you tight."

"Lootchee, I don't think so."

"Come on, we are both grown."

She didn't know why, but she let him in. He kept good on his word by not trying to touch her in a sexual way the entire night, and if the truth was told, she was surprised to find that she was kind of disappointed. Déjà vu!

$ $ $

The next morning she was awakened by the loud ringing of her hotel room phone. "How are things going down there in the Lone Star? Good to hear that everything is going fine down there. That's one of the finest pieces of property!" he boasted.

"I love it, the décor is simply beautiful," she said, thinking, *If you've seen one you seen them all.* Then she decided to cut to the chase. "To what do I owe this call?"

"Have you ever heard of the rock band Deader than Dead?"

"No, I haven't, but I will research them and make sure that I'm informed if you like."

"That won't be necessary. They're the hottest band on the rock/heavy-metal circuit and they're going to be staying at our property in Charlotte to do a concert at the Verizon Amphitheater. They rented the entire top floor, and of course they want nothing but the best, so I'm assigning them to you along with the actress slash gold digger Fiona French."

"Now, I've heard lots about her."

"She's promoting her new book and will be staying with us one night while on her book tour. And of course, you still have Natalia."

"She's actually out of town and won't be back until Thursday."

"Good for her, but because she's out of town that doesn't mean that you won't hear from her. You know that," he joked.

"That's so true."

"So anyway, I know whatever the case, you will make each of them as comfortable as possible."

"Of course. Not a problem at all," Beijing assured Thaddius. "When do they arrive?"

"Check-in is on Wednesday for both Fiona French and the band, and I have assured both of their managers that they will have the best hotel host attending to their needs when they arrive." He added, "Nothing less than the best for the best."

"You can count on me," Beijing assured him before hanging up.

CHAPTER 15

Keep Your Hands to Yourself

The stadium was filled to capacity for the NFC matchup. The Redskins and Cowboys always got everybody's motor roaring. The energy was electrifying. It was a low-scoring game, but all eyes were on every snap of the ball.

Lootchee had told Beijing during the national anthem that nothing but the best was good enough for her, and he intended on proving it. Beijing was impressed with the skybox but bored with the game. Though she knew the skybox was the best accommodations that money could buy, she felt boxed in

Lootchee was a big football fan and was deep into the game because right at that point, the game was deep down in his pockets. It was the fourth quarter. The Redskins were winning seven to six, but the Cowboys had the ball. When Lootchee told Beijing that he had a bundle riding on the game, he meant it. If Dallas didn't find a way to score, and fast, he would be out fifty grand,

and to make matters worse they probably wouldn't make the pla-offs.

"I have to go the ladies' room," Beijing said. She saw that there were private restrooms in the skybox but needed to stretch her legs and get some air. The game had been going on for three hours with only a fifteen-minute break for halftime.

"Do you want me to go with you?" he asked, never looking away from the game.

"No, I think I can manage. I just want to get some air."

"You sure?" he asked, only glancing up at her because the play had not started yet.

"I'm a big girl. I can take care of myself. Plus I'm not going that far."

"There isn't any question on whether or not you are a big girl; I just want to make sure you are comfortable on my watch."

"Enjoy the game, I'll be back in a sec." She kissed him on the cheek.

Lootchee instructed Steve, "Man, go with her to make sho she good."

Beijing was dressed in skintight blue jeans and a white top trimmed in rhinestones with a pair of blue, gray, and white studded cowboy boots and the necklace Lootchee had bought her. It might have been her beauty or her exquisite necklace that commanded the eyes of men and women as she strolled by the concession stands. She saw a restroom sign on the left beside a guy selling pretzels and made a note to get one on the way back.

As she walked into the stall, she did not notice that a guy had slipped in behind her. Before she realized what was happening, she felt something hard hit her in the back. She stumbled and felt someone trying to snatch the necklace off her neck.

"What da fuck?" she screamed out loud.

Beijing grabbed his arm, swung around, and kicked him in the nuts, forcing him out of the stall. She had been practicing this maneuver for a year, ever since she learned it in self-defense class. She anticipated that this trick would come in handy, but she always imagined that she would have to use it behind a building on a dark street or in an alley. But it didn't matter where it was, because she had her can of whip-ass out.

When she kicked the attacker in the nuts, she heard him grunt in pain. "Ah!" His groans only fueled her.

"Bitch-ass," she screamed. Her adrenaline started going. Beijing swung her purse, beating the dude silly upside the head with intense punches.

"Motherfucker!"

An older white lady with bright red hair started to enter the bathroom, but when she saw what was going on she ran out, screaming at the top of her lungs, "Oh he's got a gun! BOMB! BOMB! Help!"

Steve burst into the bathroom as if he were Superman without the cape, but Beijing didn't need any assistance. She had the entire situation under control. She had managed to get the villain on the floor and at that point, she was stomping him with her new boots, drawing blood.

The police arrived shortly after but not before Steve got a few punches, kicks, and stomps in himself. Once the police took over, Beijing went to pick up her necklace off the floor.

The police had the guy in handcuffs, and Beijing recognized him as the man at the mall that day.

"Damn, it's Owen," Steve muttered.

The police emptied Owen's pockets right there in the bathroom and found six different ladies' wallets. Owen glared at Beijing.

"That's my damn necklace," he said. "That shit is mine."

"That's enough out of you," one of the officers said, yanking Owen by the collar, dragging him out the door.

"Well, it's on my neck, and that's where it's gonna stay! Whether you like it or not," she said with spunk.

"You sure you okay?" Steve asked.

"I'm a little shook up, to be honest, but I'll be fine," she admitted, "and my ankle is hurting really bad."

"Cool," Steve said. "But can I ask you a favor?"

"What is it?" She looked puzzled.

"When we tell Lootchee about this, can we tell him that I was the one who knocked Owen out?"

"Fine by me," she joked. "I don't want him to think that I'm some gangsta bitch, no way!"

"Too late," Lootchee said from behind her. "Let's get your ankle checked out."

CHAPTER 16

Shoveling Shit

The weekend in Texas was refreshing and invigorating. Even though she came back with a twisted ankle, Beijing wished she was still there being wined and dined and living the life of luxury, but reality had called. And her reality meant getting her butt back to work fulfilling the desires and needs of other people.

Beijing spent the next day and entire night alternating between heat and ice trying to get her ankle together for the upcoming big days. When she came to work that morning at six thirty, she noticed about thirty girls milling around the lobby. Most were bearing gifts: flowers, stuffed animals, whips, chains, condoms, lotions, panties. Name it . . . if it was naughty, it was there.

The heavy-metal group Deader than Dead was due to arrive that day, and they were going to be more than a few handfuls. The band had had the top heavy-metal song in the country for the past fifteen weeks and counting, and they were a boatload of trouble, noise, and excitement all at the same time. They had booked the entire seventeenth floor for two days.

"What in the hell is going on?" she asked April.

"Groupies," April answered, as if they ought to be ashamed of themselves. "I really hope I don't look like that when I am chasing down a rich man."

"You do," Beijing half joked.

By noon the collection of people sitting in the lobby had spilled out into the parking lot and swollen to around two hundred—and it wasn't just girls anymore. Grungy-looking guys trying their best to look cool and nonchalant and not being successful at all joined the slutty-looking girls. By five o'clock when the band was supposed to arrive, there must have been six hundred people outside the hotel, and the party was on! A huge four-by-four pulled onto the premises with a Deader than Dead promotional wrap front-to-back and their number one hit blaring from the speakers. The fans were out of control as they sang and danced to the music. *What are the other customers going to think,* Beijing worried.

April was acting as Beijing's assistant this week, and together they were going over a checklist to make sure that all of the band's needs and wants would be fully taken care of.

"April, was the paperwork for the eight extra security guards taken care of? You know we need them in place to make sure no one makes it onto the floor unless they are invited guests of the band." Beijing had hosted a few other rock bands before and knew that it would be smart to have the extra manpower on hand.

"Check. I also contracted the off-duty police officers for crowd control in the lobby."

"Ten cases of Jack Daniel's sent up to their rooms."

"Check."

"Access to twenty-four-hour room service?"

"Check."

"Remove all Bibles from their rooms," Beijing read off, then thought about what she had just said. "What the hell is that about?"

"No clue, but it's been taken care of."

"All I know is we need to say a prayer to help us through this one. Girl, give me your hand." Beijing took April's hand, closed her eyes, and said a few words.

"If only Ms. French's requests were that simple."

"Now, she's another story."

Ms. Fiona French's latest claim to fame was dating an Arabian billionaire. She had co-starred in a few movies, was in the process of shooting a reality show, and had just released her new book, *How to Land a Billionaire*. The media could not get enough of her flamboyant, outlandish personality. She was in town promoting the hardback.

She had checked in already, and somehow Fiona had mistakenly thought that Beijing was her personal go-fetch-it girl. She'd arrived first thing that morning and was scheduled to leave in two days, which wouldn't be soon enough for Beijing.

Fiona called the desk next morning acting as if it were Beijing's fault that she hadn't packed the proper amount of undergarments. She insisted that Beijing run right out to buy three pairs.

"I need a late checkout and I only wear Claire Pettibone, and I don't want you to send another soul. Do it yourself," she demanded. "Because I don't want anyone else to see what goes on my tanned hind parts. It'll be in the magazines by the end of the week. You are my hotel host. Not those stupid people who can't seem to get a damn thing right."

"That's not a problem, Ms. French," Beijing assured her. "Have you had an incident with any of our staff?"

"No, but they just look like peons, like they are waiting to mess something up. Now, for the third time I need a size one." *This skinny bitch needs to eat something, instead of constantly complaining about the tea being too hot when room service delivers it,* Beijing thought as she stood in line at the mall waiting to purchase the silky unmentionables. *But if doing this will get this anorexic, neurotic bitch off my back and out of the hotel, then by all means let me get this done.*

Beijing's cell phone broke her thoughts.

"Hello?"

"Girl, you ain't gonna believe this." It was April, calling from the hotel.

"I'll believe the pope's a pimp right about now. Anything's possible," Beijing half joked.

"Are you sittin' down?" April asked.

"I'm on my way to the car now." She was walking out of the air-conditioned store into a Charlotte fall evening. "What's up?"

"I've been calling upstairs all afternoon trying to get the band out so that we can get those rooms turned around quickly."

"Is that all?" Beijing chimed in. "That's why I blocked those rooms for any check-ins until after nine PM. I had a feeling they would be late getting out after a long night of partying, booze, and broads."

"Well—" April paused. "—it looks like we're going to need a little more time than that."

"Don't tell me they're still there?"

"Actually, they're gone, but . . ."

"But what?" Beijing was too fed up with all the drama.

"You're going to have to see it to believe it, girl."

"Try me," Beijing insisted, just reaching her car, pushing the button to release the lock and getting in.

"I started calling upstairs at about two PM. I wanted to try to help as much as possible before you returned. I knew you were stressed from dealing with all Fiona's constant bullshit-ass demands. Anyway, I finally caught up with their manager around four."

"Rick?" Beijing asked, hoping April would move the story along a little quicker.

"Yes, Rick da Dick."

"Yeah, you ain't never lied, girl," she agreed.

"He promised that he was on top of the situation and that he would have everyone up and out shortly."

"And . . ." Beijing sighed, pulling out of the crowded parking lot. "Sounds like there's more."

"Oh, there's more. He got on top of it all right," April concurred. "When Rick could not get them out of the room, he took matters in his own hands. He sprayed the fire extinguisher under the bottom of their room doors, and now that white shit is all over the place."

"You're kidding me?" Beijing was in shock.

"That's not all," April added. "They moved furniture out of the rooms, barricading all the exits, I guess to block girls from coming up the stairs."

"That's a fire hazard. Thank God no one got hurt."

"Yup, and I forgot to mention the chair that was thrown out the window that almost hit one of our other guests."

"What?"

"I can't make this stuff up. They also broke most of the mirrors and some more shit. Like I said, girl, you gotta see it for yourself."

"Well, I'm on my way." Beijing's phone beeped, and she looked at the call coming in. "Go ahead, April, it's just Fiona."

"Okay, well I don't mean to continue to piss in your cereal, but the place is a wreck. They're saying it may take a week to get back in order, and that's with everybody working overtime."

When Beijing returned to the hotel she got Justin to deliver Ms. French's items, then put together a team of people consisting of management and housekeeping and set out to survey the damage. Since these were her clients, she wanted to be there. The second she stepped through the sliding doors of the elevator onto the seventeenth floor, a horrible stench hit her in the face.

"Oh God! Something smells like shit!" she screamed, covering her nose with her left arm to keep herself from vomiting. Nobody could fault her outburst, because the smell was undeniable and unbearable.

Deader than Dead made sure that the hotel was deader than dead before they left. They had treated the entire floor as if tearing up the rooms were an Olympic event and they were competing for the gold medal. All the mattresses were dripping wet and smelled of urine. Beer cans, liquor bottles, empty condom wrappers, food, and drug paraphernalia covered the floor. They even left a three-foot-long pipe that they'd been smoking sitting in the middle of the floor with a note on it that said, *Tip.*

Beijing was surveying what was over a hundred thousand dollars' worth of damage when her cell phone rang.

"Excuse me," she said to her colleagues, taking the phone from her waist. It was Lootchee. She stepped out of the room.

"Baby, I can't talk right now." She sounded exasperated. "I'm having a real shitty day. Literally."

Lootchee barely got a chance to say "Okay" before she ended the call. Beijing really wanted to talk to Lootchee, to tell him how much she appreciated the visit and quality time they had spent together and how much of a gentleman he was and how she couldn't wait to see him again. But that would have to wait, because the issue at hand was taking all the energy she had.

Before she could step back in the room, her phone went off again. This time it was from Fiona.

"Didn't I tell you that I didn't want you to send some damn bellhop to bring me my things? And you forgot to bring me the Golden Delicious apple I asked for? And also some hot tea. Not flaming hot, just hot?"

Beijing was steaming hot herself. "Can you give room service a call for that please?" she said in a calm voice.

"Are you my hotel host or am I yours?" Fiona asked.

Beijing was quiet for a second. She took a deep breath, but Fiona spoke. "Do you want to say something? Because *God* only knows what you are thinking."

"I will call them for you," she said. "Will there be anything else?"

"Yeah! Where are you that you can't deliver my things and cater to my needs concerning my tea and my Golden Delicious apple?"

"I'm dealing with a major situation in the hotel."

"I think you are avoiding me. I'd like to come to where you are, to see what's so important," Fiona pressed.

"No, that's not a good idea," Beijing said. "I will have your requests sent right up to you."

"No, I think I want to come and see what exactly is so pressing before I demand your boss fire you for your insolence."

Beijing ignored her remark. "I'm on the seventeenth floor, but I don't recommend that you come up here." Beijing knew it was wrong to let her see the hotel in that condition but she wanted Fiona to see that she had bigger fish to fry than a goddamn Golden Delicious apple and some warm tea.

"Oh my God," April screamed.

"What is it?" Beijing asked as she stepped back into the room.

"Those trifling-ass bastards shitted in the every last one of the dresser draws."

Another scream came from the hall. The manager and Beijing rushed out. It was Fiona, looking down at her shoe with a horrified expression.

"And apparently in a few other places too," Beijing said with a grin.

"This is despicable. Who lives like this? My fucking Chanels are all shitty. I'm checking out of this piece of shit, and this hotel will replace my Chanels and I mean it!" Fiona screamed as she stormed out tracking size-eight feces footprints all through the hotel.

CHAPTER 17

After a Long's Day Work

After working fourteen hours a day for the past two days, Beijing was beat. Housekeeping was pulling in lots of overtime trying to restore the rooms on the seventeenth floor to their original condition. Beijing felt bad because her clients had created this mess. She helped as much as she could, but it was time to get a good night's rest.

As she headed to her suite, she heard the elevator alert that meant it was stopping on her floor. Soon after she heard someone call out to her, "Ms. Lee. Please sign here." Maxine, one of the housekeeping supervisors, handed her a clipboard. Over the past forty-eight hours Beijing had gotten used to being passed the clipboard, having to sign off on everything that had not been accounted for in the initial walk-through of the mess that the band had ruined or broken. This time it was the icing on the cake.

"Twelve sixty-one?" she asked.

"Yes." Maxine shyly nodded.

That's Fiona's room, she thought. Beijing read off the list: towels, coffeemaker, robe, slippers, umbrella, and iron. "Not the sheets?" Beijing said out loud, surprised.

"Please don't shoot the messenger!" Maxine said.

"Oh, I won't. I seriously need a drink." She put her signature on the dotted line. "It looks like she took anything that wasn't bolted to the floor."

Maxine said, "Sorry to be the bearer of bad news."

"No, you are just doing your job. Again, I apologize that you all have to deal with this." Beijing handed the clipboard back to her.

"Just the nature of the beast." Maxine walked off and called out to Beijing, "Take a long bubble bath and try not to stress over it. It's not your fault. You can't control other people's actions."

Beijing ran her card through the swipe-pad of the door; the light turned green, and she pushed her way into her suite. All she wanted was a shower and a good night's rest. All the lights were down, the room was faded to black, but there was a sweet familiar aroma in the air. She slid her hand down the wall in search of the switch. Got it! A fluorescent hue flooded the living room. The first thing she saw was a gorgeous vase filled with every color rose imaginable arranged beautifully. Single rose petals were strategically placed on the floor, creating a trail of loveliness. The trail ended in the bedroom atop the mattress, forming a big heart with L & B in the center. She couldn't help smiling as she felt her troubles start to melt. *There is always light at the end of the tunnel.*

She dialed Lootchee's number immediately.

"How sweet of you," she gushed the moment he picked up. "Thank you, baby. It was just what I needed after such a long day."

"Don't thank me, thank the gods for creating such a beautiful lady," he said.

"I don't know what to do about you. You do all the right things at all the right times."

"Well, you did say you were having a bad couple of days and I was too far away to give you a hug, so I did the next best thing, ya feel me?"

There was a knock at the door. Not expecting anyone, she peeked out the viewer and saw Su-Yung, the Tabby's head massage therapist.

"What are you doing here, Su-Yung?" she asked, hoping he didn't need her to come and put out another fire. Lord knows she wasn't in the mood for that madness.

"You boyfriend," Su-Yung said in broken English.

Lootchee laughed and said, "I didn't get a chance to tell you that I also arranged for you to have some well deserved R and R."

Beijing was speechless for a moment and then managed to say, "Thanks, Lootchee."

"Enjoy yourself, baby! I'll be counting down the minutes and hours until we see each other again," he said before they ended the call.

"I've been sent to give you a full-body massage," Su-Yung said. "Let's start." He rubbed his magic hands together.

"Okay, Su-Yung, give me about fifteen minutes to wash off the work dust and I'm all yours."

"Excellent, madam." He agreed to come back then.

Right on schedule, skin still soft and wet from the shower, Beijing waltzed back into the front room wearing a bathrobe. There were candles burning; a cushioned table sat smack-dead in the middle of the floor, draped with white sheets.

"All right, get undressed," he said. "Lie facedown on table and cover self. Be back couple minutes."

Beijing did as she was asked: disrobed, lay on the table face-down, got under the sheet, and waited for Su-Yung to come back. When he returned, he put on some relaxing music. Beijing closed her eyes and imagined a lazy, perfect sunset.

She nodded her head back. Next she heard the splattering of oil being squirted onto his palms. He rubbed his hands together, and the room smelled like lavender. Once his magical fingers found her neck, all of her aches, pains, stress, and cares melted away into his touch. She was like butter.

"You like?" he asked.

"What?" She was feeling so good she'd missed what he said.

"You like?"

"I like," she murmured.

Twenty minutes into the massage Beijing was sound asleep, feeling like a lottery winner. Then she could feel his hand lingering on her butt a little too long for her comfort.

"What da fu—" she said, about to jump up and duke it out with Su-Yung.

"Whoa, baby, it's me," Lootchee said with a smile.

"How . . . where?" She was so relaxed, she felt delusional

Lootchee silenced her with a kiss. "Relax." Then he put his finger to his lips before giving her another kiss.

He picked her up, carried her to the bed, and placed her on the silk sheets. He gently pulled her bottom lip between his own and softly sucked on it, giving her a long, hot, and juicy tongue kiss. After half a dozen more pecks, his tongue moved between her lips and teeth, going in for the kill. She could put up a fight or accept it, but Lootchee was prepared to conquer her either way. He was met with a reticent yet insistent suction. She was roping him in like a cowboy at a bull-riding rodeo.

Before long their tongues were attacking each other like swords used by two professional fencers. Her hands rushed down to the bottom of his shirt, pulling it over his head. Lootchee's hands dropped down to her butt and squeezed it like it was Charmin.

He dragged his tongue over one breast, rubbing the other with his hand. As if his tongue had a mind of its own, it trailed down her stomach till it reached the spot between her legs, leaving wet footprints as it was marking its territory. With his free hand he spread her legs and his tongue dove in like a scuba diver looking for lost treasure. Beijing gasped then relaxed as he probed for the goodies.

When he was done, Beijing got on him and rode him like a stallion, making him call her name.

"Beijing, Beijing, Beijing!"

The next morning, Lootchee and Beijing slept in and ordered room service. "I'm so glad I don't have any special guests in town."

"Me too," Lootchee added.

"So, today I think I'm going to take you on a picnic and we can sit by the lake and appreciate the small things life has to offer us, like the natural wonders of the world."

"I'm cool with that."

Lootchee gave himself a tour of her posh suite.

"This place is cute," he said, nodding.

"Isn't it?" She was glad that he liked it.

"Nothing like indulging in luxury, but you are my woman now and my lady lives a little bit more extravagant. So we need to find you a place."

"But I stay here free of charge. Free room and board and food. I don't have to pay for anything."

"And you won't have any bills at your new place either." He gave her a long French kiss. "After the picnic, let's go look at condos."

Beijing didn't want to argue with him; nor did she want to give up her place at the Tabby. Still, she reasoned with herself, maybe if she did, she wouldn't have to take her work home with her. So it seemed like Lootchee's thoughts did make sense.

"Ask your boss for a vacation," he said.

"It should be okay with him. Before I met you, I hadn't really taken any vacation. I've always been a workaholic so he shouldn't have a problem."

"Even if he does, you need to just take one." He got up, went into his bag, and pulled out two envelopes. "Choose one. Do you want door number one or door number two?" he teased, holding them both above her head.

"Depends on what's behind the doors."

"I can't tell you, you have to pick."

"I don't know." She carefully examined both envelopes.

"No peeking." He playfully hit her. "Stop torturing yourself and pick one and get it over with."

"Okay, so let me get number two," she said excitedly.

She opened it and could not believe the contents. A trip to Rio de Janeiro. She was too excited, and the flight would leave in only two weeks!

CHAPTER 18

Is It Love? Or Intoxication?

As the jet touched down in Rio de Janeiro, a Latin man leaned over and said, "Rio is the most beautiful city for a love affair. Whenever I leave I am filled with *saudade*."

"What does that mean?" Beijing asked.

"Um, it's like longing, unbearable longing, the way you long for a lover when she is away from you." The Latin man's eyes glinted, looking over at Beijing and Lootchee.

"Really?" Beijing said. Then she looked over at Lootchee, who wasn't even listening. His eyes were glued to the scenery outside the window by their first-class seats.

"Have a wonderful trip," the Latin man said.

And it was wonderful. They spent days lolling around on Ipanema Beach or watching soccer matches that Lootchee just had to bet on, nights dancing in the clubs, and mornings having sex in the king-sized bed of the luxury suite at the finest resort in the city.

One afternoon Lootchee had to meet with somebody on some business. He wouldn't say what it was, and Beijing was pretty sure it wasn't legit. It didn't matter what he did, she thought. A lot of men earned their money in underhanded ways and then went on to turn their cash into legitimate businesses. Her own daddy had done that, turning his ill-gotten gains into a prosperous towing and transport business. Lootchee could do the same thing when he was ready.

In the meantime he gave her a wad of cash and told her to go shopping in Rio, and she wasn't about to say no. In fact, she found it was damn near impossible to say no to anything Lootchee wanted.

So that night when he looked into her eyes over a dinner of tender Brazilian steak in a restaurant overlooking jungle water-falls and said, "Baby, I want you to move to Dallas," she was at a loss for words. Her job was her world; everything that she had been busting her butt for.

"You want me to quit my job?" she asked. What a choice, she thought. She loved her work. It defined her. Would she give it up for Lootchee? She might finally have to say no to him after all.

"Did you forget they just opened a brand-new Tabby Hotel in downtown Dallas?" Lootchee asked. "I wouldn't tell you to give up your yoke. I know how much that means to you. Shit. I just want you to be nearby so I can take care of you when you ain't taking care of others."

Beijing melted.

"I'll call Thaddius as soon as we get back," she said with a smile.

Thaddius was glad to reassign Beijing.

"It's a new property and we could use your expertise," he said. "Maybe even take on an understudy. No one can be as good as you, but if you could train a mini you, of course I would be most appreciative."

It took her a week to get things packed up and get the Charlotte staff set. April said she was sad to see her go, but happy to get a chance to do some of Beijing's work. Greta even said she'd help her get moved and maybe she'd stay in Dallas for a while to keep her company. Rayna sulked.

"Girl, you can't just up and leave us," Rayna said over drinks at Scorpio, the hot new gay club where even straight girls loved to go and dance.

"Rayna, I have so many frequent flier miles I can come back anytime I want. And you can come down to Dallas. Hell, this ain't the horse-and-buggy era. Lootchee will be happy to fly his boo's best friend down once in a while. Plus I'll have to come up this way to check on Chyna and make sure her drug-addict momma isn't trying to peddle her pussy for crack," Beijing added.

"Paris isn't that bad," Rayna said.

"I hope not. As long as Willabee takes her medication, Chyna should be okay, but believe me, I'll be back on the regular to check on my family. We can hang out then."

Beijing got along great with the new staff. There were plenty of oil barons and dirty politicians who needed her discreet help in so many different ways. There was a famous preacher who liked to invite homosexual prostitutes to his room and do crystal meth with them, never mind that he was spearheading a campaign to prevent gay people from having the same rights as everyone else. Then there were private meetings between politicians so high up that Beijing had to scurry around making sure Secret Service agents didn't shoot someone. It was an exciting place to be, but her job was no longer her whole life.

Thaddius gave Beijing a suite at the new hotel, but she hardly ever slept there. She stayed with Lootchee when she was off duty in a place he got for the two of them nearby. Even though she loved her job, as the weeks turned into months, she found that she spent less time worrying about her clients and more time taking care of Lootchee's needs. It was overwhelming, but she loved to take care of her man.

One morning Beijing lay in the big mahogany bed watching Lootchee sleep and realized how much she missed him when they were apart. She ached for him. What was the word that Latin man had said to her on the airplane: *saudade*. That was it. She was filled with an unbearable longing. She sat up and looked at herself in the mirror over the dresser. Damn, she was hooked just like Teflon the Don had been on his drug of choice. She lay back on the fluffy down pillows. Now she understood what it felt like to be under the complete control of something—or someone!—else. She was jonesing for a man: Lootchee.

CHAPTER 19

She Loves Me . . . She Loves Me Not

Then Lootchee stretched and turned his head toward Beijing.

"Good morning, my love," she said.

"Is it love?" he asked, staring into her eyes and waiting for the answer.

"Of course it is." She paused and then asked him, "Don't you think so?"

Beijing never mentioned love because she knew that the discussion was like a double-edged sword. Beijing's father had put her up on this game, and she took heed. If she spoke on it too soon, it could run a man away or give him the wrong idea. On the other hand, some men used the L-word loosely to get whatever an emotional needy woman was willing and able to give.

"This may sound crazy to you but all of this is new to me. Before now, I simply didn't love women," Lootchee admitted.

"What? Huh?" Beijing was confused. How could he go through

thirty years of life without romantic love? "Please don't tell me that you did men?"

"Do I look like a switch-hitter to you?" Not waiting on an answer, "Between my mother's bullshit and me seeing so much in the streets, I decided a long time ago that in this business, I don't have time for any distractions.

"Sure, I thoroughly enjoy the company of beautiful women, but I always remembered that line Robert DeNiro used in that movie *Heat:* Never get too close to anything that you're not willing to part with in thirty seconds. I didn't have time to engage in deep relationships. They were too time-consuming, and in my mind women were trouble, only good for three things: helping me get to the next level, busting a nut, and as an arm piece, in that order. Plus, a lot of women are nags and want to keep tabs on me."

"Wow!" Beijing was stunned. "Are you kidding?"

"I'm coming clean with you because I can. For the first time in many years, things feel different. Having you in my life was something that I genuinely wanted and needed. Do you love me?" he asked her.

"I have very strong feelings for you," she answered slowly.

"I think I love you too," he admitted.

"You think?" Beijing shot back.

"I do," he corrected. "I never thought I'd be here feeling this way, but I do and here I am."

Beijing took Lootchee into her arms. "I love you, baby, and I hope the feelings I have for you will never go away."

"Then what should we do about these feelings?"

With her eyebrows raised, she asked, "What do you suggest?"

"How about marriage?" He took her hand. "Will you marry me, Beijing Lee?"

Beijing's mouth dropped wide open. She began to feel light-headed and disoriented, unable to speak.

Hoping her reaction didn't equate to a rejection, he said, "A simple yes or no will do."

The next four words rolled over him like hot butter on an ear of corn. "I'll be glad to." Then she smiled the most beautiful smile Lootchee had ever seen.

"Then it's official," he said, showing all thirty-two teeth. "When do you want to make it happen?"

"I'm ready when you are," she said.

"How about tomorrow?" Lootchee had no reservations or doubt about what he was asking her to do. And he always got what he wanted . . . when he wanted.

He got up, went into the other room, and returned with a red velvet box and handed it to her. She couldn't contain her smile as she opened the box.

"OH MY GOD!" she screamed, covering her mouth when she saw what was inside: a seven-carat flawless solitaire engagement ring, surrounded by seven carats of smaller diamonds. "This ring is gorgeous," she said.

"Seven carats for the seven months we've been together."

They made love for the rest of the morning, and they both dozed off until Lootchee woke Beijing up. "Baby, get up. We need to go get everything together for tomorrow," he whispered.

"Tomorrow?" she asked. "What's going on tomorrow?" She was scheduled to work in Charlotte the day after tomorrow for a big conference.

"Our big day. Me and you. You becoming Mrs. Cazelle."

"Like within twenty-four hours tomorrow?"

"Yes, my dear." He planted a kiss on her forehead.

"That's too soon, baby. Can we push it to next month?"

"Why next month? You said whenever I was ready. I'm ready today, but I will settle for tomorrow."

"I want to plan a real wedding, a wedding where everybody can make a big to-do about me; the flowers, the guests, the ruffles, the invites. I know a fabulous wedding planner that can pull it all together." She went on and on, excited.

"If that's what you really want," he relented.

"Just give me a month or so and though I am all yours now, then I will be all yours legally."

"You got forty-five days." He sealed the deal with a kiss on the lips.

The next day he dropped her off at the airport to head to Charlotte. As usual, she called him once she got to her departure gate and talked to him while boarding her flight and up to the time that the FAA required her to shut off her phone. Once Beijing landed, she called Lootchee back. He answered immediately, "Hey you made it safe?"

"Yup, and I miss you already." She was filled with joy.

"I miss you too," he said. "Can I call you back, though? I got a few important matters that I'm trying to take care of. I'll hit you later when you get home."

"Of course, hon. I'm going to stop by the CVS and grab some bridal magazines so I can get a few ideas."

On her ride home, Beijing begin to make calls to touch base with a few of her clients, promising that she would have all of their requests taken care of over the next couple of days.

As soon as she walked in the door to her beautiful condo in the ritzy Ballantyne neighborhood of Charlotte, she kicked off her shoes and called Lootchee. He answered on the first ring. "Yeah."

"Hey, babe, I just wanted you to know that your blushing bride-to-be is home."

"Okay, baby. But still I'm trying to get this shit over here under control. Today is hectic, I'll call you back."

"I'll be waiting."

While she waited for Lootchee's call, she browsed through several bridal magazines and a couple of different wedding websites. The more ideas she ran across, the more ecstatic she became about her own wedding plans. She got so caught up she hadn't realized that it was almost midnight and Lootchee hadn't called her back.

This is odd, she thought. When she called him and he didn't answer, she was sure that he would return her call, but he didn't. As the night got later and later and sleep eluded her, she began to think the worst: Had something happened? Was he okay? Had he been hurt somehow? Gone to jail? She called several more times and still got his voice mail. She began to look up all the local hospitals and the jails in his area and gave them a call. Part of her was hoping to find him at one of the places and another part was hoping that she wouldn't.

After two days, she didn't know what to do, so she took it way back to high school: She called Seville and told her to call Lootchee on a three-way call. He answered on the second ring. "Yeah."

"Baby, are you okay?" She was so worried.

"Yeah, I am cool."

Then why hadn't he returned or answered her calls? she thought. "I've been so worried about you."

"I'm good, could never be better, but I'm in the middle of something. I'll call you back as soon as I'm done."

"Okay, I am here. Try not to keep me waiting too long."

"Yup," he said before hanging up.

Beijing couldn't focus on the call with Seville, because she was too busy replaying the conversation over in her head with Lootchee. It didn't sound right to her.

"Is that right?" Beijing said. She was staring out the window at the Charlotte skyline.

"What the hell do you mean, is that right? Are you listening to me or are you looking at porn on your Internet?" she joked.

"I'm sorry, Seville. I'm thinking 'bout this conversation I had with Lootchee. Something isn't right, and I can't figure out exactly what it is."

"He's just busy, that's all," Seville assured her. "You know his nose is wide open for you."

"That's just it, girl," she said. "I don't know that. I don't know anything!"

After she hung up, she tried to call Lootchee again to get to the bottom of things.

"Hey, there, leave a message and I'll get back to you when I get around to it," the voice mail answered.

She didn't even bother leaving a message. What the hell was so important he couldn't answer his dang phone? What was going on?

She decided to get caught up on some paperwork for Thaddius. She needed to fill out expense reports for the past three weeks or she'd get so behind, she'd never get caught up. But all the while her stomach churned. Two hours and two weeks of reports had passed and she finally picked up the phone again. This time she would outsmart him. She blocked her number.

"Yo, wassup?" Lootchee said after the first ring.

"Wassup? You really want to know what's up," Beijing huffed. "I want to know what's up, too, Lootchee. How come you only pick up the phone if you think it's not me?"

"Ah, baby, you're just imagining things. I've just been really busy," he said. "I'll call you later. Promise."

"Okay," Beijing said, disappointed. She didn't believe him but it seemed there was nothing she could do. He held all the cards.

It was like her father always said: The truth of the matter was the person who loved the least controlled the relationship, and right now Lootchee was in the driver's seat.

CHAPTER 20

Joke's on You

The following morning Beijing was charged and ready to get to work. The day was filled with lots of small requests, causing the hours to fly by and her not to focus on the call that never came from Lootchee. Before she could get out the door of the hotel to head home, she got a call from her niece.

"Hey Chyna doll," she answered. Her only niece always brightened up her day whenever she spoke to her.

"Hi, Auntie. I need you to get over here quick. It's Gram. She's out of control. Hurry up. She's having a real bad day, and I'm worried that it might get worse and there's no telling what she might do."

"Did she take her meds?"

"She hasn't taken them in a few days."

"Ah hell." Beijing knew it was serious. "Why didn't you tell me when she first stopped taking them?"

"Because she promised she would take them the next day and then promised again the next day, but she didn't and now I think there are going to be big problems."

"Okay, I'm on the way. Now, it'll take me a couple of hours to get there, but don't worry, I'll be there."

"Just hurry, I really need you."

Her niece's cry for help made her forget about everything else. In no time flat, she was out of the door and headed to her pride and joy's side.

Once she got in the car Beijing called Greta and said, "Ma, I need you."

"What's going on, baby? Are you back home?" Greta could hear the panic in Beijing's voice.

"Yes, I got in two days ago and I've been meaning to call you but I got a little caught up."

"You've been caught up with that new boyfriend, huh?"

"Not hardly. That's a whole other story; I will have to tell you about that later." She sighed, then got back to the reason she called. "Chyna just called me sounding really scared and she says that Willabee is off her meds again. I'm headed over there now."

"I can meet you over there," Greta offered.

That's the kind of person Greta was. Without any hesitation she always had Beijing's back and genuinely wanted to help anybody in need. People in the church, the neighborhood, it didn't matter to her; she just wanted to be a blessing to folks.

"That would be wonderful."

Greta was always happy to help wherever her stepdaughter needed her, even if it meant dealing with Willabee. She'd once despised Willabee, because Willabee could have children and Greta couldn't. She knew it wasn't her place to ask God why, but she couldn't understand why God would give a person like Willabee chance after chance to have baby after baby but not give her one. Through the years, her feelings transformed from hate to more or less pity. She knew Willabee, so she only prayed for her to get better and be a positive person for Beijing and especially Chyna.

When Beijing pulled up, she couldn't believe her eyes. Her fifty-four-year-old mother was outside in a black Wonderbra and a pair of big black bloomers, hollering and screaming, "Where the fuuuccckkk is my goddamn eggs? You said you were going to give me my damn eggs back on the first of the month and today's the twenty-fifth and a whole new month is about to come in this bitch and you ain't gave me shit, not a goddamn thing." Willabee was screaming at the top of her lungs at Marsha, her next-door neighbor of seven years.

"Willabee, I'll give them to you next month, on the first," Marsha tried to explain. Marsha was a big, burly, light-skinned lady who looked to be scared for her life.

"No the hell you won't! You need to give me my shit right fucking now or else I am going to take them out of yo' stankin' ass." She rolled her neck around.

"Willabee, please calm down," her neighbor begged, embarrassed by all the commotion.

"Calm down, my black ass. I don't think so." Willabee was dead serious. "Easy for your freeloading, food-stamp-getting ass to tell me when you done got my shit, cooked whatever the fuck your non-cooking ass done cooked with my motherfucking eggs and ain't think enough of me to give me my shit back." She was walking around the fence to attempt to attack her neighbor. "And a matter of fact don't invite me over for that bullshit-ass meat loaf anymore."

Beijing parked her car, jumped out, and ran over to try to defuse the commotion. She caught her mother before she got all the way into the neighbor's yard.

"Willabee, what's going on?" she calmly asked her mother.

Willabee noticed Beijing for the first time.

"Who in the gates of hell called you?" She looked around and didn't even care about the crowd she was drawing. She turned her attention back to the offending culprit. "Motherfucking snitching-ass bitches, oh they gonna get it now. Bitches wanna run and call my fucking daughter from a few cities over to come and rescue you from this ass-beating, huh?" She was bending down to pick up a stick but Beijing was quicker, tossing the stick out of the way to the other side of the yard.

"Nobody called me to come by," Beijing explained to her mother. "I came by to check on you and to bring Chyna some things I bought for her when I was out of town. Now, why are you out here with no clothes on ready to fight?" Beijing continued firmly. "You know good and well that ain't right."

"Check this shit out, Bay, this bitch is gonna come and get my shit and then don't wanna pay me back."

"Gram, can we go in the house please." Chyna came running out of the house and handed Beijing a housecoat for Willabee to cover herself up. Beijing tried to wrap it around her mother.

"Hell naw, not until this bitch gives me my shit."

"Okay, well let's work it out, but first, Ma, put this housecoat on." Beijing tried to put the housecoat on her mother again. She calmed her mother down a bit: "Ma, we going to get all of this worked out. Don't worry. Now calm yourself down before you give yourself a heart attack." Beijing began to button up the muumuu.

"This shit is too damn hot, you don't understand." Willabee snatched it open. "I'm hot and these flashes keep hitting me." She raised her voice, pointing her fingers, "And this trifling, begging-ass bitch needs to give me my shit back."

Thank God Marsha wasn't fueling the fire. Most of the neighbors knew that Willabee wasn't working with a full deck.

Greta called Beijing to tell her she was less than a minute away, and Beijing asked her to stop and pick up a carton of eggs. Greta was there in less than five minutes with a twenty-four-pack of eggs in her hand.

Everything appeared to be under control until Willabee spotted the eggs in Greta's hand. "Thank you so much," she said to Greta with a smile. "You are such a thoughtful woman and I appreciate you so much."

Then Willabee turned back into her former self and began to throw the eggs at Marsha. Marsha had quick reflexes and managed to duck the first ones, but the last one Willabee threw fell right on her head. The yolk slid over her ear in a thin yellow line. Beijing grabbed the rest of the eggs and gave them to Chyna to take inside.

Woop-woop! It was the familiar sound of the police. A green warrant had been issued to take Willabee down to the mental hospital so she could be evaluated. She could be released once her meds were back in her system.

Meanwhile Beijing talked to Greta and the police, working out all the details on what psych ward Willabee would be taken to and who was going to take care of Chyna. Greta agreed to be responsible for Chyna, getting her to and from school until Willabee got herself together.

Willabee had calmed down. She reached into her bra and retrieved a pack of cigarettes and lighter. As Beijing looked over at her mother, she wanted to cry but she just shook her head.

CHAPTER 21

The Birthday Blues

Four months had passed. Beijing's twenty-ninth birthday came and went and there wasn't much of a celebration except as usual with her father and Greta. She had flown in the day before from Texas to spend her special day with her family. Beijing's birthday was one of the few days, if not the only day, that Sterling would take a day off work. Though both Greta and Sterling had gone to great lengths for her, the gathering somehow turned into a disaster.

Beijing and Greta had been out all day—half a day at the spa followed by lunch and of course shopping. Sterling had the house smelling like a prizewinning restaurant as he prepared a surf-and-turf meal: shrimp and crab fondue for appetizers, and for the main course filet mignon, prawns, and his famous meaty crab cakes. He also made his famous homemade sweet potato french fries as well as steamed veggies.

"A man with many talents," she said to her dad as he put the finishing touches on everything. Beijing knew there was nowhere else in the world she could get home-cooked food this great. "Daddy, you can do everything: run a business, tow, fix, transport, repossess a car, cook as good as if not better than any five-star chef," she said, admiring the way her father was putting the garnish on the plates. "And you raised a very thankful daughter who loves you with all her heart."

"Is there a price tag on all those honey-dipped words?" he joked. "I haven't heard you give me that many compliments since you talked me into buying you that Honda Prelude on your sixteenth birthday."

"No, Daddy. I'm not trying to flatter you, it's the truth," she said.

He shook his head. "It's so hard to spoil you like I used to because you make so much money that you run out and buy yourself everything you want. I remember a time when you used to have a list as long as my arm for your birthdays and Christmas. Now you're so independent. What you making, six figures now?" he proudly asked.

"Something like that, Daddy." She switched the subject, because the last thing she wanted was to spend her birthday taking one of her father's financial workshops, which he tended to give her on a regular basis. There was no denying that when it came to managing and investing money, he had it down to a science. She valued all the information Sterling gave, but tonight wasn't the time or the place. "But seriously, Daddy, you really did a wonderful job raising me and I love and appreciate you for all that you did."

"Hey, hey, hey, he can't take all the credit," Greta interrupted.

"I know you helped, but you know he's the reason why I am even here, because he had his stuff together and enough good sense to rescue me from my momma."

"Speaking of which, did your mother call you to say thank you for the flowers you sent her?" Sterling asked. Before she could answer, they heard a loud commotion and then glass shattering.

"Go hide right now," Sterling directed Beijing and Greta. He ran upstairs for his pistol. Beijing and Greta hid in the closet. From the sound of things, someone or a few someones were in the great room throwing around furniture. But why would anyone want to destroy the house?

"Do you think it's someone who had their car repossessed by Daddy?" Beijing asked Greta.

"Naw, I think it's someone high on crack," Greta whispered.

"Holy shit!" they heard Sterling yell. Beijing couldn't help it. She stuck her head out the closet door and saw Sterling standing on the table with his gun pointed at a three-hundred-pound deer. Their dinner he'd slaved over all afternoon was scattered all over the floor.

The deer was tossing his head around wildly and jumped over the leather couch. Beijing and Greta came out of the closet as the animal dashed desperately down the hallway.

"Oh my God," Beijing exclaimed, startled by the sheer size of the beast. This was something that her self-defense class had not prepared her for.

Sterling put a clip in his gun while directing Greta to call 911.

"There's a deer running around in our house. Yes a deer, a fucking deer like Rudolf," Greta screamed into the phone, clearly annoyed that the operator didn't seem to believe her.

"I don't know how he got here; I didn't invite him for sure. Look, just get someone out here in a hurry. He's trying to destroy everything in his path, including us."

Sterling had his trusted Beretta in hand, ready to defend his family and his house from the deer. Beijing was on her father's heels. When they heard the sound of lamps and glass being knocked around from the back of the house, they took off for the guest room. Beijing got there first and stared at the buck that was backed into the room. He looked so scared that for a second she thought she saw herself in his large dark eyes. He was lost, in the wrong place, and completely desperate as he stood there, huffing and closed in by four walls. She knew exactly how that animal felt. Trapped and alone, because that's how she had felt without Loot-chee in her life.

Sterling stepped in the doorway beside her and turned his gun on the animal. He was about to squeeze the trigger when Beijing slammed the door, trapping the animal inside and impeding her father's shot.

"Don't kill him, Daddy, he doesn't know any better," she said. "Let the animal control people get him."

"As long as his ass stays in there, he's okay, but the minute he comes out and we're in any danger, he's a goner!" Sterling stated, dead-ass serious.

Sterling looked around at the destruction the animal had done to their house. His wedding picture and Beijing's high school graduation picture that had been hanging on the wall were on the floor shattered.

"Fuck that! He has to die." He was reaching his hand out to turn the knob when they heard sirens coming up the driveway.

"Okay, baby girl, we'll let the police deal with it."

Moments later, the animal protection people were all over their house. They herded the buck outside, where it ran off into the woods. Still, the creature left lots of damage to Sterling's house, so they got a two-bedroom suite at the Tabby in Raleigh.

Through all the excitement and drama of the day, Beijing had not received a single call from Lootchee to wish her a happy birthday. Although she hadn't heard from him in over four months, she thought for sure that he would have at least called to wish her a happy birthday. Wishful thinking! She would have liked to tell him the story of the deer, the crazy buck that had somehow wandered into their house.

Her father came in to say good night and couldn't help but notice her long face. "Baby, why do you look so sad?"

"No reason."

"You know you can't lie to me, girl. Tell your father what the problem is."

"Just wished I'd heard from my friend, that's all."

"That guy that you transferred your job to Texas for?"

"Yes." She nodded, not really wanting to discuss it with her dad.

"Well, you know, when you let someone into your heart, it's so hard to get them out."

"You are right. Well, I just wish I could get him out of my system."

"Only time can." Sterling took his time to choose his words because he knew by the look in his daughter's eyes how volatile the situation must be. "You two met and you fell for him really quick. Always remember two things when you deal in matters of the heart: fast and fragile but slow and sturdy." He then added, "Some men don't appreciate a good woman until she's gone."

"That's what I keep telling myself, but it's been four months since I've heard from him."

"Do you want me to call him? Because I will."

She thought to herself about how the conversation with Lootchee and her dad would go, and then she smiled. "No, Daddy. That won't be necessary."

Sterling took her in his arms. "I love you, baby."

"I know you do." She realized how blessed she was to have a father to love her the way hers did. She had a father who had his shit together, a job she loved, and now she was about to start her own business. She knew she had to focus on putting the plans in motion to make her passion and the job she did at the hotel work for her.

Before allowing the birthday blues to set in, she took a hot bath, drank a glass of red wine, and went to bed. Alone. Deep down she felt a little bit of guilt because she did have a fabulous life and her sister Paris didn't have a crutch to stand on—and Paris didn't have Sterling when Willabee fell to the wayside. Thinking back, she wished that they'd shared the same father or that her father had rescued Paris as he had saved her. But that still didn't excuse Paris's actions.

Beijing got up the next morning and went to work. The day was pretty much uneventful, except for a call from Fiona.

She looked at the caller ID. *No, this ain't that crazy bitch.*

Beijing answered the call in her coolest professional voice, wondering what in the hell that woman could want with her.

"Hello. Beijing speaking," she said.

"Oh, thank God you answered." Fiona let out a sigh of relief. "I need your help immediately!"

"May I ask who this is?" Beijing said, though she knew that voice from the get-go. She just felt like toying with the woman.

"It's me! Fiona, your client, your guest, the author, and I need your help. You are the only one who can get me out of this mess," she said in a desperate tone.

"Oh, hello, Fiona," Beijing replied. "What seems to be the problem?"

"I'm at a store in Seattle."

"And that's a problem because . . . ?"

Fiona whispered into the phone, "I'm in the security office. Beijing, they've got me on videotape and they've left me alone in the office. I wasn't intending to steal anything. I just could not resist."

"You mean you got caught shoplifting?" Beijing said.

There was a long pause on the other end.

"Well, I wasn't really shoplifting. That wasn't my intention." She rambled on and then finally said, "I have a problem, Beijing. It's psychological. I'm sure you'd never understand because you're so goddamn perfect, but I have a compulsion to take things. I can't help it." Fiona sounded so pitiful that Beijing finally wiped the smirk off her face.

"How can I help you, Fiona?" she asked.

"Don't you know anyone who can convince these people to let me go? I'll pay whatever I need to pay. I have a few thousand on me. But I can't go to jail. Imagine the field day the press would have. It would be like that Winona Ryder fiasco. I can't face it. I'll kill myself."

Beijing didn't think the world would be any worse off without Fiona in it, but she couldn't be hard-hearted enough to turn the woman down. One thing she was sure of, though, and that was Fiona would be reimbursing the hotel for all her past compulsions.

"Tell me the name of the store, the address, and the value of the things you took. I'll make a few calls for you," Beijing said.

Fiona gave her the name of the store—the most exclusive place in town, of course. And the value of the items? A purse, two blouses, a pair of shoes, and a fox fur coat all totaling up to twenty-six thousand dollars.

"You've got to be kidding," Beijing said in disbelief.

"Afraid not," Fiona said and laughed bewitchingly. "I would have gotten away except the saleswoman asked for my autograph."

"Fiona, I'll get you out of this, but I want your credit card number on file. And not the credit card you gave us last time—that was over the limit!"

"Okay, I will give you my boyfriend's card."

Within thirty minutes Fiona was free. And promised Beijing that she would be forever in debt to her.

"Beijing, I owe you big-time. If there's anything I can do for you, please let me know. I'm in debt to you."

When Beijing got home she cut on the radio and cooked herself something to eat. She was deep-frying some shrimp and french fries and out of nowhere she suddenly broke out laughing, thinking about how the deer got in her father's house and destroyed the dinner.

Then the laughter turned to sobbing. Was her mother rubbing off on her? The tears wouldn't stop flowing. She was thinking about Lootchee, how he did her. How he had cut off all communication with her and even changed the locks on the doors to the house in Texas, how she had been staying in the Tabby of Dallas for the past four months working and had not seen or heard from him. How could he be so cruel? He had deserted her, and she felt trapped and so sad and unhappy. There was no way she could go back to Texas, and as stupid as it might sound it was the deer that had made her realize that she was alone and confused. She had been neglecting her clients, her job, and herself. Though her clients or boss hadn't complained, she knew that she wasn't living up to her own expectations.

Father knows best! It's time for me to get out of Texas!

$ $ $

The phone was ringing for what seemed like the hundredth time. And like the last ninety-nine, she didn't answer it. She wasn't in the mood for talking to anybody about anything. It was probably one of her annoying clients like Josie Ross. Again! She was the persistent assistant to a woman desperately seeking the brand-new Hermès bag, which had a six month-long waiting list. Or Lamont Rowe, a pro athlete planning a bachelor party; he needed some exotic dancers who didn't mind going above the call of duty to entertain him and his guests. All of these were things that she could make happen at the drop of a dime, but for some reason over the past few weeks she was dropping the ball, not focusing on work or anything else that really mattered in her life.

Or maybe it was even Thaddius himself, wanting to know what was wrong with her. Why hadn't she done whatever stupid damn thing they wanted her to do now? Why couldn't they just leave her alone?

The phone stopped for a moment and started ringing again. The caller ID indicated it was a private number.

What if it was Lootchee? Deep down she knew it wasn't but what if it was? Sure, she was still furious at him for the way he had done her, but she still wanted to speak with him.

"Hello," she said, waiting and hoping.

"Happy birthday to you!" It was Don, a day late and a dollar short to wish her a happy birthday. He sang before going into a special birthday rap that he had written just for her. As well-thought out and executed as it was, it should have cheered her up, but it didn't come anywhere close. She only could give him a dry thank-you for his efforts.

"Damn, I know shit ended on a real foul and sour note between us but I hope you can accept my apology."

"Um-hum," she said without much emotion at all. "Whatever."

"That's water under the bridge. I'm back now. I was under the influence of so many drugs, I couldn't see clearly then." He was waiting for her to say something, but she didn't. Of all the people in his life, he'd expected her to be more thrilled about his successful trip to rehab.

"Good for you," Beijing said.

"Beijing, what's wrong?" he asked. "I thought you would have more to say."

"Nothing," she murmured, her voice cracking.

"That nothing sounded a little weak to me. B, are you crying?"

"No," she lied. It was none of his business. He'd had his chance to be in her life, but he chose drugs over her.

"Yes, you are. Tell me what's wrong."

"Nothing you can fix," she shot back.

"Try me?" Don pressed.

"Look, I don't want to talk about it, and I am really glad you went to rehab. Now I will talk to you later." She hung up.

Don could not believe she'd left him listening to Mr. Tone. He kept calling back until she finally answered again.

"What is it, Don?"

"Obviously, there is something bothering you," Don stated. "Is the family okay? Your dad? Greta? Chyna? Your mom? Your sister?" he asked in one breath.

"Yup, they all fine."

"You're not sick, are you?"

Lovesick, she thought, but said, "No, I'm fine."

Don tried to think what could possibly have his friend, ex-girlfriend, and manager down like this.

"Are you pregnant?"

"Hell no," she answered a little louder than she meant.

"I mean if you are, I can stand in as the baby's father. We don't have to tell anybody anything different."

That made her chuckle.

"How noble of you, but it's not that." Tears were falling from her eyes. "I just need to get my shit together and concentrate on me and my business, that's all—how to build my multimillion-dollar empire."

"I know the feeling. I had to get a clear mind. A cloudy mind will block a sunny forecast. Now that I got my shit right, I'm about to get ready for this big tour."

"Oh that's so wonderful, Don." She was really genuinely happy for him, but his good fortune wasn't good enough news to stop her tears. "I'm so proud of you."

"Maybe you should get away," he suggested. "Come to Atlanta."

"For?" She had no intention of getting back with him.

"An escape. Remove yourself from your usual surroundings."

"I'm not escaping with you . . . or whatever you want to call it. Not happening."

"Get yo' mind out of the gutter, girl."

"You said come to Atlanta." She was puzzled. "That's where you are, right?"

"Right, but no strings attached. I just want to show you a good time, get you away from whatever it is that has you feeling the way you feeling. Look, you held me down at a time when I didn't even know if I was coming or going. You saved me when I was unable to save myself time and time again doing the same crazy-ass shit day in and day out. Through all my bullshit you've been nothing less than a real friend to me from Day One when I walked into the hotel and four hours later you were driving the getaway car for me. You didn't know me from a can of paint, yet you treated me like a friend." He paused for a brief moment then continued. "For that reason alone, you will always be my nigga. Straight up! So, if I can help you in any way, shape, or form, I got you! If it means you coming to A-T-L is the way to help, then it's settled. You need to be on the first thing smoking to the A."

Beijing was touched by Don's feelings. "How sweet," she softly said. "But thanks but no thanks."

"Please, come to A-T-L baby!" he urged. "Sun, fun, relaxation, plus I know you could network your ass off here. This is a good place to get your business popping."

She was thinking about what Don was saying, about the contacts she could make in Atlanta. Her father always said, *Success is the best revenge.* She smiled when she saw a future where her exclusive concierge business could be launched and she could be working for no one but herself. And how one day Lootchee would see her again and when he did, she'd be living a life of luxury; her business would be booming louder and more legitimately than his shady ventures. Don snapped her out of her daydreams.

"My label got me set up in this mansion, so I can be near the rehearsal site by day and mingle with the A-town moguls by night. You can have your own wing if you want. It ain't costing you shit. Just two friends in a big house trying to get their A game right, tight, and back on track. Maybe you could transfer to the Tabby down here for a while."

"I don't think I'm going to transfer to Atlanta, but maybe I would see if I can work there for a couple of weeks to help out. My boss has been asking me to go down there and help out."

What did she have to lose? Maybe a new atmosphere would help her get Lootchee off her mind and her money and business back on it.

CHAPTER 22

God Don't Like Ugly!

Beijing stopped by her mother's house and could not figure out what was happening on Willabee's block. It was so packed that she had to leave her car a couple of blocks down the street; there was no place to park. As she closed the distance on foot to the house, she discovered the source of the crowd.

Momma's having a party and didn't even tell me, Beijing thought to herself as she caught the eyes of a few people hanging out in the yard in the cold, drinking cocktails. As she was walking up the sidewalk, she passed another couple with Styrofoam carry-out trays of food in their hands. Once Beijing hit the porch she could smell the fried chicken. Willabee loved to cook and she made the best soul food Beijing had ever tasted in her life, so her mouth was watering just thinking about what her mother had cooked up.

Beijing walked into the house. Everyone seemed to be having a grand ol' time. People were sitting and standing around, stuffing their faces, drinking, smoking cigarettes, and placing orders for liquor and food.

Beijing moved around the crowded smoked-filled bungalow, putting drinks on coasters and picking up empty beer bottles and abandoned cups while all the time trying to find Willabee. She spotted her mother across the room interacting with her guests acting like she was some rich lady entertaining the likes of dignitaries and diplomats. Beijing was tickled by Willabee's ensemble: a long electric-blue sequined gown with the same-colored heels to match, with a sequined beret cocked to the side and a long fox boa thrown on her shoulder. She looked like she was from the Roaring Twenties. Even in her fifties, her mother was as beautiful as ever.

"Momma, what's going on?" Beijing approached her mother.

"Just having a little social, that's all." She was holding a plate filled with fish, greens, corn bread, and macaroni and cheese.

Beijing was used to her mother having card games, going to bingo, and even taking trips to the casino, but not all of these people at her house. "You always told me that you didn't like a bunch of people in your house."

"And that hasn't changed. I don't normally, but I'm not dealing with the norm right now."

Before Beijing could comment, Willabee continued, "I have to raise money for Chyna." She exchanged the food with a lady for a ten-dollar bill.

"Raise money for Chyna?" Beijing was baffled. "Momma, why? I gave you money for Chyna's spring break program already. That wasn't enough?"

"It was more than enough," she informed Beijing and then turned to someone else. "Marvin, did you pay for that drink?"

"Yeah, Willabee. I paid Sharon," he said.

Willabee turned back to her younger daughter. "I just ran into a little problem and I'm trying to fix it. Now let me go entertain and make this money."

"Momma, you don't have to do this. How much do you need?" Beijing went into her bag and flashed out her checkbook.

"I don't want your money, baby." She patted Beijing's hand and gestured for her to put the checkbook away. "I just can't take it. It wouldn't be right for you to have to pay for one program two times."

"What do you mean two times? Momma, what happened to the money? Did you have to pay a bill or something with it?" Beijing asked, curiosity getting the best of her.

"Harry, you want another one?" Willabee asked a guy who was standing nearby.

He nodded as he passed her a five-dollar bill.

"Go in there and see Sharon," she directed him as she went in her bosom, pulled out a bankroll, and added the five spot to it.

"Momma," Beijing pressed.

"No, I didn't. I would never do that to the baby, you know that." She added, "Not even off my meds." Willabee shot Beijing a look.

"Then what?" Over her mother's shoulder, Beijing could see Paris coming in the front door and walking toward the kitchen.

Willabee sat down in an aluminum folding chair that one of her patrons had just gotten out of and dropped her head in shame. "Paris stole the money and smoked it up."

"She did what?" Beijing raised her voice and put her hand on her hip.

"Yup, doing the same bull . . ." Before Willabee could finish, Beijing stormed into the kitchen and was up in Paris's face.

"The damn baby's money? You know you should be ashamed of yourself, Paris." Beijing was so mad that she wanted to take her sister out in the backyard and kick her ass.

Paris raised her hand palm out. "Talk to the hand 'cause I don't want to hear no fucking lecture from your Goody Two-shoes ass."

Beijing looked at her and if looks could kill, Paris would've been six feet under. "How could you steal from your own child?"

"I didn't. I took the money from Momma, not Chyna," Paris said without remorse.

"But it wasn't yours to take and furthermore how could you steal from your own damn mother?"

Willabee came in between them. "Please don't do this here. I'm begging you, Beijing."

"Why you gotta say something to me all the time, when I ain't stole a goddamn thing!" Beijing asked her mother.

"Watch yo' mouth, I'm talking to you because you are the only sensible one," Willabee answered her daughter.

" 'Cause she don't want me to whip your ass in here, bitch," Paris said, sounding more like a boxer at a press conference, than a crackhead.

"Whip my ass?" Beijing pointed around her mother, trying to reach Paris. "I'd like to know how you intend to do that. When you a junkie who probably ain't even ate 'cause you jonesing."

"Beijing. Please Beijing." Willabee was trying to keep the punches from flying.

"You right, Momma, I wouldn't even fight this trifling-ass bitch. What would I look like fighting a stone-cold druggie bitch? I've got the upper hand, simply because I eat three meals a day and I drink milk. The only thing this bitch done had to drink is cum!"

"No you didn't. Meet me outside." Paris started taking off her earrings.

"No problem, crackhead, but not until you come back from rehab. I wanna beat yo' ass fair and square."

"Beijing! Beijing! Beijing!" Willabee looked at her with the evil eye, surprised that Beijing was even entertaining Paris's bull-shit.

"You better get yo' daughter, Momma, before I treat her like a bitch in the streets," Paris said, adding fuel to the already burning house.

Two friends of Willabee's helped to keep the girls apart.

"Beijing, you know better," said Sharon, Willabee's friend.

After Beijing had calmed down, she decided to leave—but not before going into Willabee's room and putting a check on Willabee's dresser.

On her way out, she stuck a finger in Paris's face and said, "God don't like ugly and anybody who can rob a fucking kid ain't shit and damn sure ain't gonna have no good luck! May God have mercy on your soul when it comes back to you!"

CHAPTER 23

Business as Usual

The next day when Beijing's flight touched down in Atlanta, Don sent a car to pick her up and take her back to the mansion, since he was busy at rehearsal. To her surprise Don had given her the master suite; he had selected one of the smaller bedrooms for himself.

After taking a shower, changing clothes, and putting her things away, she looked around the place. Don had clearly finally cleaned up his act. He was back to the Don she'd known and loved at one time. She was so glad. She couldn't understand how someone with so much talent could throw his life away the way Don almost did.

She had set up a meeting with Lamont Rowe that evening, but she was supposed to have dinner with Don before. Then Don called and threw a monkey wrench into their plans, telling her things were running a little longer at the studio than he had anticipated and that he would probably make it in by ten or eleven.

It was only six now, and Beijing was growing hungry. She wanted to get out and see the town.

She decided to call Rayna, who was supposed to be in Atlanta for a few days chilling out with York. Maybe she could get out from under him for a few hours and hang out with Beijing. Beijing hit the button to speed-dial her girlfriend's number.

The phone rang three times.

"Hey bitch, what's up?" Rayna answered, glad to hear from her girlfriend.

"I'm in Atlanta," Beijing said, sighing. "Tell me you're still down here."

"So you did make it down to see that dope fiend rehab going muthafucka," she said. "Yeah I'm in the A."

"Then what it do, girl. I'm in this big-ass mansion the record company has Don staying in and I'm bored to death. I would've stayed in Charlotte if I wanted to be by myself."

"I know that's right, girl," Rayna agreed. "Where's that dust-head fiend of yours anyway? Only he would invite a muthafucka to come in town to visit him and not be home to greet them."

"Don," Beijing said, ignoring Rayna's dig, "is in rehearsal. He sent a car to scoop me from the airport, but it's going to be a while before he's home."

"Say no more. I mean, we still celebrating your birthday and all, right? You can't stay there alone. Give me the address and I'll be by to grab you," Rayna said. "We can go out for something to eat. It'll be a belated birthday dinner. Just you and me."

"You don't have to twist my arm, girl." Beijing rattled off the address, and asked, "How long before you show?"

Rayna was pushing the coordinates into the navigational system. "According to the Tom-Tom—" She paused for a moment to allow the machine to calculate. "—seventeen minutes."

"Wonderful, darling, I'll be waiting out front," Beijing declared before hanging up to get ready.

Rayna arrived right on schedule. Beijing was slipping out of the mansion when her friend pulled up in a midnight-blue Benz 600.

"This shit is plush, girl," Beijing gushed, getting into the luxury vehicle. "I thought you like to keep it plain Jane?" She looked at Rayna with a shocked expression.

"I do," she admitted. "York got this for me." Then she lowered her voice in a conspiracy whisper as if someone else were in earshot. "This bitch does ride sweet, tho." They both erupted with laughter, giving each other high fives.

They ended up at a trendy, upscale steak house in Buckhead. Valet parking, nicely dressed waiters wearing black shirts and pants with a white stripe down each leg, capped off with a fancy red jacket with gold buttons.

"Smoking or nonsmoking?" a gorgeous female attendant asked.

"Nonsmoking, please." Rayna took the lead, following the hostess to their seats.

After directing them to a cozy table, she said, "Your waiter will be here to greet you shortly. Here are your menus."

"Thank you," both Rayna and Beijing sang in unison.

Before the attendant was out of earshot, Rayna squealed with wide eyes, "Did you see the ass on that bitch? I bet she used to be a stripper. I can tell by the way she struts."

"You don't know that girl from a ham sandwich," Beijing playfully said from over the top of her menu.

"Believe me when I tell you," Rayna insisted, "if that child ain't never worked a pole you can best believe it's in her future."

"You are terrible."

"Maybe so, but I know what I know."

"Let's just order, girl." Beijing shook her head with a smile.

"Whatever. Don't get mad at me because I know the business."

"Aight, Madame Adult Sex trade," Beijing joked.

They both decided on the eight-ounce steak cooked medium

well, and broiled butterfly shrimp with a baked potato. Rayna ordered an apple martini while Beijing sipped on a glass of pinot noir. The food was delivered quickly, and it looked delicious.

For the next twenty minutes there was nominal chitchat and an abundance of chewing. The food was even better than it looked. The steak was tender enough to cut with a fork, and the shrimp tasted like it had been pulled from the ocean minutes before they ordered. Both dishes were prepared by either a master chef or a magician.

Beijing was musing on how thoughtful Rayna had been to bring her to a fabulous restaurant to celebrate her birthday until she heard Rayna ask, "You got the check?" Beijing was patting her slightly protruding stomach.

"Excuse me? You would really make me pay on my birthday?" Beijing exclaimed incredulously.

"Well, technically . . . it's not your birthday," Rayna said after wiping her mouth with a cloth napkin. "It's not your birthday today."

Beijing rolled her eyes and smacked her lips. "Bitch, you're scandalous." She was not really surprised. After all, this was Rayna, who was as tight with a dollar as the hinges on the gates of hell.

"You are right," she admitted with a slight laugh. "But goddamn, I ain't balling like you. I don't have filthy-rich clients that give me big tips or a paid-out-the-ass rich boyfriend like you."

"Rich boyfriend?" Beijing questioned. "The last time I checked, my bed was empty."

"Oh, he'll be back," Rayna assured, picking up Beijing's glass and drinking down the last bit of wine.

After splitting the tab, Beijing fished her cell phone from her Jimmy Choo purse

"Girl, is that the same bag you gave me?"

"Yes, but yours is black."

"I think I like mine better. And I feel that was the least you could do being that I afforded you the opportunity to meet Lootchee."

"The least I could have done was nothing or just given you a simple thanks."

"Glad you got me the bag." Rayna laughed a bit. "And bitch, best believe I appreciate it."

After finding the name she wanted stored in the contact section of her phone, she thumbed the button to dial. He answered on the fourth ring. "This is Monty. What's up?"

Lamont Rowe played basketball for the Atlanta Hawks. This was his fourth year on the roster, and he'd just received a sixty-million-dollar contract.

"Good evening, Lamont." She spoke in a professional manner. "This is Beijing Lee, how are you today?"

Lamont Rowe was six foot three; his skin was the color of hot coffee with barely a thimble of milk and a smile that belonged on a toothpaste commercial. The brother was fine and married.

"I can't complain." She imagined him smiling. "Even if I did it wouldn't change a damn thing."

"Depends on who you are doing your complaining to, Lamont." Beijing steered the conversation back to business. "Are you still available to meet this evening?"

"Just tell me when and where."

Rayna was sitting across from Beijing trying to figure out who this Lamont cat was that Beijing was talking about meeting somewhere. The suspense was eating at her.

Beijing was looking at her watch. "How about at the Velvet Rope in . . . let's say about an hour."

Lamont agreed.

"Who the fuck is Lamont?" Rayna blurted out as Beijing disconnected the call.

"My business," Beijing playfully taunted her, "and none of yours."

"Come on, B?" Rayna begged. "I thought we were girls."

"He's just a client, so get your panties out your ass. I'm supposed to get a few girls for his boy's bachelor party. Maybe you can use your Madame Sex Trade eye and pick me out a couple of the must-book-hers."

After answering a few more of Rayna's who, what, and wheres, Beijing invited her friend to come along if she wanted, since Rayna was driving anyway.

The Velvet Rope was the newest, biggest, hottest strip club in Atlanta. Both males and females partied there. The dudes flexed by throwing money at some of the most accessible beautiful bodies in the city, and the women came there to meet and see which of the fellas had the money to burn.

"Damn right I'm going." Rayna smiled devilishly.

$ $ $

Inside, the club lived up to all the hype and street promotion that it was getting all over the city. The place was huge and tastefully adorned. There was one main stage and six smaller stages with three crystal poles and four enormous bar stations. Most of the walls were mirrored, giving the downstairs area the illusion that it was even larger than its already enormous size.

Girls of different nationalities worked each of the stages. They all had great bodies, Beijing noticed. She smiled thinking of how her girl Dazzle would put them all to bed on a bad day.

Beijing was still evaluating the broad selection of eye candy when Lamont got her attention from across the room by sending the waitress over to tell her where he was sitting.

Beijing sashayed across the club with the grace of a runway model. "Sorry I'm late."

"I'm just getting here myself," he confided. "Please" he pointed to the vacant booth—"have a seat."

She smiled as she made herself comfortable. It was hard to keep her mind on business; seeing Lamont's diamond-and-platinum wedding band made her think about Lootchee, but she redirected her focus back on the matter at hand.

"Let me see if I have this straight," Beijing said to Lamont. "You want the presidential suite at the Tabby here in Atlanta. The actual party is scheduled for eight hours give or take." She smiled before continuing. "It's conceivable and doable to have at least four fresh dancers arrive to the room every hour. And of course they will have their own private rooms on the floor for the duration of the party for any 'extra' celebrating that may arise." She added, "Tips for the ladies are not included in the fee."

"What about refreshments, food and drinks?" Lamont asked her.

"It'll all be catered by the hotel."

Lamont was throwing a party for his first cousin and had invited the whole team, plus some other family and friends. His friends were going to be talking about this party for years to come; the memories would probably outlast the marriage. It was definitely worth the hundred grand.

"Then I'm happy to be doing business with you, Beijing."

They shook hands, closing the deal.

Beijing stood up from the booth, allowing her eyes to walk the club in search of Rayna. There she was in the middle of two well-dressed guys. She had a drink in her hand and a smile on her face. The girl knew how to have a good time.

Beijing was about to dip in her friend's mix for a second when somebody grabbed her elbow from behind.

That was one thing she hated: a drunk or arrogant chump putting his hands on her. Spinning on her four-inch Jimmy Choo pumps, she snapped, "Watch where you put your—" She stopped mid-sentence. It was Corday. They had met about a year ago. He owned the club.

"How were you gon just come up in my spot and not let me know you coming or holla when you get here?" Corday was wearing a gray Armani suit with a black silk shirt and Italian loafers.

"I was just looking for you, Corday." It was only a partial lie, because she definitely had plans of politicking with him before she left. "I need a small favor."

Corday raised one brow. "All you have to say is one word and I'm yours," he said loud enough to be heard over the Trick Daddy cut the DJ was blasting over the speakers.

"You know it's not that kind of party with me." She playfully tapped him on the shoulder. "Besides, I'm sure you get more pussy than you know what to do with in this place."

"That's true," Corday said. "But I'll give away a hundred well-painted copies of the *Mona Lisa* for just a chance of acquiring the original."

The man definitely has a silver tongue, she thought. "I'm sorry," she replied with a feigned sad expression. "I'm going to have to keep my art to myself until I find a permanent buyer, but I do have a proposition for you."

"I'll take what I can get. What you got on your mind?"

Beijing ran it down: She was going to need to lease some of his girls for one night. After he agreed to the terms, she told him about Dazzle. They drank a glass of Cristal over the rest of the small talk ironing out the details. "It's so late, I have to get out of here," she finally said. "Thanks for everything."

"Anytime. Let me walk you to your car."

"No, I'm good, going to give my card to a couple of people as well as say my good-byes. Plus I have to get my friend who is having such a good time, she probably won't want to leave."

She shook Corday's hand, glad at what she had gotten accomplished.

When all was said and done and they were walking out of the club, Beijing had the girls she needed for the bachelor party and Dazzle had a job making a thousand dollars a week plus tips, minus her 25 percent cut.

"Girl, that place was off the meter."

Rayna was a little tipsy as she tried to remember where she'd parked her car.

"I know that's right," Beijing concurred. She had closed the deal with Lamont Rowe for 100K, convinced Corday to let her get the girls at the nominal rate, and met a couple of other potential clients and contacts in the process. "I must say it was a pretty good outing."

CHAPTER 24

Let Me Get That

Rayna churped the lock on the car door while heading in its direction. Beijing was feeling satisfied by the evening's results and looking forward to being able to relax for a while.

"You heard from Lootchee?"

"Nope," she said nonchalantly, wishing she had.

"And who was that dude you were talking to in the well-fitting Armani suit?" Rayna was being nosy, as usual.

"Why you always up in my bizwax?" Beijing asked just as a black Range Rover sped up to them and then slammed on its brakes, bringing it to a screeching halt.

The Range Rover's black-tinted windows stopped the girls from seeing inside until the doors flew open on both the driver's and passenger sides.

Two men bounced out like panthers stalking an unsuspecting gazelle in the jungle of Africa. They were wearing black jeans, black T-shirts, black fitted baseball caps pulled low over their eyes, and black Nike sneakers. Their clothes were fitting for the urban jungles of the city.

Both men were strapped with nine-millimeter semiautomatic Glocks, so it quickly became apparent they hadn't pulled up to exchange phone numbers or offer to take the girls out for breakfast.

The driver spoke first: "Follow instructions and you won't turn a simple message into a complicated matter." His words were sharp, clear, precise, and to the point. "We gonna politely take the keys to that there 600, and any and all valuables you may have on your person. It's just that simple. So, don't make this shit too hard."

"Fuck that shit," Rayna began, "how we supposed to get home?"

Beijing could not believe that Rayna was willing to get shot rather than to tell York that someone had taken his new pride and joy. York loved that car more than he loved her.

"Bitch"—the passenger was talking this time—"you can give dat shit up by choice or force. Either way you gonna come up off it. And your time is running short." There was no mistaking the malice in his words or tone.

Beijing gave her a look that said, *They ain't playing and do what the fuck they say.* There was no point in them trying to fight back. There was no self-defense class that could help them with this. Then she put her hand in her purse to get her wallet.

"Don't do nothing with that mitt of yours. If you lift it out of that purse wrong you won't live to regret it."

"I—" she stuttered. "I'm just trying to give you what you ask for." Beijing passed her wallet over to the passenger, but all she could think of was that she wished Lootchee would have popped up and saved them.

Rayna didn't hand hers over as quickly, and the guy snatched her handbag off her arm with so much force she thought he'd separated her shoulder from her arm. Tears were in Rayna's eyes as she rubbed her shoulder. "I think . . . you broke my shoulder."

The keys were still in her hand. The driver reached toward Rayna with his palms up. "Let me get them joints," he said as if it were a request and not at gunpoint.

Rayna had no choice but to do what she was told.

"Tell that nigga York 'bout this," the driver said to Rayna, after tossing the keys to his boy. Then he looked to Beijing and said, "Sorry, baby, but you got caught up at the wrong place, wrong time, with the wrong peeps."

He gave her a look like if he'd seen her at another time, they could've gone out together or something. Then he jumped back in the Range and gunned the engine. His partner followed in York's Benz.

Rayna's heartbeat had slowed down some now that the immediate danger was over—but her anger and hate intensified. "I can't believe this shit. All because of York and some bullshit he did. Why the fuck I gotta go through this shit? I really wish he would stop taking peoples' money and not pay them back."

They stood in the spot where they'd been parked just moments ago. "What you plan to do about York?" Beijing broke the silence.

Rayna thought about the question her friend had just asked carefully before she answered. She knew York was involved with a lot of shady people and even shadier scams. She'd been a part of a few of his schemes herself. "I don't know," she muttered, "I don't know."

CHAPTER 25

Strip

Paris strolled into the convenience store in Columbia, South Carolina, on the arm of a trick that she had been dating for the past three months.

She noticed a lady named Lucy trying to buy some cigarettes with food stamps. Paris smiled at the lady and looked her over.

Lucy Roach had been born and raised in Columbia with four older sisters. Money was tight in their family of seven, so it was pretty customary for the Roach girls to wear one another's hand-me-downs. By the time the tattered outfits made their way to Lucy, they were just about old worn rags. Despite being teased on a regular basis throughout her school years, Lucy made pretty good grades. After graduating, she landed a good job at a franchise bank as a teller. Before long, Lucy made branch manager.

With new clothes, a new car, and her own apartment things couldn't have been better. Then she met a friend who told her about this incredibly sexy new drug called crack. That was fourteen years ago, when Lucy was thirty-four. The drugs robbed her of her money, her job, her car, and her self-respect. Now at almost fifty, her body had deteriorated to skin and bones. Her skin was oily, scarred, and wrinkled, and her creaky brittle bones made her resemble Skeletor. Her vagina smelled like a twenty-four-hour Chinese fish market, and Lucy couldn't give it away if she tried.

She noticed she had caught the eye of Paris and took the opportunity to engage her.

"Hey, girlfriend," Lucy said. "Can I borrow a smoke from you?"

Paris looked like a hood beauty queen compared with Lucy. In fact, Paris looked better than a lot of chicks who went out to clubs and bars chasing men, and didn't use drugs.

"I don't smoke," Paris said, leaning in and lowering her voice. "Cigarettes anyway." She snickered. Paris had just made two hundred dollars off the trick and was itching to get decent. "You know where I can buy some coke, though?"

Lucy smiled. "The best in the city," she said. "And it's close by too."

That first day they got high as the *Star Trek* Enterprise together. As they were taking turns sucking on the glass dick, they got to know each other somewhat better. Paris shared the details on how she'd met that particular trick. "I like fucking with him 'cause the country muthafucka kicks the Benjamins and he's not from my area. When he sends for me, it gets me out of town away from my environment for a while, and he pays for the bus ticket. I get two hundred a pop plus travel fee."

Lucy went on to share that she had the numbers of ten to fifteen more working married men who liked to dip out on their wives and buy sexual favors. A friendship was formed, and after that haphazard meeting Paris started visiting Lucy in the rundown shack she stayed in at least twice a month, sometimes staying the week whenever she came to see her trick.

Paris was rocking an electric-blue miniskirt and a Bebe top that she had stolen out of the car of one of her tricks. She had a pair of thigh-high boots that matched her leather jacket, which was lying over on the chair. She had been at Lucy's house for a few days, turning some private tricks, and she had eight hundred dollars stuffed inside her small purse to show for it.

Lucy looked Paris over. Even when she was the manager at the bank, Lucy never looked half as good. "Where are you going to all dolled-up like that?" Lucy was trying to put a leash on the jealousy that was eating at her. Paris didn't really care 'cause hell, if she was Lucy she'd be jealous of her too.

"You know what they say?" Paris was primping in the mirror fixing her makeup and putting on her lip gloss. "If it doesn't make dollars, it doesn't make sense. I gotta look the part if I want to keep these tricks lined up shelling out cash, you know."

"Yeah, I know," Lucy agreed, wishing that the day was back when she could use what she had to get what she wanted.

"I got three dates lined up. And them niggas pays off like a rigged-up slot machine. I get their lever so hard in this hot wet-ass mouth of mine," she bragged, "by the time I pull on it, bells and whistles are going off and dem niggas start spitting money out they ass."

Lucy rolled her eyes when Paris wasn't watching. "I know that's right. You want me to call Lil Jon-Jon over before you set off on your mission. I seen 'im earlier down at the store and that nigga say he got some good shit, and I believe him too. I can call him if you want me to."

Paris's mouth watered up when Lucy mentioned coke. "Why not?" she said.

Jon-Jon showed up ten minutes after he received the call. They started with a gram. Lucy hadn't lied—the shit was good, so good that after about five hours they had smoked up the eight bills Paris had in the purse and owed Lil Jon-Jon five hundred more.

"That's all the flav I had on me," Jon-Jon said when the coke was gone. "Let me get that five you owe and I'll go to where that came from and bring you back what you want."

Lucy and Jon-Jon were staring at Paris. "Uhhh . . ." She was trying to figure out the best way to say it. "I don't have it right this minute. But I can go get it," she added.

"Fuck I look like to you? Sam-sausage-head? That's one of the oldest tricks in the crackhead survival manual. Bitch, you need to get somebody to bring my paper over here."

Paris turned to Lucy. "Tell him I'm good for it." Then back to Jon, "I just gotta go get it. My friend don't know I get high. He ain't gon give it to me unless I meet 'im."

Jon acted like he was thinking it over. "Nah, I ain't feelin' that shit. You gon stay right here till I get what's mine." He reached under his shirt and snatched a small handgun from his waistband. "I don't care if you have to have it wired, but yo' life is depending on it."

Jon was a small-time neighborhood hustler who dreamed of making it big in the drug trade. Like most young cats who fell prey to the streets, he wanted to look tougher than he really was—but that didn't mean that he wasn't dangerous.

He passed Paris his phone.

"You would kill me," she asked in a frustrated voice, "over five hundred dollars? When it's a known fact I ain't no slouch! I make money and I will be one of your best customers to you as long as yo' shit is good."

Jon's eyes locked onto hers. "I'll bust a nigga's head for a piece of candy if the chump thought he was taking something for me, ya dig."

There were only two people Paris could possibly call to get that type of money.

First she called Willabee, but before she could get the words out, Paris heard a lady's voice calling out "B-12" in the background. "Baby, I'm at bingo. Call me back later," Willabee said, then hung up before Paris could get a word in.

There was only one other person to call.

Beijing had just gotten out of the shower. Not only had she been robbed at gunpoint, but she hadn't been able to reach Don when she called for a ride, so she'd had to hail down a cab to get back to the mansion. If her clothes, computer, and the rest of her belongings hadn't been there, she would have gone to a hotel. The sun was rising and she was massaging lotion onto her legs when the phone rang.

"Who in the hell is this?" she said out loud.

Beijing had been up all night, shocked at what her first night in Atlanta had turned out to be. At this point she was just plain sick and tired of all the bullshit, from the cigar-smoking cab-driver, to Don's inconsiderate ass, to the robbers—and her list was going on when the phone interrupted.

"Beijing, Beijing, oh my God I am so glad you answered the phone." She could hear a frantic Paris on the other end of the line. She had not spoken to her sister since the altercation at her mother's house.

"What? Paris!" she snapped, still mad at her from the other day. "I swear I can't deal with none of your scheming right now. I've done had a fucked-up night. Call me back tomorrow, I might be in a better state of mind."

"Look, I know you still mad at me about the Chyna thing but I'm in deep fucking trouble. I'm going to keep it real wit you. No bullshit. I was down here in Columbia getting high and I owe this guy five hundred dollars and he won't—"

Beijing's first thought was that it might have been one of her sister's stunts. "Paris, come now, you can do better than that,"

Beijing cut in. It would not have been the first time she'd lied to get what she wanted.

Until Jon snatched the phone from her. "And you got four hours to Western Union me my motherfuckin' five hundred or I swear to you on my grandma's holey drawers I will kill this bitch."

"What? Who is this?"

"The nigga she owe, that's who."

"So you going to kill her over five hundred dollars?" she questioned, entertaining this silly guy on the other end of the phone.

"If you want this bitch to get out of the house breathing, you need to be asking 'bout the info you need to send the paper."

Beijing was quiet for a second, thinking how she would really feel if her sister was killed, how it would affect her mother and Chyna. "Goddamn! Shit! What name you want me to put it in?" She sucked her teeth, knowing for sure this was some bullshit but not wanting to gamble—after the bittersweet night she'd had, the odds were not in her favor.

"Lucy Roach." He laughed. "Good to know that the bitch is worth the paper and don't take all day either, 'cause I do feel a lil trigger-happy."

"Just put Paris back on the phone. You gon get your fucking money for Christ's sake."

"Hello."

"I'm sending the money. Call me once he lets you go."

"I will, and . . . Beijing?"

"Yes. What is it?"

"Thanks, Sis."

Pleased with the way things were going, Jon lit up a blunt. "Now," he said, lusting at Paris. "Strip, bitch."

"Strip?"

"Ain't no echo in here." He put the gun to her head. "I'm ready for some of that good ho pussy of yours."

With the pistol cocked back, Paris had no choice. She stepped out of her skirt, standing there in a thong and the top that she had stolen.

"Ev'rything. Don't make me say it again."

She peeled off the thong and pulled the shirt over her head.

Stroking his dick, "Damn you a phat-ass crackhead bitch," Jon huffed. "Bend over the chair so you can put this here monster I got for you. I might even give you a few mo' crumbs when I'm done."

"Why are you doing this? My sister's going to give you the money."

"This is what they call an inconvenience fee," he said pulling out his three-inch fully erect penis.

"Can you at least use a condom?" Paris pleaded.

"Fuck a condom." He rammed it straight into her butt hole with no lubrication. Paris hardly knew he had entered her.

He pushed back and forth about five or six times before he came.

"Now suck it," he said, breathing heavy.

She did what she was told. For a split second she thought about biting it, but she thought twice when she felt the cold steel against her head. Out of the corner of her eye, Paris caught Lucy laughing as she watched Paris suck the little-dick-thug off. *This jealous-hearted bitch set me up,* she thought.

It was less than an hour until Beijing called Jon back. The money was at Western Union.

Once Beijing sent the money, Lucy and Jon threw Paris out of the house, tossing at her a T-shirt and some flip-flops that Lucy's dog had chewed up.

She had no cash and had to beg someone to use their cell phone to call Beijing to pick her up. All Beijing heard was her sister crying on the other end of the phone, asking for a bus ticket. It touched her heart, because in all of Paris's years of going back and forth to prison, on and off drugs, and to and from rehab programs, she had never heard or seen her sister cry. Instead of getting the ticket, she drove in Don's car to Columbia to pick up her sister.

When Beijing pulled up in the powder-blue Aston Martin, she saw her sister sitting and shivering by the side of a convenience store. Someone had been nice enough to give Paris a raggedy blanket to wrap around herself. She looked so pitiful that despite everything they had been through, at that very moment Beijing's heart went out to her sister.

She got out the car and hugged Paris. They embraced for what felt like a lifetime, until they both lost their grip but were still crying. Paris sobbed in Beijing's arms. "I'm sorry, I'm sorry. That's the shit I get for leaving you dem years ago and stealing from Chyna, it's like you said, payback's a motherfucker!"

"No, that ain't got nothing to do with that. Look at me, Paris." She removed her arms from around her sister. "That doesn't have anything to do with nothing. The guy still should not have done what he did. That was foul."

A few people started looking their way so they got into the car.

Inside, Paris said, "That dirty dick sucker kept my stuff, my jacket, my boots, and all those other lil things."

"Fuck him, I brought you a sweat suit." She reached into the back and handed her sister the outfit and a toiletry bag so she could clean up a bit.

"I need to take a shower, and go to the doctor. I hope dat nigga ain't have shit, running up in me raw," she said before flip-flopping to the bathroom on the side of the store.

Beijing was getting madder by the minute after hearing what had happened and glad that she had come to her sister's rescue. Paris poked her head out of the bathroom. "And they had the nerve to take yo' money and my clothes and . . . my pussy," she informed her sister again.

"I can't believe that," Beijing said from the other side of the door. "I am plain sick of motherfucking men taking advantage of us women. Just sick of them!"

"But I think the bitch whose house I was in had something to do with it."

"Hurry up and get yourself together the best you can." Beijing walked away from the door over to the car.

Beijing was at the back of the Aston Martin slamming the trunk down when Paris finally came out of the restroom and got in. Before Beijing got behind the wheel, she reached down and tied her Prada sneakers.

Paris had gotten it together. "Then she had the nerve to be laughing."

"Who's the lady you think set you up?"

"A no-teeth bitch name Lucy!"

"Show me where that bitch Lucy live."

"How come?"

" 'Cause I asked." Beijing shot a look at her sister that meant business.

"What if Jon is still there, Beijing?" Paris looked over at her. "He got a gun."

"All I want to do is give Lucy a firm message before we go, that's all. I plan on busting in on the backstabbing bitch and kicking a mud hole in her dingy ass."

"Yeah and you know I'd be game, but we can't take a knife to a gunfight—and hell, we don't even have a knife."

"We don't need one; just show me where she lives."

"Turn right at this light."

Beijing jumped from the far left lane over to the next one, and then cut off a Corvette. He honked and she gave him the finger.

"Bitch! Who taught you to drive? Hell, do you even have a driver's license?" Paris clutched on to the hook on the ceiling. "Damn, I know Sterling is gangsta but he shouldn't have taught you how to drive no getaway car."

"You crazy. A girl gotta do what she gotta do."

"Turn right and it's the third house on the left."

Beijing bent the corner and stopped in front of a shack. "Is this it?" Beijing frowned up at the house.

Paris assured her that it was.

Beijing popped the trunk, slid out of the car, grabbed a brick from the trunk that she had taken at the store's parking lot, and hurled it through the front window, shattering the glass.

The stone took a fortuitous route, cracking Lucy upside the dome while she was sitting in the chair by the window smoking coke that Jon had given her for looking out.

The note attached to the brick read:

Where there's smoke . . . there's fire!
This ain't over, Bitch!

The girls decided to stop at a diner right off the highway before hitting the road to head back to Atlanta. They sat in the diner and laughed at the incident, replaying it over and over again for a while until Paris said to her sister, "I'm done for real. I want out of this shit. Wanna be clean."

"That's good, Paris! It's about time! And I'm proud of ya!" She smiled. "I will help you along the way."

"I know you think I'm bullshitting you."

"I didn't say that, did I?"

"See, I've been to programs in the past," Paris confided, "because the judge or my PO sent me but never because I wanted help. I don't want to be like that bitch Lucy. That can't be me in ten years. Just can't. Not happening. I'm tired of that life and now I am ready."

"I believe you, Sis." Beijing's eyes watered. "And I got your back, as long as you are serious. I got your back."

"Thank you. I won't disappoint you," Paris assured her sister. "Anyways what's up with you and your boyfriend?"

"What boyfriend?"

"Dude from Texas."

"Lootchee? Girl, too much to fill you in."

"Talk to your big sister, maybe I can help. You know I've always had my way with men."

"Nothing really to talk about. I'm not feeling him like that anymore." Beijing tried to convince herself.

"Well, if you ever want to talk about it, you know I'm here." Paris continued, "I'm going to keep saying it: I can't believe that you showed your ass for me."

"You are my sister. What'd you expect?"

As soon as Beijing said that, she heard gunshots behind her, and they dove for cover under the table. When everything was clear, they got up and realized that the Aston Martin had been shot up and saw Jon pulling off in a Delta 88. "Shit," Beijing said, "what am I supposed to tell Don?"

$ $ $

When they arrived back in Atlanta, Beijing got Paris a room at a hotel near the bus station so she could take a shower and get herself some rest. The next day they went to breakfast and then Beijing put her sister on the bus. Paris was going to stay with Willabee until they could find her a rehab program.

Then she decided that she'd had enough of Atlanta. She'd cut her stay short after she met with Lamont in two days, but in the meantime she would work on the plan for her concierge business.

Beijing pulled in front of Don's beautiful mansion. On her way she thought of a couple different explanations that she would give him about the car—but when she got inside she saw two other girls walking out of the kitchen, one in cheap lingerie and the other in a too-small bra and thong. Before she went into her room to regroup from all the events that had occurred in the past

twenty-four hours, she stepped into the great room. Don was lying back on the oversized leather couch with his feet on the table, smoking a cigar in a robe that had been stolen from the Tabby Hotel. Beijing tossed him the keys to his Aston Martin. "Now we're really even on the car situation."

CHAPTER 26

A Mishap

The month of February was taking no prisoners this year in Charlotte. The month's average temperature was twenty-one degrees. Today was no exception.

Beijing was in her office working, making phone calls and trying to keep her clients happy. She couldn't wait for seven o'clock to roll around.

"Hello, this is Beijing."

"Seth Soberman. I'm glad I caught you, Beijing."

Seth was Natalia's super-rich boyfriend. He allowed her to do whatever she wanted, whenever she wanted. Nothing was too extravagant for her.

"I hate to bother you with little things like this," he said, "but one of my accountants gave me a call concerning a forty-seven-hundred-dollar charge on Natalia's invoice under miscellaneous."

"Yes." Beijing lowered her voice. "That was for a little mishap that took place."

"Mishap?" Seth asked, curious. "Would it be too much to ask for a few details concerning this mishap?"

"No problem at all," Beijing said. "Natalia was in a little fender-bender. No one was hurt. She just wanted it to disappear."

"What do you mean by disappear?"

"We didn't want to leave any kind of paper trail that the missus could somehow see, so I knew someone who would make it disappear."

"You mean like there is no record of it ever happening?"

"Yes, I had it taken care of," she said casually, like it was no big deal. "This type of thing happens all the time. But it does incur a fee."

Seth was quiet for a moment. "Let me get this right: Natalia was involved in a hit-and-run and you made it go away? As if it never happened?"

"That's correct, sir."

"Impressive," he commended her. "You're definitely the right person for the job." Beijing smiled at the compliment. "Now I know why Natalia speaks so highly of you."

"Thank you, sir. If you have any more questions or if there is anything at all I may be able to do for you, please do not hesitate to give me a call."

She exhaled after ending the call.

"B," April said, interrupting her thoughts, "can you hold us down while I go take a smoke?" She already had her coat folded across her arm.

There wasn't much traffic at the desk. Beijing looked around the lobby; the only person there was an elderly lady reading a romance novel by the fireplace, drinking a cup of coffee.

Beijing agreed to handle the check-in desk.

"You don't know," Beijing exaggerated, "it's ten below out

there. You gon have icicles hanging from your ass before you get done. I hope it's worth it."

"Ain't no ice sticking to this." April slapped her butt with her palm. "My shit be smoking hot, ya hear."

Beijing couldn't help but laugh at her conceited colleague as she slid into her winter coat, then sashayed through the lobby to the exit.

Beijing was hanging up the phone when she heard a familiar-sounding voice. If she hadn't known any better, she would've thought it was her cousin Seville. It was another month before Seville and her boyfriend, Jack, were due back in the States, but Jack's job ended a month early.

Looking up from the phone, Beijing thought she was seeing a ghost—or Seville's identical twin sister that she didn't have—standing in front of her, holding two cups of hot chocolate.

"Oh my God," she screamed, forgetting that she was at work. "When did you get back and why didn't you tell me you were coming?" Beijing was all smiles.

"Jack and I got back today and I wanted to surprise you." Seville passed her one of the cups of cocoa. "Surprise!"

Beijing was stunned. "Damn right I'm surprised, girl! I get off in another hour," she said. "We can go to dinner and catch up. Have you eaten?"

"I wish I could. Jack and I have to take care of a few things. We haven't even been home yet," she added. "He's in the truck waiting for me. By the way, he said to tell you hey. I just had to come and see you first."

"You better had."

"Or what?"

"Or when I had seen you, I would've had to whip that red ass of yours."

"You got to bring one to get one," she joked and then said, "I need a favor, Cuz."

"Depends on the flavor of the favor."

"Okay, Lil Kim." She went on, "Seriously, do you think you can get one of the weekends off within the next two weeks?"

"I've been taking a lot of time lately, so it would definitely have to be on my days off. Is everything okay?"

"No, nothing is wrong. I just want to take you to Miami with me for a belated birthday gift."

Mentioning her birthday made bad feelings resurface for Beijing. Lootchee never had called. It had been over eight months since she had heard from him, since he'd promised to call her back and now Valentine's Day had come and gone. "Fuck Lootchee," she thought, mad at herself for even thinking about him.

"I don't want to talk about my birthday—that's another story, for another day. And since when did my shopaholic cousin start holding on to enough money to get us to Florida and back?"

"Girl, Jack got an enormous bonus for getting the project finished ahead of schedule." Seville took a sip of the hot chocolate. "And he broke me off real decent too," she almost whispered. "Please, I've been saving."

Beijing found the saving part hard to believe. Seville was the type to buy anything and everything she saw because it was on sale or because she just had to have it. When the girl needed a gift for someone, all she had to do was go in her closet and pull out something fabulous.

"You know I love South Beach," she confessed, unable to think of a reason not to get away from the cold spell Charlotte was going through.

"Then it's settled," her cousin said. "Pack the skimpiest, flyest shit in your closet and we going to graffiti our names all over the city, my treat."

"But I pay my own way," Beijing insisted.

"No deal. You can pay next time. This one is on me."

"At least let me use my discount for the rooms."

Seville knew her cousin like a pair of broken-in shoes. Beijing wasn't going until she agreed to at least some of her terms. "You can get the discount, but that's it, that's all, that's final. And when do you want to do it? This weekend? Or next?"

"Let me check my schedule and get back to you on that."

"Trust me," Seville said, "we're going to have a blast!"

Beijing was sitting in a lounge chair by the hotel's pool reading the novel *Gorilla Black,* by Seven. Seville was relaxing checking out an *O* magazine.

They had arrived at South Beach the day before at a little past noon. They had soaked up the sun, rode mopeds on the strip, and had drinks at a couple of clubs that night.

Beijing put a bookmark between the pages of the novel. "I kinda wish we would've invited Rayna," she said to Seville. "That bitch would have loved this." She spread her arms wide.

"I called her and filled her in on everything that I had planned for you. But she couldn't make it."

"She's a trip. You would probably like her in person; I really kicked it with her while you were in Germany."

"I would love to meet her. Especially since she is really like your only outsider friend that you really deal with."

"I know," Beijing agreed, thinking about Rayna. "It's so crazy how we just managed to hit it off at my class, the chitchat turned into girl talk and then to lunches and dinners—and then she even convinced me to hook up with Lootchee, but I won't hold it against her."

They both laughed, but Seville could tell that Beijing really missed him.

"I guess she earned your friendship, whereas since the incident with P, you don't normally let women in. I'm glad you have her, because I know how hard it is for you to make friends."

"So what's on the agenda after we leave the pool?" Beijing changed the subject.

Seville gave her a look that said, *What else,* then in unison they shouted, "Shopping!" And high-fived each other.

"One of my favorite pastimes," Seville admitted.

"You are not alone." Beijing flipped her oversized white sunglasses in place to block the sun as she lay back in the chair to relax, hoping to catch a catnap.

The guys next to her were carrying on a conversation a little too loud for her not to hear them.

"I had the worst night's sleep in my life," one of them said.

She assumed the voice was the tall one with the athletic body.

"The mattress was hard and the bed squeaked."

"Where are you staying?" a different voice asked, farther away by the sound of it.

"Some piece of shit off the strip. My secretary and I called around everywhere to find another spot but everything is booked solid," he complained. "The lights are so dim in my room, I could barely write my speech last night."

"Damn, man, I'm sorry to hear that," the friend teased. "Who would have thought the mighty Malcolm Clarke would be slumming it in a do-drop-in." After some laughter, he added, "You can always stay with me. I know that shit has to be miserable."

"Nah, bro, I'm not trying to cramp your style," Malcolm replied. "I'll just have to rough it out, I guess." He took a sip from a bottled Corona.

"No, I insist."

"Man, you snore; I still wouldn't be able to sleep."

Beijing rose from the chair. It was hard not to notice her. She was rocking a white two-piece swimsuit to perfection, stretching the breathable material in all the right places. "Be right back." She twisted the matching wrap around her hips, tucked her feet in a pair of flip-flops, and gracefully sauntered into the building.

The two men were still talking about how fine she was when Beijing returned five minutes later holding a plastic room key.

"Mr. Clarke?" Beijing approached the fellas.

Malcolm looked up at the beautiful dark chocolate lady in her white bathing suit and big white straw hat standing in front of him. She was even more stunning up close and personal. "Yes?" He stood up. "Yes, Clarke. Malcolm Clarke, how can I assist you?" He would have rebuilt the engine in her car right then and there, if she had asked.

"My name is Beijing Lee, and I'm the hotel host at the Tabby in Charlotte; it's my responsibility to make sure that our guests are happy. I happened to overhear that you are not happy with the less-than-adequate hotel you're booked in, and I decided to help." She handed Malcolm the key. "I managed to wrestle up one of our special reserved rooms—if you want it."

"Of course, yes of course." Beijing had caught him totally off guard.

"If so, you can give Thomas here"—she nodded to the uni-formed bellhop—"the information he needs. He'll retrieve your bags from the other hotel and bring them to your room."

Malcolm's friend was envious, wishing he was the one that was residing in the fleabag hotel, only to be rescued by a beautiful woman. He stood up. "I thank you for accommodating my friend," he said, whipping out his card. "We'd love for you to have lunch with us."

Beijing smiled. "Thank you but I have plans already." She let him down easy then redirected her attention to her newest client. Malcolm was ecstatic and stunned by what was going on.

Beijing handed him her business card. "If you ever need any-thing, or are in the Charlotte area, give me a call and I will assist however you need me to."

He took the card but was shocked. "Thank you, Ms. Lee! How can I repay you?"

"No need, just you getting a good night's rest would be grand for me."

"Will do." He dug in his pocket and handed her his card. ATTORNEY-AT-LAW. "And, Ms. Lee, your kindness is appreciated. If there is anything at all I can do to return the favor—now or in the future—please allow me the luxury."

Beijing accepted the card. "I'll keep that in mind."

The guys were both lusting after Beijing and she knew it as she walked back over to her pool chair. Too bad she no longer had that effect on Lootchee as she did so many other men who came into her life.

Another hour of sunbathing, then Beijing and Seville left the pool and hit the mall for a round of shopping, getting ready for the evening festivities.

They had dinner at Houston's on the ocean. Afterward Seville suggested that they go to the hotel to freshen their makeup.

"Girl, thanks so much for everything. I love you and appreciate you and there are no words that can express my gratitude for this weekend. Like for real. I can't tell you."

Seville dropped her head. "I have something to confess to you."

"What?" Beijing had a big smile on her face, but Seville looked embarrassed. "What's wrong, Cuz—why you look so down?"

"I feel like . . ." She paused; the words were stuck in her throat.

"You feel like what?"

"I feel like . . ." She tried to get it out again. "I don't know how to say it."

"Just say it."

"I feel like I've deceived you," she blurted out.

"Deceived me? How?" Beijing asked, confused and stunned that her cousin and best friend would say or do something so horrible to her.

"Well, misled you."

"Misled me how?"

"All of this . . ."

Beijing looked in her cousin's eyes. "All of what?"

The hostess peeped into the restroom. "You guys are the Lee party, right?"

"Yes," Seville answered, and then took a deep breath.

"Your chariot awaits," the hostess announced.

"Thanks, but give us a minute," Seville said to the woman then looked at her cousin. "All of this, well really none of this, was my idea."

"Huh? What do you mean?"

She breathed deeply again. "None of this was my idea. It . . . he . . . He called me and told me that he wanted you to have a marvelous birthday and how it was up to us to make sure that it would be the best thus far."

"Who? Don?"

She shook her head slowly. "Lootchee, and I feel like I've set you up in some sort of way."

"Lootchee? What do you mean?" She was confused.

"Ms. Lee," the hostess interrupted again. "We've got other people waiting to dock. You all have to get going so we can get our others in and out."

"Two minutes and we're out of here," Seville said to the hostess. She started to talk fast. "Long story short, I'm excited and I need you to be too. Please don't be mad at me. Lootchee called me and asked me to set this entire thing up, the entire weekend, the shopping, everything! The only thing I did do was to make sure you looked amazing when he saw you."

"See me?"

"Yep, he's waiting on the boat along with Greta, your mom, your sister, Chyna, April, and a few more people. It's supposed to be a surprise, but I wanted to make sure you were on your A-game, to make him sorry that he ever left you. Now let's get this lip gloss on and get out there."

Beijing felt crazy; she didn't know what to say. "Are you kidding me?"

"Nope."

She hit her cousin. "I should smack the shit out of you."

"Hug me or fight me later, but for now we are going to continue to enjoy the night on Lootchee's dime."

"We'll see" was all that Beijing had to say, not knowing what to really do.

There Lootchee stood in an all-white linen suit, looking better than ever. He had begun growing short dreads that made him look amazing, and she didn't even like dreads.

He embraced her. Beijing wanted to resist and ask him a lot of questions, but she didn't, not yet anyway.

"Let's just enjoy the night and I will tell you everything tomorrow," Lootchee said, after kissing her on the cheek. "I promise."

$ $ $

Sterling had just boarded the boat when he saw a guy he assumed to be Lootchee embracing his daughter. He asked himself what in the hell he was even doing there. But he answered his very own question by reflecting back to the phone call he'd had with Lootchee the day before yesterday.

Sterling answered when the man asked, "May I speak to Mr. Lee?"

"Yes."

"This is Lootchee and I'm calling about your daughter, Beijing."

"Yes." He was concerned that something had happened to his only child.

"As you know, I'm throwing your daughter a surprise birthday party and I noticed that your name wasn't on the final RSVP list that Seville gave to me."

Without any hesitation Sterling said in a cold voice, "Because I'm not coming. I already celebrated my daughter's birthday on the day of her born day, which was months ago."

"Yes sir, I just happened to be out of town and wanted to throw her a belated celebration. If you'd reconsider coming to the party,

I'd book you on a first-class flight to Miami." He added, "I know it would mean a lot to her."

Sterling thought to himself, *This clown really thinks that I'm jumping on a plane because he snapped his fingers. He got another think coming.* "Me not coming has nothing to do with my daughter; I'm simply not the kind of father who conspires with a guy who is trying to play with my daughter's heart after breaking it once already."

Lootchee thought about Sterling's comment for a moment. Then he said, "You know, you are the most important man in her life and I'm just trying to be a distant second. That's all, sir. Please don't fault me for that. Now, we both know it would make Beijing's night if you attended. Please reconsider attending for your daughter, sir."

"I'm not making any promises, but I'll check my schedule."

Now here Sterling was on the yacht of a man who had toyed with his daughter's heart, who he'd come to meet eye-to-eye. Greta stood beside him in a beautiful green silk sheath dress.

Beijing turned around and screamed with enthusiasm, "Daddy!" A big smile covered her face. "I'm so happy you are here. What a surprise." She gave her father a big hug.

Her smiled remained as she made the introductions between her two favorite guys.

"Dad, this is Lootchee. Lootchee, this is my father." Lootchee extended his hand for Sterling to shake. Sterling accepted, but their eyes met and Sterling shot Lootchee a bullet-ridden stare. Lootchee met his stare beat for beat before finally saying, "Nice to finally meet you."

"And this is my stepmom, Greta," Beijing said. This time Lootchee smiled and took her hand, but Greta pulled him in and gave him a quick hug as if he were family.

Seeing his daughter as happy as she was, half of Sterling's work was done. Now he had to finish the job.

Greta knew what time it was and called Beijing over, pretending to have to tell her something so that the two men could be alone.

After sizing the man up who had been playing mind games with his baby girl's head, he said, "You know that's my heart."

Lootchee nodded. "I do, sir."

"And I love her dearly." Sterling didn't blink nor cut anything close to a smile whatsoever.

"Yes sir."

"More than life itself, especially yours," Sterling added, still maintaining the same hard cold stare.

"Well, that makes two of us," Lootchee tried to convince Sterling.

"That's what I need to hear." Satisfied he had made his point.

Lootchee knew that Sterling was dead serious and wanted to lighten up the mood. "Well, we got the particulars out of the way. Let's party," he said, rubbing his sweaty hands together. "With moderation."

"In moderation," Sterling added under his breath.

CHAPTER 27

The Sun and the Moon

The Atlantic Ocean shimmered under the stars like a black velvet blanket. The guests were dancing and drinking, and Beijing was happier than she had been in months. This was the first time that Lootchee had met all the people she loved. He meshed well with everyone and they all seemed to love him, even Willabee.

Beijing felt Lootchee tug her hand.

"C'mere," he whispered. "I want to show you something."

Beijing looked around. It didn't seem like anyone would miss her for a few minutes. She followed Lootchee down to the end of the yacht, which was gently and slowly passing over the Atlantic water.

"This is so nice," she said. Lootchee stood behind her and wrapped his arms around her. She felt him pressing against her body, and warmth flooded through her.

"Look at the moon," he said. "I ordered that just for you."

It was full and as shiny as a new silver dollar.

"I thought you'd forgotten about me," she said.

"No, you the only thing I think about," he said. "Most the time."

"You have a funny way of showing it," she said and jabbed him with her elbow.

"Nobody's perfect. I was going through something. And working mostly. I have a present for you. Baby, a man's got to work sometimes so he can buy stuff for his boo. Ya know, diamonds and shit like that." He reached around and opened his hand, revealing a pair of teardrop diamond earrings.

Beijing gasped.

"They're gorgeous, Lootchee." They wouldn't get him off the hook for the stunt he pulled, but it was a nice start.

"Put 'em on," he said.

She slipped the earrings she was wearing off and handed them to Lootchee, then fastened the diamonds in their place.

"Perfect?" he whispered.

They were about to consummate the gift with a long wet kiss when Seville called her name.

"Beijing, your daddy wants to raise a toast to your birthday," she said. "I've been looking all over for you."

Beijing smiled and said to Lootchee, "I got something to give you too . . . later."

That night on the yacht would be remembered by all who attended for a long time to come. Lootchee had thought of everything. The seafood buffet was catered by a private chef. There was live entertainment with a team of bartenders preparing every type of alcoholic refreshment known to man or woman. And Lootchee had been at her side the entire time, making her feel like the queen of the night.

It was the next morning and already half past noon when Beijing turned on her side to look at the clock on the night table. For a brief moment she didn't know where she was. *This is why I don't get drunk,* she thought to herself. Then she made out the familiar decorations of the Tabby's suite.

"Now I know why Seville insisted that we get two rooms," she said.

Lootchee was under the covers of the king-sized bed next to her with a smile on his face.

"You had it all figured out, didn't you? Down to the final detail," she said to him.

"I just wanted you to have a good time," he said sheepishly. "Did I at least succeed in doing that?"

"You did okay," she said. If she was to be honest, she had to admit the entire weekend was thoughtful since he had missed her birthday. The party on the boat was fabulous and the sex they shared afterward was amazing. "But now you have some explaining to do, mister." As emotionally famished as she had been without him around, she had no intention of being played for anybody's sucker. Not again.

"I promised I would, didn't I?"

Although she loved the way she felt when they were together, she was prepared to move on and never see him again if his explanation was bullshit. What could he possibly say that could justify acting so callous and cruel?

"I'm ready to hear it, then," she said, sitting up in bed, giving Lootchee her undivided attention. "No time like the present." She gazed into his eyes.

"Okay." He sighed before continuing. "Remember when I told you that both my parents were dead?"

"Of course," she said. She reflected on how he sounded so cold when he told her. How could she forget something like that?

"Well," he said. He seemed to be trying to come up with the right words. "That wasn't the truth. Not exactly anyway."

"Then what exactly is the truth?" *There goes the neighborhood,* she thought. *If he would lie about something like that, then the truth isn't in him.*

"It's not like it sounds."

It never is, let you tell it, Beijing thought and was about to tell him so, but he put his hand up and stopped her.

"My father loved my mother unconditionally. He worked twelve to sixteen hours a day, six days a week, sometimes seven, in order to afford all the clothes, jewelry, and other material things my mother insisted she had to have." His eyes saddened like a little child who had just witnessed his first puppy getting crushed by a speeding car.

"But she could never get enough," he went on. "She never really loved my father. She was only there for the ride. However far it would take her. Even as a little boy I used to see the heartless looks she gave him when his back was turned. After a while she started giving him that look to his face. My father thought her unhappiness was due to him. He wasn't working hard enough, wasn't giving her enough of the things she said she deserved to have."

Beijing knew that this must be really hard for him to talk about and was grateful that he was opening up to her. She reached out to put her arm around him for support.

"Things got so bad," he said, "my mother started rejecting him totally. She wouldn't cook or clean, and she barely talked to the man. They even started sleeping in separate bedrooms." Lootchee closed his eyes for a moment. "The only woman, besides his own mother, that my father ever loved didn't care if he was dead or alive. I know for a fact she wished that he would die. I think that's what my father thought too. Heartbroken and depressed, my father decided to do the only thing he knew how to do when it came to my mother. He gave her what she wanted. They found him with a self-inflicted gunshot wound to the head. He was slumped over in the car in the driveway of our house."

"Oh my God, Lootchee."

With tears in his eyes, he continued, "There was a note left on the passenger seat. Six words: *I hope you are happy now!*

"He gave her his life, and her only concern was whether or not he had the kind of insurance that would pay off the house. Though she did not pull the trigger, my mother murdered my father by being selfish and greedy. As far as I was concerned," Lootchee muttered with steely eyes, "my mother died that day, too."

"*Wow,* baby, that's deep. I'm so sorry you had to live through that." Beijing kissed him on the top of his head. "That's such a sad thing to witness."

Lootchee didn't speak; he just stared off into space.

"Thanks, baby, for sharing such an intimate part of your life with me."

"You know I've never told anyone about that."

"I'm glad you chose to share it with me. I feel closer to you."

There was silence, and though it felt awkward to ask at this moment, curiosity was killing Beijing. "I don't want to seem selfish but I still don't understand what any of this has to do with you not calling me for months at a time?"

"When you said you thought it was too soon for us to be engaged it reminded me of my mother . . . rejecting my father," he said. "Whether it was wrong or right, the only thing I knew how to do was fall back. But I couldn't stay away. I want to make you happy, the way you make me happy."

All of the built-up animosity she'd harbored toward him over the past months was wiped away by the time he finished. How could she stay mad after he opened his heart to her, pouring out its contents?

She wrapped her arms around his strong upper body. Truthfully she was so happy just to be back in his arms that she wasn't sure she would have cared no matter what his reason was. At least he had a good story. She could save a little bit of her pride.

"So, let's live happily ever after."

CHAPTER 28

My Troubles Are Yours

Six weeks of romance had sped by since Lootchee's heart-wrenching confession to Beijing. Since that time their relationship had taken on a life of its own and they had grown even closer. Beijing felt that same rush she had at the beginning, every time they were together.

The two lovebirds were doing a little shopping, and Lootchee even picked out a few outfits for her.

"How do you like this one, baby?" Beijing held a low-cut black cocktail dress under her chin, posing for him.

Lootchee studied her for a few seconds. "I think the dress is beautiful," he finally said. "But with you rocking it, I think it would be drop-dead gorgeous."

"I agree," she said with a smile. "Now all we have to do is to find you something to complement it and I'll wear it next week when we go to the NBA All-Star Game. My friend Teflon the Don is opening the event with a performance. I want us to be there to-gether, to show support."

"I'm going to pass on that one. I've been consuming too much of your time. Between your working and spending time with me, you've been out of the loop with your girls. This is something I think you should do with them," he suggested.

She raised an eyebrow.

"But you love sports," she said. "You're not going to the All-Star Game at all?"

"Naw, baby, I'm going to pass."

"But I really want you to go with me."

"I think I'm going to stay here or shoot over to Atlanta. I need to make the money to pay for my boo's dream wedding," he said, pulling her closer to give her a soft kiss on the lips.

"But you know you don't have to do that. My dad will pay for the wedding. He's been putting money away for that day since I can remember."

"Whatever you want, baby girl." He smiled. "You think you got enough stuff yet?" He changed to an easier subject.

"Just about," she said.

While she was picking out a few more things, Beijing's cell phone went off. It was Dennard. He told her he was coming to town for a few days.

"Are you staying at the Tabby?"

"If I can get a room," he hinted.

"Stop it, I will make sure that you get all squared away. What's the date that you arrive?"

After noting the date of the arrival, she told him that she would make sure he was taken care of while he was in town for his con-vention.

In the car, on the way back to their condo in Charlotte, Loot-chee was unusually quiet.

"A dime for what's on your mind," Beijing said. "It seems like something heavy is on your mind."

He never took his eyes off the road. "Nothing to trouble you with, just my own problems."

"Your troubles are mine too."

"I'm just trying to come up with a proper solution to a small inconvenience."

"Tell me about it," she said, turning in to face him. "Maybe I can help."

"Thanks, babe, but it's not your problem. I'll figure it out."

"You don't have to always be Superman with me. I love you just the way you are," she told him. "If you got a problem, then I have one too."

"If you insist," he sighed. "I got some money that I need cleaned up."

Beijing knew exactly what he meant by cleaned up. Making dirty money clean.

"How much?"

"Three, maybe four million."

"Dollars?"

"No, pesos," he joked. "Of course I'm talking about dollars. I live in America, don't I?"

"That's a lot of money, but I can make some phone calls and check to see if I know of someone who can take care of it."

"Really?"

She nodded. And at the end of the day Beijing always made it happen, didn't she?

CHAPTER 29

Spaghetti for Dinner

Houston was bubbling with energy and it was only two thirty in the afternoon. Some folks on the sidewalks were taking advantage of capitalism, selling everything from sports memorabilia to accessories to sexual favors. You could scoop up almost anything your heart desired for the right price if you knew where to look.

The All-Star Game festivities weren't scheduled to take flight until six thirty, but the restaurant and lobby of the hotel were filled to maximum capacity.

Beijing was in the midst of it all, having a ball. It was the first time she, Paris, Seville, and Rayna had all been out together; neither Paris nor Seville had ever met Beijing's newest friend.

Beijing noticed that Rayna and Seville seemed to hit it off right away, but Paris was cold and indifferent to Rayna.

"I've been meaning to tell you, B," Rayna said, "you looking too good in those jeans and pumps."

Beijing was rocking a pair of figure-hugging jeans, four-inch purple pumps, and a fitted top.

"Just a lil somethin'-somethin' I threw together," she said. "It don't look like you slummin' none either."

Rayna had put on a few pounds since the last time they were together, but she was tall and carried her weight well.

"I relapsed to my bad eating habits and slacked on my workout for a minute, but I'm trying to get back on track," Rayna confessed. "That ordeal in Atlanta kind of threw me off point," meaning the robbery.

"I wouldn't even have noticed it, if you hadn't said anything," Beijing lied.

"I wish I would've brought Jack with me," Seville said as she checked the fellas out. "All these fine brothers are gonna push my temptation to the limit." She chuckled.

The four girls definitely were not going unnoticed as they waltzed around the star-studded lobby. They looked like money. Even in a room filled with various industry people, actors, musicians, professional athletes, and models, Beijing, Seville, Paris, and Rayna turned heads.

"I don't like that bitch," Paris told her sister as she looked Rayna over. Rayna was talking to some rapper who was way too short for her. But what the entertainer lacked in height, he made up for in bank.

Beijing asked, "Why? What did she do to you?"

Paris shook her head, "The bitch ain't do nothing to me. I just don't like her vibe. I've rolled in the grass long enough to know a snake when I see one. I can be got, but not too often." She then added, "Just don't give that bitch your full trust."

A few months ago Beijing would have dismissed Paris's ramblings as drug talk, but she'd been drug-free for a minute, had gone to the drug treatment program was going to the outpatient meetings, doing well for herself, the whole nine. Beijing heard the warning but didn't take heed because she thought her sister might be a little jealous of her and Rayna's relationship.

"Beijing?" a voice called out from behind. "Is that you?"

She turned around; the voice belonged to Jeff, Lootchee's friend, the one she'd met at the New Edition show.

"Where's my man?" he asked, kissing her on the cheek. Jeff scanned the area like he was looking for someone.

"He couldn't make it. We're having a girls' weekend," she told him. "You remember my sister"—she nodded to Paris, then pointed to Seville—"and my cousin, from my birthday party, don't you?"

"How could I forget Miss Seville?" He smiled. "She shot me down at least twice that night."

"Over there, getting her mack on, is my girlfriend Rayna."

Beijing saw him admiring Rayna's backside. There was no denying Rayna had booty for days. When Jeff realized he was busted, he pulled his attention away from Rayna's ample rear. "I'm surprised my man ain't here, ya heard?"

"Me too," she said honestly, "but you know how it goes."

"Yeah, I know how it goes but I would've definitely been here, ya heard."

Beijing eyed Don across the room. He was obviously trying to go incognito, wearing dark sunglasses and a hoodie over his head and most of his face. She couldn't be fooled; she knew that walk anywhere.

"Well, I'll probably see you somewhere later," she said, happy for the distraction. "I need to go say hello to someone."

Jeff tracked the path of her vision. "I didn't know you were a fan of Teflon the Don, but who isn't? I tried to book 'im at my spot before he blew up."

Beijing wasn't sure if he was asking a question or making a statement, or both.

"He's an old friend, I actually used to work with him." She explained to Jeff the nature of her and Don's business relationship before walking away. She didn't want it to be a mix-up whenever the conversation came up between him and Lootchee that Jeff had seen her with Don. And she knew that it probably would one day. She knew they were close and they kicked it a lot.

"Well, hook a brother up, ya heard."

She nodded as she hurried to catch up with Don before he got on the elevator. Beijing called out, "Hey you! Slow down."

By the look on his face, she knew that Don had been trying to avoid her.

"Hey, sweets, when did you get in?" He gave her a hug after being cornered.

As soon as the first word came out of his mouth, she knew that something wasn't right.

She pulled him away from his mob. "You okay?" she asked out of concern. "You look a little funny."

"Yeah, I'm aight," he said unconvincingly. "Just a lil tired." He rubbed his eyes. "That's all."

He's more than a lil tired, she thought. She was about to comment when her phone went off.

It was a 212 area code. *New York,* she thought.

"Hold on a second, let me get this," she said, thumbing the green TALK button. She could see the relief on Don's face for the temporary interruption. Beijing knew that he wasn't feeling where their conversation was headed anyway.

"Beijing, it's Seth."

Please not this Natalia bullshit today. She's supposed to be in Hawaii. She turned her back to Don after giving him a one-fingered *Wait* signal, but he took it as his cue to flee. She did not feel like or want to deal with Natalia's drama today but she put a smile in her voice and said, "Yes, Seth, is everything okay with Natalia?"

"Besides being off in Hawaii, spending my money recklessly, and trying hard to send me into bankruptcy?" he joked.

"You're way too smart for that to happen," Beijing shot back.

"I would hope so." He shifted the conversation. "This time it's a friend of mine who could really use your help."

"How can I be of service?" she asked as she noticed Don getting on the elevator. She walked into the bathroom so she could hear Seth.

He began to tell her about a friend of his named Amir, a prince from somewhere in the Middle East. They were traveling in a Gulfstream IV and scheduled to touch down in Miami on a private landing strip at nine thirty. If it was at all possible, Seth asked, could she manage to have someone deliver to them about a pound or so of the sticky-icky!

"Of course."

"Since you are in Miami," he said. "Do you think you'll be able to make this happen for me?"

"I'm actually in Houston, but it shouldn't be a problem at all. I will take care of it for you."

"Of course you know this needs to be done with the utmost discretion," he said.

"Of course. Give me a couple of minutes and I will call you back."

In less than five minutes, Beijing had cut a deal with another one of her clients who distributed large quantities of marijuana in his spare time and was passing on the particulars to Seth, who was so grateful to her.

In the meantime she received a call from Lootchee. "I'm lonely and I miss you."

"I miss you too, baby."

"I hear you down there looking good, smelling good, and having lots of fun." She knew that Jeff had already run and called Lootchee and told him only *God* knew what.

"The girls and I are having a ball. You should've come."

"Well, I miss you and want to see you."

"You will see me the day after tomorrow."

"But I want to see you now. Book a limo to Dallas, stay a few hours and then you can be back by morning."

Beijing thought that was rather selfish and that he should've been there with her. She said "Okay," slowly, but she didn't want to say it to make him mad.

She went over to the concierge's desk to try to get a limo, but it was almost impossible. Besides, she didn't really want to leave her friends anyway.

She called Lootchee back, "Baby, they are trying to charge us like three grand to drive me from Houston to Dallas. It's ludicrous to pay that kind of money for me to be there for only a few hours, and then come back."

"Aight, if you think so."

"But I will be in your arms day after tomorrow; I'm still coming there just like we planned."

After the business with Seth was taken care of, Beijing let the girls know she was going upstairs for a minute. In the lobby she ran into Bill—the security guard she had hired when Don first started. He told her that Don was in room 1725 and she should go and talk some sense into him. He had relapsed again, and Bill was afraid that Don might kill himself if the leeches around him didn't.

Beijing entered the elevator and pushed the button for the seventeenth floor, not before realizing that Corday, the club owner from Atlanta, was in the elevator with Dazzle and several of his strippers he had brought out to the All-Star Game to work. She shared a few words with Dazzle and promised to get up with her later before getting off on Don's floor.

A mixture of music and talking could be heard from Don's room.

Listening for a second, unable to pick out Don's voice from the cacophony, Beijing knocked on the door.

No one answered, so she knocked harder.

This time the door was opened by a tall, rail-thin woman. "May I help you?"

Beijing had never met the beanpole blocking her entrance to the room, but for some odd reason the voice sounded vaguely familiar.

"I need to speak with Don." Beijing was polite but curt.

Macy-Rae did recognize Beijing. She looked just like the photo that Don kept tucked away in his wallet, the one he thought she didn't know about.

"I'm sorry, but Teflon the Don don't do private meetings. He'll be signing autographs and mingling tonight with groupies at an after-party."

That was it! Now she knew where she'd heard that squeaky voice. It was that girl that had called about Don a while ago. Macy-Rae was one slice of cheese from getting beat down.

"Excuse me." She pushed past into the luxury suite. "Where is he?"

A few of the leeches that had clustered around Don in the lobby were now in his hotel room. They were drinking and smoking with a gaggle of young girls in short-shorts and miniskirts, the perks of tagging along with a platinum-selling rap artist: partying, pussy, and drugs.

Beijing swept the place with her eyes like a hidden camera searching for shoplifters in a department store. It was a large room with a big-screen TV and card tables, a humongous dining room table, and four bedrooms, two on either side of the suite.

"He doesn't want to be bothered and isn't talking to anyone while he's having dinner." Macy-Rae copped a seat at the Last Supper—like table in the same spot Judas would've taken.

One of the weed-smoking leech worms pulled away from the pack of gullible girls to try his hand at Beijing.

"Hey what's your name, if you nice to me, I will get you in to meet Teflon da Don."

"What you will do is show me some goddamn respect parasite,

if you don't want your ass thrown out of this hotel and out of Don's entourage, leaving you to scrounge up pussy and drugs on your own merit. Now lil boy, don't play with me. Which one of these rooms is Don in?"

She glanced over at Macy-Rae before entering the room, giving her a look that said, *I'm not finished with yo' trifling ass either.*

Macy-Rae didn't budge.

What Beijing saw after stepping inside the adjoining bedroom wouldn't have looked so out of place if this was a cartoon, but it wasn't—this was real life.

She ran over to the small table where Don was seated face-down in a full plate of spaghetti. If she hadn't gotten there when she did, he might have been the first rapper to ever drown in a plate of meat sauce.

Teflon the Don had relapsed.

After she wiped the red sauce from his face, Don looked at her. Actually, he looked through her. Clearly he was spaced out and had dilated pupils. Beijing had seen it all before.

Later that night the performance by Teflon the Don was canceled.

CHAPTER 30

Crack Is Wack

Other than the rumor about Teflon the Don overdosing on heroin backstage, the All-Star weekend was a fun-filled, successful event. But like all good times, sooner or later it had to come to an end.

The girls were packed up, standing in front of the hotel, upset that it was time to leave. They had reserved two limos—a black stretch Hummer and a white Lincoln. Rayna, Paris, and Seville planned to be driven to the airport in the Hummer. Beijing was going to get chauffeured to Dallas to see Lootchee.

"What you going to do, girl?" Rayna asked Beijing.

She'd been trying to call Lootchee since last night to let him know what time she expected to arrive.

"I don't know. He still hasn't answered his phone." She snapped the flip-lid on her cell phone. "I don't want to just show up."

"I would go and ask him what the fuck is his problem," Paris suggested.

"Right," Seville said to her outspoken cousin. "And that's why you don't have a boyfriend; you don't know what the hell to say out of your mouth."

"Actually I have three boyfriends," Paris stated in a matter-of-fact tone.

"Who?" Seville called her out. "I thought you were chilling, trying to get yo'self together."

"For yo' information"—Paris rolled her neck—"his name is Nunya."

"Who is that? Anybody we know?" Rayna finally asked.

"None of yo' damn business." Paris burst out laughing and Beijing, Rayna, and Seville followed suit.

Beijing decided not to barge in unannounced at Lootchee's home in Dallas. She was about to climb into the stretch Hummer heading to the airport when Corday walked up with a long-stemmed red rose.

He gave her the flower and asked, "When are you going to be back in Atlanta?"

"Not sure when I'll be that way," she said, smiling on the outside but inside wishing it was Lootchee handing the beautiful flower to her. "I haven't really thought about it."

"The next time you are," he said, flashing a Colgate smile, "I would love to take you to dinner and get to know you better."

I don't have time for this shit right now, she thought, pissed off about the situation she was in with Lootchee, but she said, "Okay." She didn't want to rub him the wrong way because she knew that they were destined to do more business together.

Rayna peeped her head out of the limo door. "Beijing, come on."

"Seriously." Corday grabbed her hand. "Anytime, anywhere, anyplace, name the city!"

"I'll keep that in mind if I'm ever bored and hard up for a date—" Before she had finished her sentence, one of Corday's dancers called for him to come over. Beijing just smiled. "—with a man who has pussy parading around him twenty-four seven."

"You do that." He smiled.

Beijing tried calling Lootchee the entire way to the airport, hoping he would answer so she could head to see him as they had planned. Every time he didn't, she got more pissed.

Before she knew it, she was in the back of the limo with her sister, Seville, and Rayna, sulking, a tear or two swelling in her eyes.

Soon tears started dropping down her face.

"You need to stop that," Seville said. "Your eyes are going to get puffy."

"Cheer up, Sis. Fuck that nigga," Paris said.

"Don't get yourself twisted over a no-count nigga," Rayna added.

"The same no-count nigga you talked her into hooking up with," Paris blasted Rayna.

"All she's saying is that anybody who can make a woman cry like that is not any good for her," Seville interjected, trying to defuse the tension between Paris and Rayna.

Beijing tried to put on a strong face for her girls. Deep down, she knew they were right. She kept replaying the last conversation with Latchee to figure out what she'd said to make him shut down.

$ $ $

It had been two weeks since she returned to Charlotte from the All-Star Game, and Corday had been blowing her phone up. Most of the time she let his calls go to voice mail. The rare times she did pick up, the conversation was brief.

He finally convinced her to have lunch with him. How Corday found out when she was scheduled to be in Atlanta was anybody's guess.

The day was amazing. He started by picking her up from the airport and giving her roses.

"You do so much to take care of other people, I wanted this day to be all about you," he said as he pulled in front of a nail salon.

"That's very thoughtful of you." She smiled. Corday took her hand and helped her out of the car.

As they walked into the salon, she felt eyes on her. The Asian women greeted her at the entrance, leading her over to the spa pedicure chair. Once she was settled, a woman asked her, "What's your name?"

Beijing told the girl her name.

"You Chinese?" the woman asked with raised eyebrows after being told.

"No, I'm not." Beijing let out a chuckle. "I get that all the time. My mother named me and my sister after the places she felt that she would never see."

"Chinese dad?" she questioned.

"No." Beijing shook her head.

"Your hair so silky. Look like you could be mixed."

"It doesn't help with Lee being my last name either," Beijing said with a smile.

"Get out." The Asian woman showed surprise. The woman spoke great English and she talked so much that Beijing and Corday could not get a word in. He didn't mind as long as Beijing was enjoying herself. And she really was until she got a text from Rayna.

I HEARD YOUR BOY WAS IN ATL, it read.

After getting the full treatment for Beijing at the nail salon, Corday took her to dinner and a movie. To Beijing's surprise they got along great. The conversation was easy and he seemed sincere. He was such a gentleman that she almost forgot that he was a legal pimp who owned a strip club.

After being out all day, Beijing was back in her suite at the Tabby of Atlanta when Paris called her cell. "Hey P-Money," Beijing answered.

"Hey right back at you. Look, I know you are busy and things but just wanted to talk to you for a few."

"Shoot." She had more than a moment to kick it with her sister.

"Just wanted to let you know that I got a job at this mail-order pharmacy place, and it has room for advancement."

"That's good! I'm so proud of you!" And she meant it. Paris had been doing surprisingly well.

"Me too, but I'm a little nervous. I don't want anything to mess it up."

Beijing told her, "You have to think positive."

"Yeah, but I'm gonna need Momma for a ride and when she's off her meds it throws everything off. I never knew how crazy and out of control she can get without that stuff. I guess I was so busy medicating myself, I never really paid attention."

"She can get out of control," Beijing agreed. "That's why you have to make sure that she's taking them. And it's a little easier now since you are living with her."

"The problem is, one day off her meds, she feels like it ain't no different, then two days still nothing, and then three days and then it's really no sweat girl."

"And before you know it, shit done hit the fan," Beijing said. They both broke into laughter thinking about the crazy stuff they had witnessed their mother do.

When neither of them could laugh anymore, Paris changed the topic of conversation.

"So how's it going in Atlanta?"

Beijing thought about her evening with Corday. "Better than I expected," she said. "I had a date with the guy that gave me the rose when we were leaving Houston."

"The strip club owner?" Paris was shocked. "I didn't know that you were even entertaining his conversation."

"Hey, but what's a girl to do? He's a nice guy aside from having a strip club."

"Tell me everything. Don't hold back. How was it?"

"It was nice, and I have a meeting tomorrow that's thirty minutes away from here so he's allowing me to use his car and driver to take me there and around town afterward. He said he wanted to buy me something nice but ran out of time, so he's going to let me use his card to purchase myself something at Lenox Mall."

"Really?" Paris questioned. "That's good." She was somewhat suspicious, not used to men doing favors without motives.

"Sweet, right?"

"Yeah but be careful, you know how men can be, always want something for a lil bit of."

"At first, I was going to decline but I changed my mind. I'm just going to roll with the punches."

"I heard that. Because a bitch don't turn nothing down but her collars," she replied, contradicting herself.

"I know that's right, big sis." They giggled some more.

"Can I confess something to you?"

"Yup, you know it. Anything you want."

"I texted Lootchee today."

A few seconds of silence passed.

"Okay and . . . ," Paris pushed.

"And he didn't respond." She paused. "I thought he would."

"What did you say?"

Beijing recited the text verbatim: I'M IN ATL, HEARD YOU WERE TOO.

"Well, if he doesn't hit back, then it's his loss."

Again, neither sister spoke.

"Hello."

"Yeah, I'm still here."

"Why you get so quiet, what you thinking?"

"What I'm thinking is that I don't want you to take this the wrong way but over the years, I've always had to hear you say things to me that were hurtful, but true. And sometimes when you are caught up in a situation you can't really see things for what they are."

"I'm not really in the mood for riddles," Beijing said. "If you know something I don't, please tell me."

"I'm getting to it. Be patient. I want you to know that I'm saying this out of love and not envy or jealousy."

Beijing listened.

Though it wasn't easy for Paris, she continued. "Over the years I've been jealous of you. I can admit it today."

"Why?" Beijing asked.

"Because you had everything: a good childhood, a father who loved you enough to get his own shit together to rescue you from our mother situation—he gave you everything you asked for while I had to scramble for the little I got.

"You know I've apologized before for leaving you that dreadful day." This was a conversation that they'd avoided for years. The only time they'd ever said anything about it was during an argument. "I beat myself up about it so many days. Day after day I'd look in the mirror and ask myself how I could do a thing like that to my only sister."

Beijing's eyes got watery, and she could hear the tears in her sister's voice.

"You know it's been about six months since the day I called and you came to rescue me. I vowed that I would never put another drug in my body, so help me God. If you could at the drop of the dime, and despite everything I've done to you and said to you, come to my rescue because you heard me crying, then goddamnit I can get my shit together. Now it's my turn to help you." She paused briefly. "Lootchee isn't any good for you, B."

"Tell me something I don't know."

"He can make you feel your best but it's always only temporary. In Narcotics Anonymous, they call it highest of the highs and the lowest of the lows. Just like the narcotics, deep in your heart you know he's bad for you, but you still are willing to ignore the fact for the sensation he gives you."

Beijing listened to what her sister was saying. It was making some sense

"Eventually, you will abandon the ones you love for him, and your job. Nothing will seem to matter but him."

Beijing thought about how she'd almost left her girls in Houston and how she'd call in to work for him and how his influence had made her do things that she knew she shouldn't have, like launder money.

"I really hate to admit it." She paused. "But I think you may be right."

"I know I'm right," Paris insisted. "From this point on, I say we refer to that nigga as crack. That's his new name: Crack."

Beijing laughed but she knew that what Paris was saying had some truth to it. "So how do I kick crack?"

"You have to decide when you are sick and tired of it. What it does to you, how it makes you feel afterward, and the things it makes you do. Once you hit bottom then you will kick it. I promise. You may have a few relapses before you're able to finally kick him for good. And we use anything to prompt relapse."

The next morning, just as Corday had promised, his driver was there to pick her up for her client meeting.

After it was over, Beijing took in an afternoon of shopping, courtesy of Corday and his American Express card.

In the midst of the spree she was compelled—for reasons she couldn't have explained even if she had to—to call Lootchee. It seemed like being in a city where he'd been known to hang out drew her to dial the number.

He answered on the second ring. "What's up?"

"Hey you." Beijing was happy to hear his voice. Something

about the man just did it for her, regardless of how insensitive he could be at times. "What are you doing?"

"I'm on the highway." His voice sounded as if he didn't have a worry in the world.

He must have gotten her message and wanted to surprise her, Beijing thought.

"How long before you get here?" She was excited. "I miss you—even though you drive me crazy sometimes."

"What are you talking about? I'm on my way to Florida," Lootchee said, bursting her bubble again.

"You did get my text, didn't you? And if so," she said with attitude, "why aren't you on the way to Atlanta to see me?"

"Because I don't see a reason to waste my time driving to see anybody who's not willing to spend a couple of g's to show me some love."

Beijing was almost speechless. She didn't know what to say. *This is what this shit is about? Because I didn't spend fucking three grand to come and see him. Is he fucking kidding me?*

"You can't be serious?" she said.

"Yeah, I'm dead-ass serious. I would've ridden across the country on a moped to come and get you. Don't you know I done had bitches paying three thousand one-way to fly in to see me, and you going to cry about paying it one night to see me?"

"You said it wasn't that serious. And if it was, then why didn't you send a car for me?"

The phone was silent, and then the next thing she heard was her phone ringing. Lootchee had hung up on her and now he was calling her back. So she thought anyway, and this time she was ready to rip into his ass. But she was going to have to wait to get off her frustrations. It was Corday calling.

Beijing wanted to let the call roll over to voice mail, but how could she? She was in his car, being driven by his driver, and had just spent his money. Taking a deep breath, she thumbed the TALK button.

"Hello." Her voice was low, hesitant.

"How are you, beautiful? I hope you're finished burning the credit card up, because I have something special planned for this evening."

"Everything is good," she lied, trying to put a spark in her voice to disguise her feelings.

"You sure?"

"Totally." That wasn't even close to the truth.

"I hope you bought yourself some nice things?" He sounded as if he genuninely meant it.

"I did." She wiped away another tear.

"Well, you still don't sound like you're happy."

"I am," she tried to assure him, even though she couldn't quite convince herself.

"I tell you what. We'll talk about whatever's bothering you at dinner."

She took a deep breath, and then exhaled. "Sounds good to me."

"If there is something else you want to treat yourself to while I wrap up here, feel free." A rap video was being shot at Corday's club. She could hear the commotion in the background.

"Okay, sure thing. You don't have to tell me twice. Well, get back to work and call me when you are on the way." Beijing rushed him off the phone before she lost it.

She disconnected the call and was in tears. The driver asked, "Ms. Lee, everything is fine?"

"Marvelous," she sniffed. "Simply marvelous."

She pulled out her phone and texted Lootchee. YOU NEVER CEASE TO AMAZE ME. THANKS FOR BREAKING MY HEART AND HURTING MY FEELINGS YET ANOTHER TIME!

Back at the hotel, Beijing went to take care of her clients. She was trying to hold it together enough to work but couldn't focus at all. Still, she managed to quickly get her clients checked in to the hotel. Once they were all settled, she decided to go to her room, charge her phone, and lie down for a nap to get her mind off Lootchee—only to be awakened by her doorbell ringing.

She popped up to see who it was: Corday. *Damnit, I wanted to be waiting for him downstairs.*

She had Corday sit in the living room of her suite while she went into the bathroom to get herself ready for their dinner date.

As she was retouching her makeup, Corday called out, "Your cell phone is ringing." She dashed across the room to check the caller ID—a private number. "Hello."

"I broke your heart?"

"Hello." She acted like she couldn't hear him.

"Yeah, can you hear me?"

"Hello." Beijing kept up the charade. "Hello, hello, hello!"

"Yeah, B," he called out to her, "it's me."

"Whoever this is, stop playing on my phone." She hung up feeling somewhat recharged. It felt good to fuck with him for a change.

Lootchee called back three more times. When she didn't bother to pick up, she felt more in control.

The next day she continued spending Corday's money and even though he put a lot of effort into showing her a good time, she still could not keep her mind off Lootchee.

It was time for her to wrap up her stay in Atlanta. As soon as Corday dropped her off at the airport to head to Durham, before even checking in, she called Lootchee. Just like that her plans had changed and he was on his way to pick her up.

CHAPTER 31

Emotionally Twisted

Beijing got in the car without looking at Lootchee and crossed her arms.

"So you not speaking to me?" he asked. "You don't pick up my calls, claim your phone is broken, and now you not talking to me?"

"You got that right." She nodded. "But why should I? You dumped me without giving me a damn explanation!"

"I can't blame you. You have every right to be mad at me, baby. I'm just crazy and fucked up in the head sometimes. I felt like you were neglecting me by being out with your girls not even thinking about me. And I just thought, *Fuck it! I don't need her.*"

Beijing finally looked at him.

He gazed into her eyes. "But I was wrong. I need you like the sky needs the sun, hell needs water, and the world needs peace. I could go on."

"Really?" she asked. She felt herself starting to melt.

"Baby, I'm going to make it up to you. I promise you that. And I'm gonna start right now, right here." He removed a jewelry box from the glove compartment. He opened it up and Beijing's mouth dropped. It was a beautiful charm bracelet with gold and diamond trinkets.

"I love it," It was odd but gorgeous.

"It has a diamond Chinese pagoda charm from Beijing," he said. Then he leaned over and kissed her, and Beijing couldn't even remember the pain and hurt she had felt. She became warm and soft inside.

Beijing had been chilling in Atlanta with him for over a week now, and when she wasn't working, the make-up sex was hot, passionate, and intense. Lootchee made love to her at least twice a day, and fucked her brains out three times before the sun started pushing the rays of light through the partially closed curtains on the eighth day they had been together.

"I might have to pick a fight with you more often," Beijing said after waking up. The top of the sheets came up just above her navel. Her firm perfect breasts were rising up and down with each breath as she lay on her back. Lootchee lay beside her, watching her. "Last night was incredible."

Lootchee sported a lopsided grin. "If my memory serves me correctly," he said, "you weren't taking any prisoners either. I thought I was going to have a stroke trying to keep up with you."

He planted a soft kiss on her lips.

"You had a stroke all right. It was long, hard, and steady, and lasted all night." They both started laughing.

The two went back and forth with playful banter until Lootchee's cell phone interrupted from the night table.

He let it go to voice mail.

"What time do you—"

This time it was his pager vibrating. Every time his pager went off, Beijing smiled because Lootchee was so old-school.

"You might as well answer it," she said, trying to shield the fact that she was annoyed by the electronics and the distractions.

He sat up in the bed. "I'll only be a second."

The entire conversation was one sided, and he only asked a series of questions. Beijing ear-hustled from her side of the bed.

"What's such an emergency?" he asked. "Who was it? Which people?"

Whatever were the answers to those questions caused him to hang up with a frantic look on his face.

He immediately turned to Beijing with weary eyes. His next call was to have his numbers changed.

"What's wrong, baby?" she asked once he was finished. She had never seen him appear afraid.

"I had met this party planner chick from Virginia at my man's funeral," Lootchee explained, "when we were broken up. I was vulnerable."

When have I ever known him to be vulnerable, she asked herself but continued to listen.

"The chick's business had potential and I invested in it. And in return she helped me out with some business ventures I had going on in D.C. And now I believe that the bitch is trying to set me up."

"What's her name?"

"Bambi," he said. Something about the way he said her name made Beijing suspicious, but she decided not to probe further. He'd never admit to anything anyway. "She's trouble. I just know it. I can feel that shit in my gut, like she's greedy and conniving and will do anything to save her own ass."

Beijing was shocked. "Set you up how?" Beijing wanted to know.

"With the feds. She said they kicked their way into her business and were asking about me." He added, "I know that broad put them on me. I know she did." He punched the headboard with his fist, startling Beijing.

"I know you are angry and it is fucked up, but you have to calm down so we can think this out," Beijing reasoned. "Now, what exactly did this girl say?"

"She said, the *feds* had busted her spot and I'm next on the list. I need to get out of the country until I get a grip on what's really good. I may need your help."

"Of course, of course." Beijing racked her brain trying to figure out how she could help him. She had never seen Lootchee so frazzled. "I know some people in South America that'll put you up," she said, already scrolling down her mental Rolodex. "How soon do you need to leave?"

"As soon as possible." He seemed so nervous.

"I know things look bad, baby, but try not to panic. I know someone who can hook you up with a passport and you can be on your way in twenty-four hours. You have to trust me."

He turned to her and took her in his arms. "Sorry for getting you involved with this. But right now you are the only person I can trust. And baby, if the shoe was on the other foot you know there are no bounds."

She put her own emotions and well-being aside and looked in his eyes. "Don't worry, I got you. I promise you I do," she said.

CHAPTER 32

Thirty Escalades

Seth's friend Prince Amir was so pleased by the way Beijing efficiently and discreetly had the pound of marijuana delivered to Seth when he and Amir touched down in Miami that over the past two months he'd called on her a few more times to handle things for him. The moonlighting work was a welcome distraction from her problems with Lootchee.

With the money that Amir paid—not to mention several of Beijing's other clients demanding so much of her time—she had to make a hard decision. She thought about what she needed to do from every possible angle before deciding that it was time for her to step out on faith, follow her passion, and work full-time for herself. Beijing filled out the necessary paperwork to take a temporary but indefinite leave of absence from the Tabby, her home away from home for the past six years. She had been burning the candle at both ends for so long that she didn't want to torch the bridge down.

She called Thaddius to inform him of her decision. Thaddius was a good employer and even a better person. He told her that although he was sad to see her leave, he fully understood. Business was business.

"The door to the Tabby will always be open to you," he promised her.

Amir's latest request was to have thirty Escalades shipped to his new home in Cuba. He wanted to give the cars to a Cuban diplomat as a gift. The Cuban diplomat and Amir had been good friends for years; he was like an uncle to Amir. He loved American cars, and since the United States had placed the embargo on Cuba in '62, American automobiles had been difficult for the ol' head Cuban to obtain.

Amir didn't want to deal with customs and he wanted no documentation of him, her, or anyone around him ever receiving the vehicles, because then he'd have unnecessary headaches with the government. Beijing didn't fully understand the seriousness of the risk she was taking, but she was up for the challenge or the trouble that she could get in from sometimes helping the people she helped. This time was no different!

If she could pull this one off Amir promised to pay her enough money to send Chyna to boarding school, college, medical school, and any other type of educational institution the child wanted.

Beijing sat in her front room in an off-white suede recliner sipping a cup of hot tea, her computer resting on a pillow on top of her lap. She was thinking hard. The prince's request was odd. The man was a billionaire many times over, and what he wanted with the cars was none of her business. That was one of the reasons most of the people she dealt with returned to do business with her again: She didn't ask questions and was always discreet.

Beijing's mind was a total blank. Getting those cars overseas didn't seem within her means whatsoever. She wished she could call Lootchee and see if he had any ideas, but that was pointless. He was out of the country, still on the run. Though she talked to him for a few minutes a few times a week, she knew the reality was that she couldn't rely on him for anything.

She felt like a junkie who knew that her drug of choice was bad for her but at the same time loved to indulge all the same. She had to keep telling herself to forget him, forget him, FORGET HIM. Maybe if she kept telling herself, eventually it would come to pass.

Back to business. She had an idea. It was a long shot, but if it could be done, it would solve at least part of the problem.

She picked up the phone from the end of the table and dialed Peggy Bucotti.

"Hello."

"Hey, Peggy. This is Beijing." It had been over six months since the two last spoke. Peggy loved herself some Sterling. She and Sterling had gone to high school together, and though Sterling never gave her the time of day, she always kept in touch with Beijing.

"Hey girl," Peggy said, "long time no hear. How've you been?"

"Just working hard," Beijing said. She set the laptop on the coffee table and stood up. "You know how it is."

"All too well." Peggy sighed. "To what do I owe the pleasure?" She knew Beijing well enough to know that it wasn't a simple social call.

"I have a question for you, Peggy. How easy would it be to have a car declared salvage?"

Peggy had been working at the DMV for over eighteen years, and she had seen it all throughout her time.

"That's pretty simple," Peggy said. "When do you need it? I will just need the VIN number to get it done for you."

So far so good.

"How about if there was more than one car?" Beijing asked. "It'll definitely be worth your while."

"How many more?"

Beijing could sense that Peggy was less enthusiastic than before.

"Twenty-nine more," Beijing said, laughing a little. "Thirty in all."

"Are you serious, B? That's a lot of cars."

"Serious as a heart attack," Beijing replied. "Can you help me?"

Peggy was quiet for a few beats.

"I'm afraid not," she finally said. "If it was one, certainly, two no problem, three maybe . . . But thirty, Beijing? That's a lot. If I tried to mess with that many documents it would be like taking a red flag and sticking it in my ass for everyone to see. If we were talking about before those terrorists flew into those buildings, that would be a different story. But now, that would be my last day at work and I would be sent off to the federal prison."

"And we don't want that."

"No we don't."

It was worth a try, Beijing thought. "I knew if anyone could do it, it would be you."

Peggy told her if she needed anything else to call and said that she was sorry one last time, then said good-bye.

With no other ideas of her own, Beijing did what she knew best.

The next morning Beijing sat in her father's newly remodeled kitchen. She admired all the upgrades added since the uninvited guest had tried to demolish the entire first floor of the house. For a split second she daydreamed about what it might be like to have a house of her own as Lootchee's wifey, then she quickly shoved that idea right back where it came from.

Sterling drank a glass of juice while Beijing put together a veggie and cheese omelet and heated up a can of corned beef hash. She explained the situation to her father as she cooked.

"Well, baby," Sterling said after she finished, "I'm pretty sure it can happen, and if it can be done, you're going to want to call a guy I know that goes by the name Stash. If it can be done, dude can do it. He can get his hands on anything, so I am sure he might be able to help you. Besides, he's a good person to have as a friend with all these high-profile clients you have making these types of requests."

"What exactly does this dude Stash specialize in?" She put a plate of food on the table in front of her father.

Sterling said the grace and then jabbed a forkful of eggs into his mouth. "Anything he wants," he said, after swallowing. "The guy is so off the hook at what he does, when I hear on the news about one of those multimillion-dollar paintings turning up missing from the museum, I envision Stash somewhere selling the Picasso or the *Mona Lisa* to the highest bidder. I'm telling you, baby, this is your man."

According to Sterling, Stash would buy and resell anything of value: old, new, collectible, vintage, hot, borrowed, gifted. The only exceptions were illegal drugs, his ass, and his soul.

Sterling filled Beijing in on the background info. For almost twenty years Stash had run one of the most lucrative fence operations on the entire East Coast, providing services to some of the wealthiest and sometimes grimiest people on Planet Earth.

In Stash's eyes what he did was completely ethical. He was just a middleman accommodating both sellers and buyers. Although a great percentage of the goods he sold were hot or had been at one time, he could honestly boast that he had never stolen anything in his life—not even second base when he played softball in junior high.

Beijing was impressed with Stash's MO and that her father

knew him. "How come you haven't put me in touch with him before now?"

"Never seemed to need to." He forked some corned beef hash into his mouth. "Time and place for everything, though," he added. "And I guess no better time than the present."

CHAPTER 33

What's a Man to Do?

The sun was a ball of fire inching across the tropical sky, blasting waves of heat onto Stash's rented Dodge Stratus. The small nondescript car was characteristic of its driver: low-key and efficient. He fingered a button on the console, switching the air-conditioning to high, then signaled and made a right turn off the main street.

A young man behind the wheel of a souped-up blue Honda Civic bumped his horn at Stash after almost hitting him.

Stash cursed himself for forgetting that he was in the U.S. Virgin Islands, St. Thomas, where they drove on the left side of the road. He sheepishly waved his hand in the air gesturing to the young native, *my bad.*

St. Thomas was the place to come if a person wanted to be on vacation on a tropical beach or buy a nice piece of jewelry for a decent price, but Stash was on the compact island for neither of those reasons.

He parked the Stratus in front of the small, familiar box-shaped building on a narrow road. He smirked at the irony of the sign above the door, GOLD MINE.

He'd made a small fortune over the years dealing with the owner of this particular establishment, he thought as he got out of the car.

"Look what the cat done dragged in," the owner, Ian, said as Stash opened the wooden door and walked in. He acted like Stash hadn't called in advance to announce that he would be paying a visit to the island.

"It's been a long time." Ian got up from the stool behind the glass display case and hurried to lock the front door before a customer walked in or, worse, a tourist wanted to window shop.

"I always appreciate any business we do and I'm glad you consider me for your merchandise. I like Maurice. He's good and honest, but it's always good to see you. Don't get to see you much." He patted Stash on the back.

"It's good to see you, too, Ian." Stash shook the gray-haired Jewish's man hand. "How's business, old-timer?"

"Fantastic," Ian replied. "But I would rather talk about our business, if you don't mind." He smiled a mouth full of tobacco-stained teeth.

"That's why I'm here. Let's slide to the back and I'll show you what I have for you."

Ian led the way to his private office. Inside the tiny space, he took a seat behind the old, scarred-up desk. Stash sat in the chair across from him.

Ian's eyes lit up like a six-year-old peering under the tree at Christmastime, seeing everything he'd asked Santa Claus for, plus some. He removed an eyepiece from his pocket to get a better look. "May I?" he asked.

Stash nodded. "Help yourself. There's a hundred Russian diamonds in all. All three to five carats."

Ian held one up to the jeweler's glass and somehow his smile managed to grow even larger. "Beautiful," he murmured to himself. "I've never seen this many stones of this quality at one time in my life," he added. "They have to be worth a fortune."

"Actually," Stash confirmed, "they'll bring in one point two million, wholesale, on the open market. But for you, old-timer, I'm going to give you a real nice deal." He paused. "Seven hundred thou."

"Really? Hmmm, I don't have the whole amount now, but I can get it together in . . . let's say . . . ten days."

Stash studied the old man. They'd done a fair share of business in the past, and the man's word was always his bond.

"Not a problem, old-timer. I'll even leave the stones with you. You can get me the money the same way as the last time. If that's okay with you," Stash added, smiling.

"Your generosity doesn't go unnoticed or unappreciated, Stash. I'll see to it that you get all your money on time." Then, as an afterthought, "I have one question, and your answer has no bearing on our deal. Only so I'll know how to proceed."

"Then ask, old-timer."

"The diamonds . . ." There was no way to ask other than bluntly. "Are they stolen?"

It was Stash's turn to sport the mega-smile. "Have I ever sold you stolen jewelry before?" he asked. "I have my ways, old-timer." He added with a wink, "Besides, who ever heard of hot ice?"

They both laughed.

His business on the island was concluded, and Stash was climbing back into the Stratus when his phone woke up. It was a 704 number. He answered.

"What's up?"

"Is this Stash?" the guy on the other end asked.

"Who wants to know?"

"My bad, Stash, this is Sterling; you may not remember me, but I used to run with your uncle Benny."

Stash knew exactly who Sterling was; he had the memory of an elephant. Benny never had anything but good things to say about the man. And the one time they'd met, although more than ten years ago, had been nothing but love.

"Sure I remember you, Sterling. What's popping, my man? I thought you had completely squared up?"

"Like a box of Kleenex," Sterling joked, "but I still know what I know. My daughter, Beijing, presented me with a problem that I couldn't solve. I told her, though, if it could be done, you could make it happen."

Stash almost dropped the phone when Sterling mentioned the name Beijing. How many could there be in North Carolina?

"Uh, no problem, Sterling. Tell your daughter to give me a call and I'll see if I can be of any help," Stash offered.

"Cool. I got her right here, you can tell her what you want her to know yourself."

Stash could hear a few words in the background, and then a soft but confident-sounding female voice was on the line.

After she'd introduced herself Stash said, "It's nice to meet you, Beijing, you have a lovely voice. Has anyone ever told you that?"

"Not that I can recall, but thank you for the compliment."

"Don't mention it; I was only telling the truth. No big deal. So"—he changed the subject—"your father mentioned that I might be able to help you with something."

While Beijing explained the gist of her situation, Stash reminisced. He had always wondered what had become of the young girl with the odd name. The girl who had been partly responsible not only for him changing his name but also for probably saving his life. After he had seen how far some people would stoop to get drugs, even selling and raping a young girl, he knew it wasn't something he wanted to do any longer.

He had seen Beijing's picture in a magazine article on the most accommodating hotels in the country and fallen in love. As resourceful as he was, he could have found her, but not knowing what turns her life had taken, Stash didn't want to intrude. Maybe now he would.

"That sounds doable," he said, after Beijing finished talking. "I'll have to check a few things out and call you later," he added. "What's the latest you're comfortable taking calls? I wouldn't want you to get in trouble with your husband for having a strange man calling in the middle of the night." He was fishing for information on her martial status.

"Oh, I'm not married and no jealous boyfriends," Beijing offered quickly. "You can call anytime you like . . . I mean, when you find out what's what."

"I'll do just that, Beijing. You'll be hearing from me real soon," he promised.

When Stash hung up, he smiled. He had so many extravagant things at his fingertips and never really took advantage of any of the luxuries he provided to other people. Now, though, it was time for him to go after something that he wanted for himself.

He had an interesting dilemma to deal with of his own. Should he follow his instincts and stay out of the picture? Keep it all professional and deal with her from afar? Or should he follow his heart and pursue the young girl he'd never stopped thinking about, who had grown into a beautiful woman?

CHAPTER 34

Pushing the Pedal to the Metal

After the giant aircraft taxied the runway, Beijing shouldered her carry-on and Louis bag and stood in the aisle by her seat. Once the flight attendant gave the go-ahead, she hurriedly tried to exit the plane. A few of the passengers who had seats ahead of Beijing voiced their annoyance at her rush. "Excuse me, please," she said while inching by a lady who was taking too long getting her things together.

Dallas International had its usual army of traffic. People were flying to and from destinations all over the world. Normally Beijing would spend a minute or two wondering where some of the passengers were going or where they may have been. But today she had a one-track mind: getting to the rental car counter and getting to her destination.

As she stood in line, she remembered the phone call from Rayna that morning.

"York told me he seen Lootchee in Dallas yesterday," Rayna

had said casually. "Why didn't you tell me he was back? When did he return?"

"What?" Beijing had asked, stunned. Lootchee had been in South America for the past three months. He and Beijing usually talked over the phone three to four times a week, but she was so caught up with trying to take care of the many, sometimes complicated demands of her clients that more than a week had gone by since she had last touched base.

"Are you sure it was Lootchee?" Beijing asked, thinking it had to be a mistake.

"Pretty sure," Rayna replied. "York told me he thought he saw him last night in Club Celestial. He said they were shouting him out on the mic and he described him to a T."

Confused and dumbfounded, Beijing kept her cool. "Girly, I'm going to call you back in a while." She had an international call to make.

When she called the cell phone that Lootchee had acquired while south of the border, the operator came on and said the number was no longer in service. Thinking she had somehow dialed the wrong digits, she tried again and got the same recording.

Her confusion quickly turned into anger. As a last resort, Beijing called Julio, the man who had helped get Lootchee safely out of the United States and into the jungle and promised to personally see to it that Lootchee was taken care of as long as he was there.

"¿Julio, como esta?" she asked.

"Bueno, señorita," he answered. "How are you?"

"I'm good, Julio. But I'm just wondering where Lootchee is."

"I take him to the aeropuerto last week," Julio said, and then asked, "Why? He no call you?"

"He no call me, all right."

· · ·

Beijing drove the rented Dodger Charger down the highway at least ten miles per hour over the limit. *I can't believe that the no-good nigga didn't have the decency to tell me he was back, after all the bullshit I went through to get this motherfucker out of the country. Harboring and abetting a fugitive. After all I've done! That inconsiderate bastard!*

Beijing tapped the brakes to slow the Charger down enough to veer onto the exit that would take her to Lootchee's house. It didn't matter if he was home or not; Beijing was determined to stay staked out in front of his house until he returned. She wanted to look into his mendacious face when she told him where he could go and how he could get there.

Afterward, she could turn her back on him and walk away from his callousness for good.

A black Mercedes S550 blew by Beijing going in the opposite direction. Lootchee had one just like it. Beijing jerked her neck around to get another glance. It was him all right. Before she knew it, Beijing skirted through a red light and busted an illegal U-turn.

The back end of the rental car almost went out of control before straightening up. She stomped the gas pedal and the high-performance car lurched forward and was on Lootchee's bumper in no time. She blasted the horn, nonstop, motioning for Lootchee to pull over. For the first time, Beijing noticed a female in the Benz with him.

Lootchee checked his rearview mirror to see what all the commotion was about. When he realized that it was Beijing, waving her arm around gesturing for him to stop, he sped up.

Unfortunately for Lootchee, Beijing had been taught to drive in one of her father's tow trucks when she was twelve years old. By the time she was fourteen she was more than efficient at handling anything on wheels with the confidence of a professional driver. Beijing mashed the pedal to the floor, causing the Charger to bump the back of the Benz.

"Pull over you son of a bitch," she screamed as if he could really hear what she was saying. The woman in the car with Lootchee was looking back, her features revealing both fear and shock.

Lootchee kept it moving until he reached an intersection with a red light. Beijing could tell he wanted to run it, but there were too many vehicles in his path. He had to stop, and when he did Beijing rammed right into the back fender of the Benz. The tire burst. She was in such a rage that she backed up and rammed the car again for good measure.

"What's the matter with you?" Lootchee shouted as he hopped out of his smashed-up Mercedes. "You done gone crazy or something?"

Beijing was unfazed as she met him face-to-face in the middle of the street, not one ounce of fear on her face.

"Yeah," she shot back, "for believing in a no-good, selfish, lying-ass bastard like you! I hope you had fun with your childish games and your beyotch over there." She gestured to the girl in the passenger seat of Lootchee's car, speaking in a controlled, calm voice. She paused a second before continuing screaming, "Because I'm done with yo' trifling ass. You don't have to worry about getting the time of day or all the shit you can eat out of me," she added with an acid tongue.

"I'm sorry" was all Lootchee managed to say.

"I know you are, you sorry bastard." She took a bottle that was on the curb and hummed it at him. "Sorry motherfucker!" Beijing walked over to her rental car and got in it. As she drove away the bumper of the Charger fell off.

CHAPTER 35

Happy Birthday

Beijing drove back to the airport but was not able to get a flight back to Charlotte, because everything was oversold, so she had no choice but to spend the night in Texas. As she made her way across town to the Tabby it seemed like every single radio commercial was promoting Lootchee's birthday bash. She would have never known anything about his birthday extravaganza had she not popped up into Texas unannounced. Tears formed in Beijing's eyes at the thought that Lootchee had planned on celebrating his birthday without her.

From the time she left Lootchee he kept calling but she never did answer his calls, not one time. Once she was in her room, she kept listening to the song by Miles Jaye, "I've been a Fool for You," thinking of Lootchee but she didn't call him. After crying herself to sleep she woke up with a new perspective. No longer did she want Lootchee to love her, now she only wanted revenge. She sat up in the middle of the bed and the wheels began to turn.

First she decided to check her messages. There were a couple of calls from clients that she had somehow missed and the rest were from Lootchee asking her to please call him. The final message was from Lootchee: "I'm sorry about everything that has happened but I just wanted to apologize for all my bullshit. Everything you said about me you were right and I want to apologize, for real." He sounded sincere. "I know shit doesn't look good for me right now but I know if you gave me another chance to do right, I would. I really hope you allow me to prove myself. If you ever cared about me, I'd ask you to give me just one more shot to prove myself."

Beijing listened.

"I'm having a birthday party at Club Celestial, a real party this time and it would mean the world to me if you could come."

Beijing listened to the message several more times and could hear the humbleness in his voice.

It was a catch-22 situation; on one hand she wanted to get all dressed up and be knockout gorgeous and go to Lootchee's party to make him regret that he ever crossed her but on the other hand she didn't want to give him the satisfaction.

She was beyond mad or angry, then an inner voice spoke to her, "Why in the hell are you crying like a punk? Don't get mad! Get even." And that's exactly what she planned to do. She jumped up and called Dazzle to put her plan into motion.

"Hey girl, I need a favor."

"Anything for you."

"Look, I need you to get on the first thing smoking to Dallas."

"No problem," Dazzle agreed.

Mon and women alike were staring at the beautiful beauty as she walked up to the velvet rope wearing a one-piece jumpsuit. It was hugging her curves like a wrapper on a Hershey's Kiss. She sashayed with grace past the block-long line, with a big, gorgeous gift-wrapped velvet box in her hand, straight to the man holding the VIP list.

The guy looked her over and said, "Ain't no doubt you fine as a motherfucker but if yo' name ain't on the list, there is nothing that I can do for you. What's your name?"

"My name ain't really important, I'm with Beijing Lee."

Everybody who worked at the club and who worked the event knew that Beijing was at the top of the VIP list and knew that Lootchee would be elated that she showed but Dazzle held her own. The guy looked her up and down. As scrumptious as she looked, the guy would have let her in regardless. But he told her, "Y'all at the top of the list. I'm glad I didn't have to turn you away." He motioned for her to be let past the velvet rope and into the club.

Turning heads the entire way to the exclusive VIP, she kept asking people where Lootchee was. Lootchee had been notified the minute she stepped foot into the club. It didn't take long for them to cross paths. He approached her.

"You must be Lootchee," she said in a sensual voice. "My name is Dazzle. I'm a friend of Beijing's. She asked me to bring a gift to you."

Inside Lootchee really hoped that Beijing would have showed up but in his heart he knew she wouldn't. In spite of her not coming, he was satisfied knowing that she was still thinking of him and sent a gift. That was at least a start. He was eager to see what she had sent him. He set the box on the table. The people in the VIP area were intrigued either with the beautiful box and its contents or the shapely lady who was presenting it to Lootchee. People begin to surround the table as Lootchee removed the big bow.

As he was opening the box, Lootchee thought about the way he had treated Beijing and promised himself that he'd treat her better. Though he didn't always show it he really cared for her.

He opened the box like a kid at Christmas, excited to see what his parents had gotten him.

When he took the lid off the box, it was the biggest pile of shit he had ever seen. Half of the people beside him held their noses and looked at the person beside them wondering who farted and what had they eaten. And the other half of the people turned their heads out of respect for Lootchee.

"Read the card, read the card," Dazzle insisted excitedly with what looked like a genuine smile. Lootchee for the first time in his life did not know what to do. In shock he thought it was some kind of prank, surely his real present was coming. Maybe the card disclosed what she had really gotten him. He took the card from Dazzle. It read:

"I wasn't going to send you anything . . . but I'm not that selfish. Here's all the shit you can eat. Happy Birthday! That is . . . if it's really your birthday."

Lootchee was speechless and there was no playing it off. The expression on his face was defeat and his attitude turned as shitty as the pile in the box. He looked at Dazzle as if he was about to hit her, as she licked her lips. "Get the fuck out of here." He put her out in one breath and then in the next, he demanded, "Get Beijing on the phone now."

She called Beijing and passed along Beijing's message, "She said she don't wanna talk to you." Lootchee snatched the phone but Beijing hung up and didn't answer again.

As Lootchee threw Dazzle out of there, Beijing laughed her butt off the entire night and for days to come. She was satisfied that she had ruined his birthday!

CHAPTER 36

Neighborhood Watch

Beijing drove her Lexus at a leisurely pace, heading east on Alston Avenue, only a few blocks from Chyna's school. She had promised her niece that if she brought home a good report card, Beijing would take her to the mall and treat her to some new shoes. Beijing loved buying things for Chyna. Hell, one of the reasons she busted her butt working was to make a better life not only for herself but also for Chyna.

Mary J. Blige's new CD was playing in the deck but the volume was turned down while she talked on her cell phone to Rayna. Beijing was in no rush since she was more than a few minutes early. As she came up to a stop sign, Rayna was dishing out her daily dose of gossip.

"Girl, I'm telling you. I was shocked when I saw him." Rayna claimed to have seen a prominent Atlanta-area rapper dating a homosexual.

Beijing wasn't sure if Rayna was putting her on or not. "You need to stop lying on people, girl."

"If I'm lying," Rayna shot back, "Tupac ain't dead."

Beijing laughed. "Then you know you fibbing. Everybody knows that Machiavelli isn't dead. That nigga in Cuba somewhere, still making music and probably pushing an Escalade." She thought with some satisfaction about how she'd gotten the trucks to Cuba, courtesy of Stash. The most fascinating thing about the whole ordeal was that he'd made it all happen with just a phone call. As thoughts of Stash crossed her mind, her phone rang. "Hold on Rayna."

"Naw, girl, I'm telling you something. Let whoever it is call your butt back."

"Nope, I can't, as a matter of fact, let me call you back."

Rayna sucked her teeth as Beijing clicked over to the other line. "Hello."

"Hello, beautiful."

"You haven't even seen me yet. How do you know I'm beautiful?" she asked Stash.

"Because you have a beautiful spirit and that makes you a gorgeous person."

"How sweet of you."

"How sweet of you to send me the Cuban cigars. I really appreciate it."

"It was the least I could do. You helped me get something to that place and I wanted you to have something from there."

"They just arrived. So," he continued, "how about let's meet and celebrate what a good team we make."

"That sounds like a plan." Beijing smiled. Although she could not put her finger on it, there was something about Stash that she liked.

"Consider it a date, then. Tell me what city, time, and place of choice," he said to her.

Beijing was secretly excited that Stash had asked her out on a date and was about to change the track on the disc when she was startled by the squealing of tires coming to an abrupt stop, making her heart skip a beat.

"What da fu—?" she exclaimed, but Stash never heard her. "Shit," she said, frustrated by the phone's reception.

When she lifted her head up to see what was going on, three SUVs had her triangled in so Beijing couldn't pull away. She had no idea what was popping off but knew it couldn't be good. To make matters worse, she had no way to call for help since her cell was in a dead zone.

There was nowhere to go: An Escalade was in front barely touching her bumper, a Range Rover was on her left, and a Denali was on her back bumper. To the right of her were the curb and a stop sign. She was cornered. Where was neighborhood watch when she needed them?

Three men wearing camouflage army pants, black T-shirts, and masks popped out of the vehicles. One quickly moved to the driver's side of Beijing's car, and the other two went to the passenger side, armed with semiautomatic weapons.

One of the pistol-wielding trio reached for the door handle.

Beijing beat him to the punch, locking her door before he could grab it. What the hell did these guys want? She started to rev the engine, but then quickly remembered that there was nowhere to go. For a split second she thought about ramming into the Escalade in front of her but knew it was a lost cause. A Lexus against a Cadi truck? No competition.

The guy on her side tapped on the window and said, "Open up the door and you won't get hurt."

With tears in her eyes, she shook her head. She didn't know how she was going to get out of this alive.

Before she realized it, one of the guys popped off a shot in the rear passenger tire.

She may have been superwoman to some, but when it came to

bullets, her flesh was just as vulnerable as a baby's. And right now she wanted to scream at the top of her lungs like a newborn. But she didn't. She didn't want these lunatics to see how scared she truly was.

"I don't want to see you get hurt, now open up," the guy said. "I'm not the crazy one, these guys are." He gestured to the men with the automatic weapons. "I'm the calm one, the Negotiator. One of the crazy ones took matters in his own hands," he said firmly.

As Beijing stared at the man doing the talking, she prayed that God would somehow miraculously send a tower signal to her cell phone so she could call 911. Or at least send another car her way that could call for help. While she was eye to eye with the Negotiator, she didn't see one of the other guys walking up on her car. He held a brick in his black-gloved hand covered by a black towel. *Pow!* He bashed in the window.

Beijing yelped, seeing the shards of glass everywhere. The same man stuck his hand inside the door and punched the button to unlock the latch.

"See, bitches don't appreciate you when you are nice," he said after sucker-punching her window. "You gotta rough them up to make them understand what the fuck you are saying. All that negotiation ain't hitting on shit," Glove-Man said.

"Fall back," the Negotiator demanded to his hotheaded friend, moving him out of the way. "Miss, let me help you out of the car. As I said before, I don't want you to get hurt. I don't want that guy over there"—he pointed to the man who had just broken her window—"to pull you out, nor do I want to be forceful with you, but as you can see these guys don't give a fuck. If you don't cooperate, I seriously don't know what might happen." He paused briefly to make sure he had Beijing's undivided attention, "Nobody here wants you dead, but they will kill you if they have to. I promise you that."

The Negotiator searched in her eyes as he reached a hand out to help her exit the car. "In fact, you are worth more alive to us. So I'm asking if you would please not make these guys rough you up."

Beijing's mind was in overdrive. She thought about Chyna waiting on her—*Under these circumstances she's better off at school than here,* she reasoned. She began to think about all the horrible things they could do to her. She wondered if she would make it out alive. Where was Lootchee when she needed him? She tried to block out all of those negative thoughts.

"Fix the tire on that motherfuckin' Lexus and bring it with you," Glove-Man said to the other two dudes.

Beijing looked back quickly at her car, wishing she were in it. Then the driver of the Escalade took off, and she realized that she was no longer in control—of anything.

CHAPTER 37

Somewhere in the Middle
of Nowhere Land

Inside the backseat of the Escalade, the Negotiator turned to his captive and handed her a mask to cover her eyes.

"You're going to have to put this on," he said. "It's for your own good."

Beijing was trying not to show how frightened she was, but she could no longer pretend. She was terrified.

"Who are you?" she asked in a shaky voice. "What do you want with me?"

The Negotiator gestured toward the mask still in her hand, "First, you do as I say."

Beijing pulled the thick silky cloth over the top of her head and everything went black. She felt the truck smoothly take off as if the driver were leisurely transporting his grandmother to a place of worship.

"Now," the man next to her began, "who I am is neither here

nor there. My job is to pick you up, deliver you to a secure location, and babysit you until someone pays to get you back."

"All this is for money?" Beijing said, mortified. But as long as it wasn't personal, maybe she would be all right. "How much money do you want?" she wanted to know.

The Negotiator pressed his spine to the back of the soft leather seat. "You'll find out soon enough. Now sit back," he ordered. "Question time is over."

They rode in silence except for the radio. She had no idea how long they were driving, but she heard Don's new song at least three times. She felt the Escalade turn and then realized by the bumpiness that they were off the main road. She could smell pine and evergreen coming from outside, and could feel the thick tires on the truck crush the small branches and leaves that carpeted the path.

Her hands were still free, and she desperately wanted to reach up and snatch the mask from her eyes, but thought better of it. It might cost her her life.

Once creeping along the trail, the SUV finally came to a stop.

After the engine shut off, Beijing asked, "Can I take this thing off my face now?"

"Not yet," the Negotiator replied. "Sit tight."

The front door of the truck opened at the same time as the rear door where the Negotiator sat. A few seconds later someone opened the door next to her. A hand was on her arm, then the Negotiator said, "Step down . . . easy . . . I don't want you to fall and hurt yourself."

He led her across a grassy surface for about thirty feet then stopped.

"Take your time on the steps," he warned. "There are three of them."

Beijing felt like a blind woman and quickly learned to appreciate her other senses. She gingerly raised her right foot and felt for the step. It moaned under her weight. The next two steps also cried out as she pushed off to reach the top.

A door creaked open, and the man led Beijing into a room that smelled of mildew.

"Sit down," she was told.

Someone pushed her firmly down onto a sturdy wooden chair. Next, another man—not the Negotiator, she could tell by his scent—roughly secured her hands and feet with plastic ties so that she couldn't escape.

Beijing heard her phone ring. "Yo," she heard a familiar voice say. "Who is this? Who are you? A friend of hers?" he questioned, and then took over the conversation. "And you want to make sure she is okay because the phone went dead when she was talking to you?"

Beijing thought hard as she listened to the one-sided conversation. "Well, nigga, she ain't aight; she's being held captive until somebody she knows or loves coughs up ten million. So at this stage, playboy, I don't know if you can get your hands on ten mil or not. I wouldn't be surprised if you can, because from what I hear she only deals with big hats anyway. Or maybe if you contact her other boyfriend—he goes by the name of Lootchee—maybe you can get that nigga to pay one half and you can come up with the other."

Damn, Beijing didn't know how this was going to end. She wasn't sure what Lootchee's money was looking like, because she knew that half of it was tied up being laundered. Or—after the whole altercation when she'd last seen him—if he would even pay that kind of money to get her back.

It hit her that this all had something to do with Lootchee. She thought about all the risks she had taken for him, but the risk that seemed to bother her most was the way he gambled with her heart. As much money as he had, he always needed to be bailed out; now that she needed to be bailed out, would he come?

Her thoughts were interrupted when she heard the guy say, "Naw, nigga, this shit is serious as world peace, cancer, or AIDS in Africa. Nobody's on joke time. I got your number and a few others we plan to alert, so you got forty-eight hours to get that money. Or I don't have to tell you what. You seem like a smart dude."

After the guy hung up, Beijing heard footsteps coming from down the hallway, somewhere. Then there was more talking.

"Were there any problems?" a voice asked.

Beijing thought she might have heard the voice before.

"A walk in the park," the Negotiator replied.

"Good, knew I could count on you." It was the familiar voice. "Get the video camera so we can get this show on the road. We about to get rich."

Ain't this a bitch? I know who the voice belongs to. Beijing had met the man only twice before, and she didn't want to believe it, but her ears and gut had never lied to her, and they had no reason to start now.

CHAPTER 38

Man to Man

Someone sent the email from Beijing's account to all the key people in her life—her father, Lootchee, Thaddius, and a couple of her other powerful clients. Thaddius was the first to receive the video with Beijing tied to a wooden chair in which she spoke with tears in her eyes, "This is not a horrible joke of any kind. I've been kidnapped and they are asking for a ransom of ten million dollars. If you don't pay them they will kill me. Please wait for a phone call." The video went black and then the words came up, "This is not a fucking game. Look forward to our call."

Thaddius was the first to receive his email and the first to call the police. The police had put two and two together when someone had reported hearing gunshots in the neighborhood near Chyna's school. A witness had seen three men in a big black SUV snatch a young African American woman, while one of the others quickly changed a flat and drove off in the Lexus. The witness didn't have much of a description of the kidnappers, but she did have the plate number of the Lexus that the girl was driving before they took her.

Because Sterling was out in the field grinding as usual, he didn't get the email. It was Greta who called him when the police had showed up on her doorstep to give Sterling the news. Sterling fled back to the house and saw for himself.

Inside, Sterling's home was rapidly filling with concerned friends, family, and clients along with police.

From his street days before the birth of Beijing, Sterling had developed a natural dislike for the police. Now as a successful legitimate businessman, he still wasn't all too fond of them. However, he'd put his own feelings aside if it meant they could help his only child.

As the police tried doing something to the computer and asked countless questions while prepping for a phone call from the kidnappers, Sterling decided to make some phone calls of his own.

He began putting word out that his daughter had been kidnapped and he wanted people to put their ear to the streets to find out where she was. In the midst of everything, Stash called Sterling to fill him in on what he knew. They agreed to meet at Sterling's shop because Sterling needed all the help he could get.

Someone stepped from the shadows as Sterling climbed out of the truck. Instinctively Sterling removed the .44-caliber revolver from his waist. He pointed it at the shadow.

"No need for that," Stash said, "it's only me." He had his hands up. "Did anyone follow you here?"

Keeping the revolver locked and ready, Sterling replied, "I don't think so.

"What do you know about the kidnapping?" Sterling went on, getting straight to the point. "That's why we here, isn't it?"

"Right now," Stash admitted, "I don't know much at all. But

I'm calling in favors from all over the country. I got everybody I know and everybody they know looking and listening for any little thing that might lead us to her. I want to get her back safe just as much as you do."

Since he was the biggest fence on the entire East Coast, Sterling was still not sure if Stash was there to negotiate the return of his daughter or to offer a helping hand. The latter would be better, but what vested interest did Stash really have in Beijing? As far as Sterling knew, his daughter had only met Stash by way of telephone just a few months ago when she enlisted his help getting the Escalades over to Cuba. Sterling knew that Stash had personally set up the formalities to get Beijing's task done. It seemed odd that Stash would go out of his way to involve himself in such a public situation. Especially since the man went to every precaution to maintain a low profile in his business and life in general. He preferred to play the role of ghost.

Sterling asked, "Why the personal interest?"

"It's a long story. And the clock is ticking, but for now we need to put our heads together to figure out as much as we can."

"I'll take the abbreviated version," Sterling told the younger man in a no-nonsense tone.

"Well . . ." Stash sighed in thought. "I was deep in the dope game, wildin' in the streets. School by day, slaying narcotics as soon as the school bell rang, until one day I was dropping off a package and saw firsthand what kind of power and perks drugs could give to the wrong person. To save a little girl from a pervert motherfucker, I murdered a man."

Sterling stood there in shock. He knew what incident Stash was speaking of. Even after years of counseling Beijing had always denied that she knew how the dead man got in that kitchen or that she had seen anything. He wanted to thank the guy that stood in front of him, but instead he listened.

"That incident changed my life and my lifestyle. From that

point on no matter what kind of money it could put in my pocket, I never sold another narcotic whatsoever. I didn't want to destroy lives anymore.

"For years I always wondered what became of that little girl with the most intense brown eyes I'd ever seen. Then I saw Beijing's picture in a magazine article a couple of years back as the best concierge in the country. Still have that article to this day. That's the day I fell in love with your daughter."

Sterling could not believe how small the world was. That the man who'd saved his daughter had been under his nose and he didn't even know it.

Stash added, "When you contacted me, the only reason I agreed to talk directly to her and allowed you to give her my direct number is because I knew she could hold water. To the best of my knowledge, she has kept our deadly secret for all these years. Though it was hard, I made up my mind that I wouldn't intrude in her life. That's why I only dealt with her by phone, text, and email. But now"—Stash leveled his eyes with Sterling's—"all that has changed. I'm going to find her, and I'm not going to let her get away from me again if I can help it."

CHAPTER 39

Blood Is Thicker than Mud

As Thelma faced the vanity mirror in the marble-floored master bathroom and applied the finishing touches to her makeup, Isador slipped up on her from behind, planting a soft kiss to the back of her neck.

"You're going to make me mess up my face," she said to him.

The two had gotten married right after high school. They had raised two wonderful kids and been happily married, give or take a few hundred disagreements, for more than three decades. This day was their thirty-fifth wedding anniversary.

"Your face is as beautiful now as it was on our wedding day," Isador said.

Thelma blushed. Thelma might not look like an eighteen-year old but at fifty three, she could still pass for a woman in her mid-thirties. She still worked out at least three times a week and tried to eat right. The rest was genetics.

"My husband is still strikingly handsome too," Thelma tossed back.

Isador ran an open hand across his full head of sandy red hair. "That husband of yours is a lucky man," he said. "Now hurry. The kids are downstairs. I just saw them."

Thelma smiled, knowing those two children of hers were never on time. Her son had suggested they have a home-cooked meal prepared by a chef before they left for the Golden Princess cruise—fourteen days to Hawaii and back—he'd given them for their anniversary. Thelma and Isador could hardly wait until morning when they were scheduled to set sail; they had been packed for over a week.

Thelma locked eyes with her son after coming down the steps. He was watching CNN with his sister. "Every time I see you," she said to Lootchee, smiling, "you look more like your father."

Lootchee stood to give his mother a hug. "Happy anniversary, Mom and Dad. You two look great. Congrats."

"Don't they?" Gia chimed in, embracing her dad.

"Let's make a toast," Lootchee suggested.

Isador went to get four glasses and the bottle of Moët & Chandon he'd been saving, and then popped the cork.

"Allow me." Lootchee removed the bottle from his father's hand and filled the flutes. "May health, wealth, and wisdom never elude you," he declared. The four glasses of bubbly kissed with a high-pitched "ting" when they touched. Then they drank.

As Lootchee sipped on the champagne, he couldn't help but think of the lies he'd told Beijing about his parents. He felt bad, but he had to come up with something to get her to come back with him. For the first time, he thought how the truth might have sounded: *I love you, B, but when I feel like you are giving me the least bit of rejection, I just get preoccupied, sometimes with my girl on the side.*

They still had a few minutes to kill before it was time to eat, so Lootchee asked his sister to get him online.

"It doesn't make no sense you still don't know how to use a computer," she teased.

"Just get me on the thing. That nigga Jeff told me he emailed me a picture of his new car."

"I ain't yo' damn secretary," Gia fussed, but she logged on to his email account. "It's easy to get on; you need to sit still long enough so I can teach you how to do it yourself."

Lootchee stood over his sister's shoulders as his email account opened. "Go to the one that says Beijing Lee," he said with a big smile. Lootchee was shocked but happy that she had emailed him. He hadn't heard anything from her since she tried to ruin his birthday

Gia did as she was told, causing Lootchee's smile to be wiped off his face, "What da fuck?" The contents of the video shattered his thoughts. Gia sat mesmerized as everything came together in her mind.

"Watch yo' mouth," his father quickly scolded him.

Before Lootchee could react, Gia gasped, "Oh my God!"

Lootchee broke a lamp in his parents' house, throwing it across the room. "Shit! I can't believe this bullshit," he screamed. His father tried to calm him down but it wasn't working.

Gia had her mouth open for a few minutes before speaking. "I think Roy may have something to do with this," she muttered

"What, why do you say that?" Lootchee asked as he took in every detail.

"I thought that motherfucker was bullshitting. Roy kept saying that he had some million-dollar heist going on. I blew it off, I thought he was in on a bank robbery or an armored truck. He left a couple of days ago to go to North Carolina and everytime he calls he talking about how he going to get us a bunch of money and I would never have to ask you to do a damn thing for me again. I had no idea that it—"

"That what?" He huffed angrily. "That he was going to snatch

Beijing? The one chick I ever gave a fuck about? Shit." He shook his head. "She don't deserve this bullshit."

Gia saw the hurt written on her brother's face. He always was so secretive about everything he did. The mere fact that he admitted to actually having feelings for someone was shocking—and now this. It hurt her to see her brother the way he was, and she especially felt guilty because her boyfriend was partly responsible.

"I never liked that dirty dog anyway," Thelma said.

Gia felt rotten.

Lootchee went over to his dad. "Dad, I need all the money I had you put up for me and anything extra you might have. This is my fault and I have to get this girl back."

Thelma came up behind them. "Son, it will be okay. Just calm down." Everything his mother said went in to one ear and out the other.

Lootchee got the money from his father and raced out the door.

Gia was on his heels. She took a deep breath, and said to her brother, "Blood is always thicker than mud, and this is what I know." She told her brother everything she could, even though it meant double-crossing her man.

CHAPTER 40

It Takes One to Know One

Paris raced into the house wearing a pink sweat suit and sneakers. She went straight over to Greta and gave her a hug.

She released her and then said in a louder voice, "Everything will be okay."

"I know," Greta whispered, even though she wasn't too sure of anything.

"Any news at all?" Paris searched Greta's teary eyes for answers. All she saw was hurt.

She took a long deep breath, lowered her voice, and said, "No news at all." She dropped her head in disgust. "But I'm prayerful that God is going to work this all out."

"Well, if it's money they want, why haven't they called?" Paris declared.

Greta didn't have an answer. "We don't know. We don't know anything. There's been nothing since that email. I keep telling myself that maybe it's a hoax."

"Maybe it is and maybe it ain't. I need answers, I love my sister," Paris said and looked around. "Who is in fucking charge around here?"

"Detective Jimmy Janks," a detective said, introducing himself.

Greta spoke up. "This is Beijing's sister." As the detective and Paris spoke to each other there was a knock at the door. Greta went to see who it was. She was hoping and praying that it was someone with some answers instead of questions. A team of caterers walked in with caviar, escargots, crab cakes and all kinds of delicacies, courtesy of Prince Amir. He had already put up a reward for anyone with information about the kidnapping and come up with half of the ransom. He said it was the least he could do; Beijing had a good soul, for an American girl.

Darkness had taken over the sky. The lights, cameras, satellite transceivers, and other equipment the reporters used to digitally transport their photographs, videos, and stories to the control room were finally off. Rayna took in a long breath of fresh air, then exhaled before pushing the doorbell.

The front door swung open, revealing a puffy-faced, tear-stained Greta. Rayna stepped into the foyer of the house and hugged Greta.

"Has there been any news? What do they know?" She bombarded Greta with questions.

Greta dabbed her eyes. "Nothing since that horrible video," she said. "Come on in. Have something to eat."

Rayna followed Greta's lead into the great room, scoping the downstairs of the house. People were scattered all over the place. Willabee was in one corner talking to Chyna. They both looked as if their best friend had died.

Rayna felt a tug at her heart. "Where's Sterling?"

"Working. You know he's one of those people who can't sit

still. Anticipation kills him, so he throws himself into his work," Greta said.

Rayna had figured he would be on post, like everyone else, waiting for the call from the kidnappers. Rayna and Greta spoke for about five minutes before Rayna made her way over to Paris.

"Hey, girl," she said. Paris jerked her head around toward the voice. "How are you holding up?"

"I'm holding." She looked Rayna up and down, and then asked, "Why are you here?"

The question caught Rayna off guard. "I—I was concerned," she answered, mad at herself for stammering. "I just want to know if there's anything at all I could do to help."

Paris was studying Rayna closely, but Rayna had pulled herself together. She knew that Paris didn't care too much for her from the way she kept giving her the cold shoulder.

"I have five hundred dollars if you all need it," Rayna offered.

Paris glared at her. "Ten million is a lot of money, but we don't need a damn thing from yo' ass."

"It's not for you, Paris, it's for Beijing."

"Look . . ." Paris had her hands on her hips. "Beijing doesn't need your money and we don't need your company. Besides, we've got the money together if it comes down to that. I don't know why my sister can't tell you are not worthy of her friendship. But you can't trick me. I've been a larceny-hearted bitch most of my adult life, it takes one to know one." Paris scanned Rayna from head to toe. "I know one when I see one." She pointed and said, "You."

"You are just jealous because I'm closer to your own sister than you will ever be."

"You wish," Paris said, unconvincingly.

"I don't know why you dislike me the way you do, Paris, I've never done anything to you . . . and I've been nothing but a friend to your sister." Rayna spoke deliberately. "I'm not tripping on you, though, because I know this situation has everyone stressed to the max, including me. But that's no reason to take your pent-up frustrations out on me. I'm only trying to help."

"Whatever." Paris walked away, leaving Rayna alone and looking stupid.

Rayna said good-bye to Greta and Willabee and shared her intentions and regrets one more time with them.

"We'll let you know when we learn something," Greta said.

Rayna drove past the camera people at the entranceway of the house, and then looked both ways before turning the white BMW X5 onto the dark road that would lead her onto the main stretch. Relieved to be out of there, she picked up her cell phone and dialed York. She set the cell phone on speaker and laid it in her lap in case someone drove by.

He answered on the first ring. "What up, baby?"

"I did everything you told me to," she said into the phone. "Nobody knows anything and everybody is shook up. They're all waiting for the call and ready to pay whatever you say. They done gathered up the money and everything."

"That's what up," York replied, sounding extremely happy with what he heard.

"I'll call you back. Later." Rayna hung up and dropped the phone in her pocketbook on the passenger seat. She turned the volume up on Teflon's new song blaring from the Bose speakers, singing it word for word as she made her way down the dark road.

"I knew you were a snake from Day One," Paris said. She had been hiding in the back of the vehicle and had now revealed herself by sliding one of the seats down. She pointed her .25-semiautomatic directly at the back of Rayna's head. "Bitch, don't give me a reason to kill yo' ass. I don't like you anyhow," she spat. "Now, where's Beijing, bitch?"

Rayna tried to regain her composure and play innocent. "What the hell are you doing in my truck, Paris? Are you crazy or something?"

"Not crazy as I'm going to be if you don't come clean. Where the fuck is my sister?" This time she made a gesture with the gun showing her she wasn't afraid to use it.

Rayna was trying to think of the right thing to say or do.

"How would I know where she is?" Her eyes bounced from the road to the mirror and back again. "Please put that gun away."

"You'd rather deal with me than the others, that's for sure. Drive where I tell you, bitch," she said and poked Rayna with the gun. Rayna followed Paris's directions until they pulled up at the double gate of Sterling's business. Paris had called him on the way over, and he was waiting at the gate. He opened the gates then shut and locked them behind the BMW.

The door opened and Stash stood there, looking down at Rayna with fire in his eyes.

"Turn off the car and get out," he said roughly.

Rayna did as she was told. They led her inside and sat her down in a metal chair.

"Don't make it harder for yourself than it already is," Sterling threatened.

"Don't take him lightly. If he has to, he will set fire to your ass to make you talk," Paris leaned down and whispered to Rayna.

"It wasn't my idea," Rayna cried. "But, honestly, I don't know where she's at. They threatened to kill me. That's the truth."

"I'm going to kill you, bitch, if you don't do better than that," Sterling shot back. He was distracted when his phone rang. He answered, "Yes."

"Mr. Lee, sorry to have to call you under these circumstances. It's about Beijing." It was Lootchee.

"Do you know her whereabouts?"

"No, I don't, but I have managed to pull together some money. A few mil. I'm on my way to your house if you don't mind waiting on the call."

"Yeah, call my wife, but if you got warrants I wouldn't go there."

"I don't even really care about that." Lootchee thought about how Bambi had lied to him about the police coming to her house just to get back at him, forcing him to South America. "I just want to be wherever I need to be to help get her back." Lootchee sounded like a sad puppy dog.

"Well, that's where the family and friends are posted up," Sterling said bluntly with appreciation that Lootchee was trying to help. "Be careful, man, traveling with all that green."

"I'm flying in private so I'll be okay."

While Sterling was on the phone, Stash went through Rayna's purse and found her cell phone. After studying it for a second, he dialed the last number Rayna had called. Stash put the phone on speaker as it rang.

"Yo, what's up?"

Rayna grimaced when she heard York's voice over the speaker.

"We have Rayna," Stash said loud enough to be heard. "You give us back Beijing the same way you found her and you can have Rayna. No questions asked."

York erupted in laughter.

"You must be kidding, man. That shit is real funny." His voice boomed out of the speakerphone. "Rayna ain't worth nothing to me. I was wondering how I was going to shake the dumb bitch after this was over anyway," he said. "With ten mil in my pockets, a nigga ain't got no need for a straggly bitch, no way. If you want Beijing back . . . it's going to take ten mil. Good try though." He was roaring in laughter. "I will be in touch with the instructions within the next twenty-four hours. Oh, and this phone will be destroyed in a matter of seconds, so no need to try to trace it."

The phone connection went dead. Rayna looked dumbfounded. She couldn't believe what York had said about her. They had a child together, for Christ's sake.

Three sets of eyes were boring down at her now.

"Okay," she said. "I'll tell you everything I know."

CHAPTER 41

Desert Storm

York Tresvant couldn't believe how well things were going. He had been running scams and cons since he was fourteen years old. He always moved around, never giving anyone his real name, until he met Rayna—and got her pregnant. That was more than three years ago.

From time to time, York involved Rayna in a few small cons, but nothing of this magnitude. The minute Rayna put the bug in York's ear to the effect that Lootchee and Beijing were an item, York started thinking of a way to make the situation profitable to himself.

York kept pumping Rayna, as discreetly as possible, for information on how the new couple's relationship was progressing. It wasn't too hard a task, because Rayna was jealous and always rubbed in York's face all the elaborate things Lootchee did for Beijing.

York found out that Lootchee's nose was as wide open as it

could be for a dude like him, plus Rayna told him about all these other rich people that Beijing befriended and associated with.

When he first devised the plan to kidnap Beijing for ransom, Rayna was feeling it. That's why York sent the two young thugs to rob Rayna that night at the strip club, planting the seed in her that York owed some strong people money—big money!

After that incident it was easy for him to convince Rayna that all of their lives were in danger, including that of his and Rayna's daughter, who was with her mother the majority of the time. She had to help with the plan to get the ruthless killers off their backs.

Scared, mostly for her innocent little girl and her mother, Rayna relented and agreed to help any way she could.

York rubbed his hands together like he was in front of the fireplace trying to warm them. He was thinking about all the cold cash he was about to put his hands on.

That's when he got the call from Stash. Now he was just a little worried.

The small dirt path that wound its way from the main road was cushioned with pine needles, moist leaves, and several seasons of decayed foliage, muting the intrusive sound of footsteps in the cool ink-dark woods. It was mostly silent, except for the occasional owl making its presence known to any possible mates in its territory. The information that Rayna had given him, along with a few words that just came in hot off the press of the streets about a guy named Jake, gave him the location. Stash had been lying on the wet ground watching the house where Beijing was being held. He tightened his grip on the MP submachine gun, which was equipped with a screw-on sound suppressor.

He had no idea that a special tactical team was also watching the old blue house from a distance. They had been following Sterling all day. With his background they figured that he'd learn his daughter's whereabouts and try to pull something crazy like this.

With a thermal-heat seeking device, they were able to discern how many people were in the dwelling and what part of the house they were in. Of the four people still inside, one had not moved from the center of the front area since the SWAT team took up watch. They concluded it must be the prisoner.

Stash could see the orange glow of fire at the end of what looked to be a blunt. As it was passed back and forth, the small torch revealed a dim glimpse of the careless smokers.

One of the men was Roy; Stash had never seen the other before tonight.

Stash stealthily moved within ten feet of Roy and the man he was with. He could hear them talking.

"I can't wait to get my hands on that money," Roy said under his breath.

"I know that nigga Lootchee is as rich as goat's milk," the other replied. "But you think he will hand over ten million for a bitch?"

Roy looked like he was thinking the question over. "Hard to say," he murmured. "Love's a muthafucka."

"Yeah," the other man countered, "but that nigga don't love nobody but himself."

Roy was about to open his mouth to respond when three slugs slammed into his chest. The impact lifted his feet eight inches from the ground before dropping him flat on his back, dead. The assault rifle he'd been holding lay by his shoes.

Jake's eyes bulged almost completely out of his oversized head. He wanted to scream but it was too late. Another trio of deadly hollow-point bullets from Stash's silent killing machine stung Jake in the face and forehead, muffling his attempt to shout for help. Jake was dead on his feet for a second or two, and then tumbled to the ground like a fallen oak tree that had just been cut at the trunk.

Stash stepped over to the dead bodies, admiring his handiwork, when he felt something hit him in the back. Turning around, he saw a man holding a gun, a mirthless smile on his face. Stash raised his weapon but was a little slow to the draw. Two shots went off. Stash fell to his knees clutching his stomach. The next shot from the Negotiator, Marquell's, army-issued .45 put Stash on his back. He never got a shot in.

The cold barrel touching the back of his head ended any celebrations Marquell might have thought about.

"Sleep with the maggots," Sterling barked before squeezing the trigger to his own silenced MP5, sorry he was too late to save his friend from his unfortunate fate.

But he did manage to succeed at what he was there to do, save his daughter.

The SWAT team commander immediately jumped on his walkie-talkie. "Shots fired," he shouted. "Shots fired. We are going in now."

Thirty seconds later the glass in most of the house windows turned into shards. York and the remaining two conspirators were not totally caught off guard. They'd snatched up their weapons after hearing the first shots.

They weren't prepared for what happened next, though. The house went completely black: SWAT had cut the power. Three shadows appeared wearing night vision goggles and ended the madness with a single shot each.

York managed to dive on the floor, face-first, just in time to avoid the fate of his colleagues.

"I surrender," he screamed at the top of his lungs, "I surrender."

Two other members of the SWAT team had their eyes on the hostage the entire time. Her father untaped her and escorted her outside. Beijing was shaken but unharmed.

She sobbed in tears trying to pull herself together until she saw Stash lying in a pool of blood. She was stunned; she could not believe her eyes. Immediately she remembered who he was, and looked as if she saw a ghost. "Oh my God." She looked at him the way she had that unforgetful day when she was ten years old as all kinds of questions ran through her mind. Her thoughts were interrupted when her father came up to her and took her into his arms. Sterling said, "You owe thanks to this guy right here. Without his help . . ."

"Mike?" she gestured to the supine man she remembered.

"Yeah," Sterling confirmed, "we also call him Stash."

Wow. Beijing was stunned, wishing that she could formally thank her angel for saving her for the second time. She had always wondered what she'd say to him if she ever saw him again, but now that she did, she feared that she might never get to say anything to him again.

Beijing returned to her father's house and was surprised by all the people who had gathered to pray her home. She was most surprised by three guests who greeted her, Lootchee and his parents. Though she appreciated that his parents had put off their vacation to support their son, and felt good that Lootchee was prepared to go bankrupt for her, she was still tired. Tired of Lootchee's games and bullshit. She turned to Lootchee, who had trailed Beijing and her father back to the house. "Lootchee, I'm done with your lies and your bullshit. It's time for me to move on with my life and find someone who understands what a healthy relationship is."

She walked out of Lootchee's life that day and knew that she would take one day at a time. No matter what lures Lootchee sent her way, she'd wouldn't relapse again.

CHAPTER 42

May the Best Man Win

Lootchee knew that Beijing was done, but he wasn't. He was used to getting what he wanted, and this was no different. He followed Beijing over to the county hospital and waited until she left. Beijing had been visiting Stash for the past two weeks, and now it was time for Lootchee to pay him a visit.

"Good to finally meet you," Lootchee said to Stash. "That was some real crazy shit you did in those woods. All joking aside . . . that was real admirable."

"That's what we do for those we love," Stash said, eyeing Lootchee with suspicion.

Lootchee cut to the chase. "So, you trying to take my girl, huh?"

"Actually she was mine first," Stash said, enjoying the fact that he was ruffling Lootchee's feathers.

"Which means you know that she was my woman? And we've been through a lot and weathered a lot of storms together."

Stash nodded. "She told me all about y'all's time together. She also told me she was done with you. Besides 'we' have history."

Lootchee raised an eyebrow. "Oh really?"

"I knew her since she was a little girl. And who would have thought that fate would bring us back together again."

Lootchee had heard of Stash. He knew he was a stand-up, respected guy, and no one ever had a bad word to say about him. Lootchee looked him dead in his eye and said, "If I heard of you, you must have heard of me."

Stash nodded.

"Then you know this ain't over, playboy, and may the best man win," Lootchee said with a cunning smile as he walked out the door.

ACKNOWLEDGMENTS

My loving children Kennisha and Timmond—I thank you both for all your understanding and for making me such a proud mother. My mom, I thank you for your unconditional love.

My dear Craig, I love you and no words could ever express how much I value you for loving me the way you do! My brothers: Damon Williams (always hustling in our squares—I truly get it), Tim Patterson and Curt Bone (you both should write books and drop some of that knowledge you got. I'd buy them one hundred times over), and Shaft Jones (Superman-the Superstar. LOL)! Though I may not be in touch everyday, I love and appreciate you all in your own ways.

To my girls who hold me down through all the ongoing madness in my life, all while pushing me to the finish line to beat the deadline. Jewel Sanchez, your name says it all; you are a gem! Natarkki, Mia Upshaw, Nikki Allen, Kia (I got on my slicker and galoshes), Rosetta (for making me breathe), and my dear little cousin, Faith aka Shay-Shay. Thanks for always hanging in there with me.

To my agent, Marc; Melody; Porscha; Jane; and all of the team over at Random House/ Ballantine for your undying support and assistance with making a conception into a birth.

To all the people in my past who have helped me to learn what addiction and relapses are all about. And most important to my readers; not one inkling of any of this would be possible without you! I love you all.

NIKKI TURNER is a gutsy, gifted, courageous new voice taking the urban literary community by storm. Having ascended from the "Princess" of Hip-Hop Lit to "Queen," she is the bestselling author of the novels *Ghetto Superstar, Black Widow, Forever a Hustler's Wife, Riding Dirty on I-95, The Glamorous Life, A Project Chick,* and *A Hustler's Wife,* and the editor of and a contributing author in her Street Chronicles series. She is also the editor of the "Nikki Turner Presents" line, featuring novels from fresh voices in the urban literary scene. Visit her website at nikkiturner.com, or write her at PO Box 28694, Richmond, VA 23228.

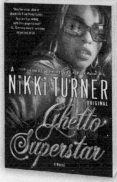
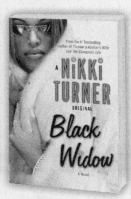

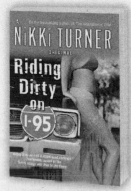
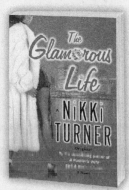